# Secrets of the Runestones

# Dennis Medbury

Trade Paperback

@Copyright 2019

All Rights Reserved

Library of Congress: 1-6635449591

ISBN: 978-0-9969593-2-2

Requests for information should be addressed to:

A Vegas Publisher, LLC.

www.vegaspublishers.com

vegaspublisher@gmail.com

First edition: 2019

Cover Design: Starcat Games

Map Design: Adam Wolters

## DEDICATION

For my wife Kim, whose love and support allowed me to chase my dream and to become the man I was meant to be.

# Publisher's Note

When Dennis submitted his manuscript to A Vegas Publisher, we were intrigued. His writing style is unique and alluring. We were instantly transported into the world he created, filled with diverse, captivating characters and creatures engaged in action-packed scenarios. Dennis has a vivid imagination and his visual writing style allowed us to picture his magical world, with clarity, just as he envisioned.

We asked Dennis how he came up with the material because it was unlike anything we had previously read. It was his reply that caught us by surprise: Dennis struggles with PTSD and suffers from insomnia; a result of his 14 years of service in the United States Navy. Not wanting to become dependent on medication, Dennis started to write this story in his head to help him fall asleep. The story began to develop and take on a life of its own. He decided to put his story into words.

We applaud Dennis for discovering a coping mechanism that works for him. It is estimated that over 44 million Americans suffer from PTSD. Dennis is a role model for those suffering with this condition. Through creative writing, Dennis can share with others how his evolving thoughts and ideas have helped him relieve some of his symptoms. Dennis encourages sufferers to discover their unique creative outlet. It can lead to brighter days.

Dennis, thank you for your service.

Joyce Spizer Foy

Virginia Clark

A Vegas Publisher

*Each case is different; it is not recommended to stop medications, procedures or treatments without consulting your physician.*

The following links contain valuable information for struggling veterans in need of assistance:

https://nvf.org/veteran-resources/

https://www.mentalhealth.gov/get-help/veterans

https://www.neptunesociety.com/resources/list-helpful-veteran-resources-support-groups

# Dorian

Interrupting the silence of the woods, the ring of steel clashing against steel sent several birds scattering into the air. Two warriors entangled their weapons to best the other. Dorian, the younger of the two, squinted after being maneuvered into the sun's setting rays. Struggling to focus his eyes, only his adversary's outline provided solace from the blinding light. He lunged toward his opponent with his sword outstretched to reposition himself, but his father blocked the advance with his warhammer and pushed his son back into the disadvantageous position. Dorian, visibly frustrated, swung his sword at his adversary, but the old-timer quickly ducked underneath the attack and drove his hammer into the young man's chest, holding his advantageous position. Clutching his breast, Dorian stepped back to recover the wind knocked out of him.

"Losing your composure only makes it easier for me. Perhaps you'd fair better if you used a dwarf's weapon like a hammer or an ax," the old dwarf said with a smug smile peering beneath his long, brown beard.

"Those are your weapons, father, not mine," he replied, returning a sly smile.

Dorian Kinsman was used to his father trying to goad him into using an ax or hammer. They were the weapons of the dwarves. Centuries of history told the tales of the short yet powerful race wielding the heavy weapons with grace and efficiency that not even humans could hope to obtain, but Dorian's blood did not belong solely to the dwarven race. Half of his lineage came from the human mother that died giving birth to him, as all women who birth a child of half-dwarven blood do.

His father, Thane Kinsman, stood in his fighting stance, his hammer at the ready in front of him. His bulbous nose and blue eyes would be his most outstanding features if not for the braided beard hanging to the center of his protruding belly. Unruly tufts of brown hair jutted from behind his ears adorning his otherwise shiny, bald head. He stood at the height of five stones, the average height for a dwarf. His thick muscles, a product of years of demanding physical labor, bulged beneath the padded leather garments that provided protection against blows from his son's dull practice sword.

Sweat poured down Dorian's face. Exhaustion washed over him in a wave, making his sword feel many times its weight. He knew his father held the advantage in experience and strength, but Dorian's superior speed gave him an edge of his own. Ignoring his body's plea for rest, he stepped in for a rapid double strike. Predicting the combination, his father blocked the effort with the blunt side of his hammer with apparent ease.

Dorian shuffled his feet to retreat into the shadows, but his father stomped on the young man's foot while driving his shoulder into his son's abdomen.

"Argh!" Dorian exclaimed. "I hate that move! There's no way to stop it!"

With a cocky smile, his father boasted, "That's why I use it, son."

Dorian dashed in for another strike, swinging his sword while his father brought up his hammer to intercept the blow. Hoping to catch his father off guard, Dorian attempted a feint by suddenly stopping the attack. The unexpected halt threw his father off balance and Dorian saw an opening. Spinning around on the ball of his foot, he brought his sword full swing in the direction of his father's skull and terminated the advance just a pebble's width from his head.

"I got you! I did it! I finally beat you!" Dorian panted with a rush of excitement. Sparring with his father began when he was old enough to hold a sword, but not once in his twenty-five years had he ever won.

Thane smiled into his son's eyes and, without saying a word, looked down, making his son follow his gaze. When Dorian broke his line of sight to his father's arm, the basis of the old man's smile shown. Thane held a dagger pointed at Dorian's stomach, the tip close enough to feel the cold of the steel.

"That's dirty!" Dorian exclaimed in frustration.

"Aye, my boy. In a true fight there are no rules. Only kill or be killed. Life or death."

Dorian dropped his sword to the ground in defeat. He stood a full head taller than his father, yet with far less girth. Possessing the identifying features of every half-dwarf, his dull gray eyes resembled storm clouds moments before releasing their downpour. His body lacked a single trace of hair, right down to the missing eyelashes. His leather garments fit loosely, allowing him to take advantage of his superior agility, including a leather bandanna around his head for protection against the harsh summer sun.

"You know the deal, Dorian. Have the stables cleaned before you come in for dinner." Thane walked toward a weathered wooden barrel that stood against the wall of a small cottage. He placed a mug under the spigot, poured the golden ale to the brim, and drank the contents in one satisfying gulp. Wiping the froth off his mustache, he entered the cottage to prepare dinner.

Dorian examined his practice sword, contemplating his father's claim about the fairness of battle as he went to the horse stable to face the consequence of losing their weekly spar.

The barn, consisting of eight stalls constructed of the same weathered wood as the cottage, provided shelter for their four horses. Dorian practiced and trained every day in hopes of avoiding the arduous chore. Sparring with his father, coupled with a hard day's work, intensified the weariness in his muscles, leaving him to long for the day he could gloat as his father endured the mucking misery. At night, he fantasized over the mocking taunts he would lay upon him when the day finally arrived.

A few hours later, Dorian walked into the cottage he called home. The sun dipped beneath the tree line and the crisp night air left a chill on his skin. The savory aromas of meat and potatoes filled the air, but not enough to mask the stench of manure radiating from Dorian. Approaching the fire in the hearth, he stopped short when the hearty laugh of his father burst forth from the kitchen.

"You smell like you were rolling around in dung! Did you clean the stables or go for a swim in them? Go wash that smell off you before you stink up the whole house."

*Did you clean the stables or go for a swim in them?* The same question was asked every time he finished the laborious chore. Thinking it was funny the first hundred times he heard it, the joke became old and tired. Rolling his eyes, he replied, "Yes, father," and went on to bathe the day's filth from his body.

Two paintings, the only decorations adorning the barren walls, hung on either side of the washroom door. Both represented the same beautiful woman with long, wavy auburn hair. The portrait to the right depicted an up-close picture of the woman. Her thin lips curled up in a sweet smile, and her bright green eyes sparkled like emeralds next to her pale skin. The one to the left portrayed the same woman standing in a long flowing white dress with her arms hugging her stomach, highlighting her unborn child. Dorian glanced at the paintings of the woman he would have called

12

"mother" as he walked into the washroom.

He removed his clothing and stepped into an enclosure in the back corner of the room. Two sliding glass panes formed a square with the adjoined walls of the room. He knew this space as the rain bath. Once inside, Dorian reached up to a copper fitting with many small perforations surrounding a carved blue stone in the center. He touched the sky colored rock, and it began to glow. Water poured from the holes as the shower started.

With the fetor scrubbed off, Dorian made his way to the kitchen. His dinner lay waiting on a small wooden table with tin plates in front of each of the three chairs. The savory aromas of his father's expert cooking perfumed the air. Mounds of food were heaped on two of the dishes, leaving the third plate empty in silent reverence of his late mother. Though she was gone, she remained a member of their family and would always have a place at their table.

"I need to go into town tomorrow. We are getting low on supplies." Thane mumbled as he shoveled potatoes into his mouth.

Comprehending the real desire behind his father's upcoming expedition, Dorian replied, "But we haven't finished the order yet. We still have four more swords to make."

"We are going to be short then. It can't be helped. We need supplies."

"You mean we need ale." Dorian knew of only one reason his father would go into town without completing a full order for his customers.

"Aye, an incredibly important supply! Dwarves drink ale, Dorian! I am a dwarf! Besides, I am Thane Kinsman, Master Dwarf Weaponsmith! People come from far and wide to buy my weapons because no one can match the quality of my wares!"

With animation, Dorian mouthed along with the words Thane spoke, as he had heard this boast countless times.

"Make sure you finish the order while I am gone. It is for that half idiot Marshal Marcus Bane. He won't mind getting part of the order late."

"Can I go with you this time?" Dorian queried sheepishly.

Thane's expression grew stern. "You know that can't happen."

Dorian fell silent and returned to eating his meal. Aware of his father's basis to deny his request, the answer to his question remained the same since first asked. *The people do not understand half-bloods*, his father had told him. *They would treat you with hate and contempt. The people would just as soon throw you in prison as look at you.* These were just some of the warnings his father had relayed over the years. Raised to fear any stranger, and remain hidden at all cost, Dorian grew weary of his solitude. No matter how many times he begged and pleaded with his father to bring him along, the same answer persisted. He offered to wear hoods, cloaks, and every manner of disguise he could think of to hide his identity, but his father insisted that it was too risky. When he was young, the arguments grew intense over this subject, but now Dorian resigned himself to his fate. Asking his father if he could accompany him into the city became more of a custom than an honest request these days.

The next morning, Dorian rose to see his father loading the wagon for his trip. Having watched his father leave for the city many times, preparing for the journey became instinctual. He walked to the stables to fetch two horses to hitch to the cart and saw his father struggling to move the wares from sore joints and a stiff back. Once the horses were bridled, Dorian helped his father load the axes, swords, spears, and maces crafted in the previous weeks.

"Do you have your bags?" The young half-dwarf asked, knowing his father often overlooked them. The bags contained clothes and a small ration of food to last for several days. Dorian knew the exploits his father would engage in after arriving in the city to open his shop. He would sell most of his wares within the first few days and spend the rest of his time drinking at the local tavern. He grew to expect his father to come home with fresh scrapes and bruises from drunken brawls.

"Who is the parent here? Of course, I have my bags!"

Thane spent a moment rummaging around the seated area of the cart before heading into the cottage. A moment later, he emerged gnawing on a leftover drumstick in one hand, and the travel bag in the other.

"Could you stop by the bookstore and get me a few new books while you're in the city?"

This question became as much of a tradition as him asking to accompany his father on his journey. Dorian learned to read when he was young, and little else pleased him as much as immersing himself into the realms of fiction and history. Books of all genres were piled high in his room. Fables, historical accounts, myth, lore, any book for that matter, were favorites. Many nights he stayed up late reading, leaving him sluggish in his duties the following day. Still, his father never denied him the small escape from the mundane life in which Dorian was accustomed. The love of reading, a trait he inherited from his mother, often consumed his senses, leading him to miss his father's call. For every instance, Thane bellowed a hearty laugh followed by how much Dorian reminded him of his mother, his dear sweet Alora.

Thane looked at his son with loving eyes. "Aye, that I can do." With a smile he snapped the reigns to begin his journey.

Dorian watched his father disappear down the wooded path. The trail twisted and turned to the north and south, while heading its way east, making the trip much longer than it would take a brave man to venture through the woods in a straight line. After a moment of self-pity over his lonely situation, Dorian went to the forge to begin his work.

Dorian and his father were not blacksmiths, who hammer out and cast common tools from soft iron. They were the far more talented weaponsmiths. They faced the challenge of producing a sturdy fighting blade hard enough to hold a razor-sharp edge and point, yet resilient enough to have the ability to flex under strain and immediately return true. They were the elite of metalworkers and wore the title with pride.

Dorian set about to work the prepared metal into a blade. A weaponsmith forges a sword with meticulous care and unfettered determination, and he and his father were masters of their craft. He shaped and mixed metals of different known qualities, some softer for the core or sides, some harder for the edge and point. The process included sandwiching harder steel around the malleable iron so the blade could flex under impact and resist deformation.

Working until dusk, he only paused for food and water. The job exhausted him, but he enjoyed it. Training to become a weaponsmith began at a very young age, and he had committed many, sometimes expensive, mistakes. Dorian believed he mastered his abilities and felt that his work matched the same high-quality as his father, although he would never tell him that. When it was time for dinner, the young apprentice would normally put out the fires in the forge and set all of the tools in their place, but without his father's presence, he would alter his routine.

Dorian went into the cabin to make a meal. His skills as a weaponsmith rivaled his father's, but his knack for cooking was no match. After eating his overcooked meat and undercooked carrots, he threw a cloak over his shoulders and returned to resume work on his secret project.

Dorian traversed to the back of the forge. Kneeling, he brushed away a small pile of leaves and dirt to retrieve a sword unlike any he crafted in the past. Few males possessed the thick, long hands of a half-dwarf, making it necessary to customize the fit to the precise dimensions of his fists, allowing comfort and ease of use. The girth of the pommel prevented the sword from slipping, and the oversized guard protected his meaty hands from opposing blades. Crafted in the style of a long sword, it held significant weight yet remained light enough to use one-handed if the need arose. In the center of the guard, two imposed stones shined like gems, one red, and the other black.

Dorian brought the secret project into the forge and began to work. Placing the sword into the hot coals of the kiln, he waited until the blade glowed red before bringing it to the anvil for shaping. Folded and forged more times than any other blade he designed, he doubted it could be refined any further, but that did not stop him from trying.

"Hello?" Dorian suddenly heard in the middle of swinging his hammer, sending a fearful tremor down his spine. With trembling hands, he picked up his sword, still glowing red with radiating heat. His heart pounded in his chest like the beat of a drum. He hadn't felt fright like this since a bear chased him up a tree when he was very young. His father had come to the rescue and spooked the bear away. On this night, he was alone and scared.

He gripped his sword with both hands as he quietly inched his way towards the door.

# Brett

Brett walked down a long dark hallway surrounded on both
sides by guards dressed in armor and carrying spears.
Shackles bound his hands and legs. He stood roughly six
stones tall with a muscular build, a shaved head, and dark
stubble across his face. His jade green eyes stood out as
much as his strong jawline. He wore a crisp white shirt with
a black leather vest, black pants, and black boots worn
beyond their intended use. The rattling of the chains echoed
in the corridor with each step he took. Before long, the stone
walls gave way to iron bars, revealing the cages on either
side.

The cage to his right appeared empty while prisoners
were tightly packed in the cell to his left. One of the guards
removed Brett's shackles while the other guard unlocked and
opened the occupied cell. Shoving him into the pen and
slamming the door shut behind him, Brett turned to watch
the guards walk away.

"Lovely accommodations. Can't say much about the service though." Brett shouted to the guards.

"Oh, a funny man! If there is one thing that doesn't last around here, it's a sense of humor."

Damp from the humidity, droplets of water raced down the stone and mortar walls. In the corner of the room stood a large wooden box that reeked of excrement, flooding his nose with the overwhelming stench of human waste. Body odor wafted in waves from the unwashed prisoners. A thin layer of liquid covered the floor that he assumed to be water, although it was likely mixed with any number of bodily fluids. Fifteen men of varying shapes and sizes filled the dank room. Four cots lined the walls, each occupied by three sitting men. The prisoners seemed either unaware or uncaring to the presence of their new cellmate.

Brett looked around his new home for a place to sit. Spotting the driest space available in the corner of the room, he sat with his knees pulled up to his chest. Folding his arms atop his knees, he closed his eyes and rested his head against the wall.

"Oi, new guy!" a voice came in front of him. Opening his eyes, he saw what he believed to be the ugliest human in existence. Sores, bumps, and dents riddled his head. His thin, straggly hair fell in tangled knots as a swarm of gnats dove in to retrieve a meal from his rank skin. His cheeks sunk deep, and his bloodshot eyes bore dark bags beneath that made them seem permanently blackened. His nose bent awkwardly, and when he opened his mouth, Brett saw what few teeth remained had turned yellow and were rotten. Short and skinny enough to see the outline of his ribcage through his veiny skin, the frail man resembled a decaying corpse. His ragged clothes hung loosely on his body, and his callous, bare feet revealed knurled toes with nails that turned a mixture of yellow and black.

The vile man spoke. "Did you bring any food in with you?"

Brett raised an eyebrow at the ugly man, "Yes, you can have it as soon as I squeeze it out."

From within the cell, a voice boomed deep and loud, "Leave the new guy alone, Skank."

Brett looked past Skank to discover the source of the voice. What he found was a being so large, he thought there was no way he possessed purely human heritage.

When the oversized man rose from the floor, his height required him to lean his head down to avoid bumping it into the eight stone tall ceiling. Nearly as wide as he was

23

tall, his barrel-shaped body resembled a dwarf more than a human. A thick mane of black hair ran down to his shoulders and looked in desperate need of washing. His jutting forehead formed a shelf above his eyes and bore a single thick brow. Walking over to Brett, he stuck out his enormous hand. "Name's Dak."

Brett rose to shake his hand, uncertain of the beast before him. Returning the friendly gesture, he raised his arm and watched Dak's giant paw engulf his hand.

"Brett Shaw. This isn't my first time getting arrested, I've never been to this part of the prison. What's the deal?"

"Prison?" Dak let out a deep laugh. "This isn't a prison. This is the arena!"

"The arena!" Bret exclaimed. "No, no, no, there must be a mistake. I didn't kill anyone. I just stole some stuff."

Brett ran to the bars of the cell. "Guard! Guard!" He screamed down the hallway. A drunk, overweight guard responded by meandering toward the cell in a swaying stupor that barely allowed him enough balance to remain upright.

"What do you want?"

Brett tried to claim his case, still hearing the mocking laughter of Dak. "There's been some mistake. I shouldn't be in here."

The guard snickered at Brett's quandary. "Mistake?" The sour smell of booze rolled heavily from his breath. "No, Brett Shaw, no mistake here."

"But I just stole some stuff! I shouldn't be in the arena!"

"No, Mr. Shaw! This is your fifth infraction for the crime of thievery. The court of the Holy Order changed your sentence this morning. You're sentenced to fight for your freedom to prove your worthiness before the eyes of the Gods." The guard slurred his speech and walked away laughing.

"But this can't be right! Don't leave me in here! I shouldn't be in here!" Brett called out in vain after the departing guard.

Brett remained at the bars of the cell, slouched over while listening to the mocking laughter of the prisoners. He returned to his semi-dry spot and sank to the floor in defeat. The sullen astonishment drove deep. He believed only murderers and rapists were sent to the arena. Closing his eyes, he hoped that he would soon awaken from this nightmare.

"Sorry friend." Dak said to Brett, wiping the tears from his face from laughing too hard. "Everybody who gets put in here reacts that way. It's funny every time. You'll laugh too if you can survive long enough."

"I can't believe this! I can't believe I'm in here!"

"Well, just win fifty straight matches in the arena, and you'll be free." Dak replied in a sarcastic tone.

Brett knew the rules of the arena, but never attended a contest. He knew that a person could earn their freedom by winning fifty straight matches, but he also knew that no one had ever accomplished this task. The days of an arena fight had always been one of Brett's favorite events. The citizens of Regiis attended these events in droves, leaving their homes empty, unguarded, and an easy mark for thievery.

Brett looked across the hall to look at the empty cell. "Why are we all in here? What's wrong with that cell over there?"

Dak's quick response revealed an uneasiness that seemed odd for a man of his stature. "That cell? That's Razuul's cell. No one bunks with him! Every time they put someone in there, he waits until the moment a guard isn't paying attention, and then he kills them. They posted a guard to watch his cell once, but Razuul reached through the bars, pulled guard's head between the opening, and crushed his skull flat as a pancake. They reset his win count back to zero after that. I heard he had already won over thirty matches at that point too."

Brett squinted his eyes to peer into the cell across the hall. In the dim light, he could barely make out the figure of a man lying on one of the four cots within.

"The Razuul?" Brett, just like everyone else in the Capital City of Regiis, knew this name. His legendary reputation spread to every ear. The undefeated arena fighter had more wins than anyone in recorded history. Renown as the wild elf whose skill and brutality exceeded any other fighter, his matches brought spectators from far and wide to witness the spectacle of fury and bloodshed. "What's his record at now?'

"Well, his count has reset a couple of times because that guard I told you about wasn't the first one he killed, but still, he won his forty-eighth last week."

"Forty-eight!"

"That's right, one more match, and then onto the king's champion. If he wins that one, he'll be the first to win his freedom. I wouldn't bet against him."

"Shaw!" A guard yelled, standing in front of the door to the cell. "Welcome to the arena. You've been selected to fight tomorrow. You're the opening act!" The guard smiled, baring his crooked teeth. He threw a small pile of papers between the bars that scattered across the damp floor like feathers in the wind.

The prisoners clamored for the papers. Dak rose, walked over to an inmate holding one of the sheets, bent over so that his eyes leveled with the man's own and growled. The man looked up at Dak with terror plastered on his face. He raised his trembling hands to present the paper, and Dak violently snatched it away.

"Hey, big man!" A voice came from outside the cell. Dak looked into the cell across the hall to see Razuul standing at the bars. "You scream like that again and I'll find a way to get over there and hang you by your intestines. I'm trying to sleep."

Brett saw Razuul for the first time. The dim light made it difficult to see, but he was able to make out some distinguishing features. About six and a half stones tall with a chiseled, muscular build, he looked abnormally large for an elf. Jet black hair hung loosely to his shoulders and pointed ears stuck out like two arrows piercing a veil. His copper skin tone reminded Brett of the statues scattered across the Capital. A tribal design tattoo wrapped around his left eye, confirming his wild elf heritage. Brett thought Razuul appeared intimidating, but couldn't fathom why the oversized Dak would react in fear of a being that looked the size of a child by comparison.

Dak walked over to Brett and sat down with a heavy thump. Realizing he made another loud noise, he turned his attention to Razuul's cell and released a sigh of relief after confirming the wild elf seemed undisturbed. Dak looked at the paper. "He's right. You got the opening fight tomorrow."

Brett reached for the paper in Dak's hands. It contained a list with two columns of names and a 'vs.' in-between each column. At the top of the list, he saw his name: "Brett Shaw (0) vs. Max Hilling (9)." Brett scanned the room. "Which one is Max Hilling?"

"I don't know." Replied Dak. "They never arrange matches with people from the same cell. If they did, the fight would happen in here instead of in the arena. Easier to kill a sleeping man than an awake one."

"There are other cells?"

"Of course. This is just one of the six halls. There are two cells in each hall, and all six halls lead to the arena." Dak pointed to a massive set of wooden double doors at the end of the hallway.

"What do these numbers mean at the end of the

names?"

"That's how many matches each prisoner has won."

Brett read all the names listed. "Well, lucky you, you're not on the list!"

"That's because I just got out of the infirmary." Dak lifted his shirt, large enough to use as a tent for an average sized man, to show the bruises that covered his rib cage. A sea of black, blue and yellow hid his natural skin tone, and a scabbed wound the size of a fist, oozed puss on the left side of his chest.

"You got that from the arena? I thought all the matches in the arena were to the death."

"I didn't get this from the arena." Dak's head sank, signaling his unwillingness to explain further.

"Nope!" Came a reply from a nearby man eavesdropping on their conversation. "Old Dak here is the only roommate Razuul ever had that lived."

"Razuul did that? That wound on your chest looks like a stab wound! How did he get a weapon into his cell?" Brett asked, glancing between Dak and the eavesdropping man.

"No weapon, he ripped the wood off the crap box." The man replied.

Dak shot a look at the man that warned him to stop talking. The man raised both his hands in surrender and went back to leaning against his knees with his elbows.

Brett looked over at Razuul's cell and saw the top of the crap box splintered into pieces. Understanding the reasons behind the terror Dak felt for Razuul, a chill ran up his spine at the amount of rage that possessed the legendary arena fighter.

# Elendor

---

In a small dim room constructed of tightly interwoven branches with thatch covering, a young elf named Elendor sat at a desk reading a book. Three tall shelves, packed with books, lined the wall. A single bed made of straw sat in the corner. The walls were bare except for one small round window that let in just enough light for him to read. His platinum blonde hair hung to the middle of his back and shined like strands of golden twine. His young, handsome face hid his age of over one hundred years, which to elves is still adolescence. Violet eyes, like the color of lilacs in bloom, darted from side to side soaking in the knowledge of the text before him. The folded and pinned left sleeve of his tunic hid his disfigured appendage that lacked the portion of an arm below the elbow. The legs of his pants were folded beneath his thighs to hide the nubs of his missing legs beneath both knees.

The door opened and a man, a head taller than the average male elf, walked into the room. His round face and pointed ears lacked the chiseled features of the typical elf. His light-colored hair did not lie straight, a fact he tried to hide by weaving it into a braid. His slouched posture and potbelly contrasted with the regal elegance and physical perfection of the elven race. The other elves of their home city, Parvus Arbor, reviled the young half-elf due to the human half of his ancestry, but Elendor considered him one of his few friends.

The gleeful guest glanced outside the hut, turned his head in both directions to spot anyone within earshot, and whispered, "Elendor...Me, Jocia and Galain are going to see Hidden Falls. Want to come?"

"Vaylon, first of all, it is Jocia, Galain and I. Second of all, no, I have studying to do," Elendor kept his gaze fixed on the book in front of him.

"Please Elendor? You love going to Forest's End, and Jocia has never seen it before!"

"I am sorry, Vaylon. I do not think it wise. Besides, if Elder Jalaana catches us, we will surely get in trouble again. Even more, if Morace is the one that catches us." Elendor forced himself to refrain from smiling. The adventure of traveling to Forest's End enticed him and would be a welcomed change of pace compared to the mundane task of studying books he had read a thousand times over.

"But look, I already have your harness." Vaylon turned to reveal a harness made of thick branches and vines strapped to his back.

Elendor chuckled at the excitement in his friend's voice. "I apologize Vaylon, but I cannot receive punishment again. Last time, you were forced to scrub the entire floor of the Grand Hall, and Morace took all of my books away for a week! Have you forgotten how much your back ached after that chore?"

"It's still worth it, but I understand. I hope we will be safe without you." Vaylon feigned defeat as he left the room.

"It is, not it's. Elves do not use contractions, Vaylon." Correcting Vaylon's speech came naturally to Elendor after many years of attempting to get his friend to speak in a traditional manner. How the habit of using contractions came to be baffled even the wisest of elves.

Elendor returned to his book. The prospect of his friends going to Forest's End without him weighed heavily on his mind. He knew Vaylon only mentioned his friend's safety to goad him into submission, but the rouse achieved the desired effect. "Vaylon!"

The young half-elf burst back in the room, revealing

his looming presence near the door. The look on his face portrayed pure joy. "Are you coming?"

"I shall accompany you," Elendor groaned. Frustrated with himself for being so easily manipulated, he wished he had the will power to resist the temptation, but the prospect of adventure defeated his common sense once again.

Vaylon squealed with excitement. He and Elendor had been to Hidden Falls one other time. Vaylon nagged to return ever since and Elendor could not blame him. The remarkable beauty left an unforgettable impression on anyone lucky enough to witness the splendor.

Unstrapping the harness on his back, Vaylon set the contraption next to the disabled elf. Awkwardly, Elandor squirmed into the harness, his half-legs sticking out from the bottom. With him in position, Vaylon squatted down, put both arms through the shoulder straps, stood, and exited Elendor's humble living quarters.

Outside, Elendor drew a deep breath. He did not leave his room often, but when he did, he loved to take in the sights and sounds of his home city. The earthy aroma of the damp earth combined with old fallen leaves filled his senses. The trees gave off their unique scents from every direction.

Some perfumed the air with a sweet aroma while others released a bitter odor, but to him, each essence combined to form a medley of forest fragrance that made Elendor feel at home.

The city, in its entirety, existed in the upper section of broad tree branches and featured miles of homes, public gathering rooms and houses of worship. Throughout the city, green banners bearing the elven sigil of a silver tree upon a field of silver grass swayed gently in the breeze. Not a single nail or plank of wood could be found in the construction of the community.

Once every generation, an elf was born with the unique ability to manipulate the growth and formation of foliage, known as an arbormancer. The child born with such an ability bore the burden of sustaining and expanding the city, thus ensuring it thrived without harming the plant life that sheltered them and provided a means of living. To be one with nature was a custom of the forest elves of Parvus Arbor. Elendor knew this well as the burden of arbormancy currently rested on his shoulders.

Vaylon made his way through the city, traversing the rise and fall of the tree branches. Greeting elves with a smile as he passed, he continued until he arrived at the designated meeting spot, The Hall of Nakaan, Elendor's favorite building in Parvus Arbor.

A large banner, identical to the smaller ones found throughout the city, hung above the entrance to the building. The branches that formed the walls had died and faded to gray many years ago. Cracks spread throughout the tree trunk, making the floor far too dangerous to walk on. Thatch drooped inward toward a massive hole in the roof, a result of the ravages of time. This was the original home of Nakaan, the founder of Parvus Arbor, and the first elf in known history with the rare ability to manipulate plant life.

Jocia and Galain came walking up the pathway. "Well met, Elendor, well met, Vaylon," Galain greeted. He stood at average height for a male of the elven race, with dark hair styled in the same customary fashion as Elendor. His blue eyes resembled the color of a cloudless midday sky, and his thin lips and nose, along with his long pointed ears, identified his pure elven heritage. His clothing looked identical to the style that both Elendor and Vaylon wore with one exception: the sigil emblazoned across the chest of his tunic identified his status as an elf born within the accepted standards of his race.

"Well met, Elendor, well met, Vaylon" repeated

Jocia. Elendor's heart raced upon hearing Jocia's voice. Her scarlet hair flowed past her shoulders and her translucent green eyes shined like imperial jade. Her beauty matched that of any elf with ivory skin and petite features, but to Elendor, she was the personification of grace and elegance. She wore a long-sleeve dress that hung to her knees with the silver tree sigil embroidered across the front. Leggings and hiking boots signaled her intentions for a long journey along with a leaf-hewn pack strapped to her back that bulged with food and water for the hike.

"I cannot believe you were the first to arrive," Galain teased. "We purposefully gave pause before traveling."

"We expected it would take longer for Vaylon to convince you to leave your room," Jocia smiled. "Before we begin our journey, I would make a short detour." With the expectation that her friends would follow, she turned to walk down the path.

Before long, they arrived at her intended destination, The Reverence Garden. Elendor knew the garden as Jocia's favorite area within the city. It spread far, wide, high, and low within the treetops. Every flower known to exist grew in Reverence Garden. The flowers that required more sunlight thrived high up in the treetops, while the flowers that needed more shade gathered scattered sunlight from beneath the branches. Some flowers grew broad enough for an elf to rest upon its center, while others bloomed barely visible, even to elven eyes. Every color of the rainbow existed within Reverence Garden, giving off a splendor unfound anywhere within the kingdom, a fact that the elves promoted with pride.

Scattered throughout the garden, wooden statues of elves from the past who contributed to the legacy of the elven race stood in reverence to their accomplishments. Euroch the Storm, Landria of the Forgotten Isles, the elegant Faimar of the Woodland tribe and many others, some of whom had names forgotten by the long history of Parvus Arbor. At the center stood a colossal statue of Nakaan, surrounded by a fountain filled with beautiful fish whose scales sparkled like diamonds in colors of bright red, yellow, blue and gold.

"Can you do it, Elendor?" Jocia asked, knowing he understood the basis of her request.

"I really should not Jocia, it is not good for them, and if someone sees, I shall receive punishment for certain."

"Please, Elendor? Please grant me this request." Jocia insisted, batting her eyes and making his heart melt.

Annoyed at how easily his friends could goad him into forbidden exploits, Elendor groaned beneath his breath. Closing his eyes, he extended his one fully developed arm and traced a runic symbol in the air with his finger. A faint rust-colored glow emerged from beneath his tunic, and within the blink of an eye, every flower within the garden opened in full bloom.

The multitude of flowers blanketed the area in sweet perfumes. The four friends closed their eyes and inhaled the assortment of scents. Opening their eyes, they soaked in the enchanting beauty of the garden dazzling in a spectrum of colors that demonstrated nature's glory.

"What are you doing?" An angry shout came from the garden. The friends did not need to look to know who called. The familiar voice harassed them many times in the past and seemed present at every transgression the young elves committed, no matter the severity. The elf marched toward them with a rageful expression. "You have been told how many times? The bloom of the flowers is not to be manipulated!" The berating elf, far older than the group of friends, poked his finger in the air as he spoke with authority. His silver hair, pulled back to reveal a wrinkle-free face, served as the only identifier of his advanced age. One of the oldest and most respected members of the Parvus Arbor council, Morace's hard stance on elven customs and traditions ran afoul with the group's adolescent curiosity for as long as any of them could remember.

"Pardons, Morace!" Jocia stepped in front of the elder to block his path. "Elendor was attempting to teach me arbormancy so that he is not the only one in the city with the ability."

"Child," Morace replied as his voice and tone shifted from annoyance to kind. "The ability is rare, and if you have not developed the skill by now, the chances are slim that you will get it at all."

"Perhaps, but attempting to attain the skill should not be neglected. The future is uncertain, and we are the Miracle Three." Jocia responded with every bit of sweetness that she could muster to remain in Morace's good graces.

The Miracle Three referred to three elves being born within the same year. An unheard of occurrence as elven children are sparse, and gestation can range anywhere between one to five years. Hearing the title spoken, Vaylon shifted uncomfortably, looking away in shame. He knew most elves considered his birth anything but a miracle.

"Yes child, The Miracle... Three." Morace shot a

look of disdain at Elendor upon speaking the final word. "Keep trying young one, perhaps you shall acquire the skill, and we can finally have an elf worthy of the power in Parvus Arbor once again."

Elendor wanted to give Morace a venomous response when a voice bellowed from behind. "Well met everyone! The smell of blooming flowers in Reverence Garden is unmistakable. The aroma reached me all the way to the west end!"

"Heece!" Galain exclaimed.

Vaylon turned to the direction Heece's voice came from, allowing Elendor to see as well. Heece stood tall compared to the average elf. His muscular build defied the timid, elegant repute of the elves. Darker than the blackest night sky, his long black hair looked all the more prominent compared to the bright silver of his elven armor. Polished to perfection, his breastplate, chainmail, gauntlets, and greaves, protected him from the glancing blows of battle, yet allowed no hindrance to the superior mobility of his heritage. The bowstring draped across his chest revealed the elegantly crafted wood of his favorite weapon, and a quiver holding dozens of feathered arrows hung from his belt. A sheathed sword with intricate designs etched into the handle hung on the opposite side, demonstrating his proficiency in both far and close combat. Considered the most respected warrior in Parvus Arbor, his sword and archery skills were known throughout the kingdom. Although many admired the high commander of the Parvus Arbor Guard, no one idolized him as much as his protégé, Galain.

"Morace, well met!" Heece declared as he walked up to him.

"Well met, Heece. I was about to tell…"

"I have been looking for you!" Heece interrupted. "The situation with the griffons has grown dire on the west end again. I would like to acquire your expertise if I may."

"Why yes, of course!" The old elf responded with giddiness in his voice. Morace, the retired Beastmaster of the village, took pleasure in harassing the current Beastmaster even more than he enjoyed berating Elendor. A fact Heece likely knew.

Putting his arm around Morace, Heece began chatting in his ear. Looking back to the group, Heece nodded his head to the side in a silent message for the young friends to escape while the opportunity presented itself. The team took the hint and swiftly departed. Jocia silently mouthed "thank you" over her shoulder as Elendor released his magical spell, returning the flowers to their natural state.

The group walked for nearly an hour before arriving at the south edge of the city. Dangerously close to the Nigereous Forest, or the Exiled Forest as it was more commonly known, the southern section of the city received very few visitors. The elves of Parvus Arbor avoided this area, allowing the young travelers to proceed on their forbidden journey without hindrance. Arriving at the edge of the branch, Elendor traced a runic symbol with his finger, manipulating the limb to lower the group to the ground. They walked further south in silence, staring at Nigereous Forest as it cast a looming shadow upon them.

The trees of The Exiled Forrest grew taller and broader than those of Parvus Arbor. Veins of a black oozing substance crept up the ash-colored trunks like a hundred black snakes, desperately slithering toward the sun. In most places, the roots and trunks of the trees raised from the ground close enough to one another that barely an arm could fit in-between, let alone an entire body. The barren branches resembled gnarled, arthritic fingers that threatened to grab anyone who dared to approach. No scent emitted from the forest, and although it appeared as if all of the trees died long ago, Elendor could feel the life burning within each one

44

through his arbormancy skill.

Beyond the trees, darkness that elven eyes could not pierce denied even a single ray of light to peak through the threatening veil. The local lore believed a curse was laid upon the land thousands of years ago, causing the dark shadow of mystery.

A source of curiosity, Elendor inquired many times to his brethren about the forest. As an arbormancer, scary-looking trees posed no threat to him and only further fueled his interest. He asked every elf that would listen about the Exiled Forest, but the same replies of "stay away from that place" or "that place is best left forgotten" came as an answer. Only Elder Jalaana, the oldest living elf in Parvus Arbor, offered Elendor more. She told him that nearly a thousand years ago, during her youth, a young elf dared to enter the Exiled Forest. No one saw the brave elf again.

Elendor believed the eerie stories passed down through the generations to be baseless nonsense. A tool used to keep young elves like himself away. For him only superstitious fools would fall for such folly. Still, being this close to the forest made Elendor uneasy, as if someone closely watched him through the trees.

The sounds of rushing water perked the group's ears.

"I hear it!" exclaimed Galain. The young elf began to rush toward the roar. Vaylon and Jocia excitedly joined in the pursuit. The rapid motion of Vaylon's stride made Elendor bounce up and down, his thighs rubbing harshly against the harness with each springing step.

"Vaylon stop! You're hurting me!" Elendor cried.

With Vaylon slowing his pace, Galain and Jocia disappeared down the embankment, making Elendor's heart jump into his throat with worry for their safety. By the time Vaylon caught up with their friends, they saw the two standing in awe at the shoreline of a small lake.

Surrounded on two sides by the trees of the Nigereous Forest, the lake's open northern bank allowed any spectator to absorb its beauty. To the south, a waterfall emptied into the lake from a cliff in the distance. The sun reflected upon the rippling waters like a thousand gems bobbing at the surface. A variety of birds inhabited the area, each shimmering with varying shades of green, yellow, pink and blue. The avian song chirping from the birds flowed in symphonic harmony, more melodious than the combined efforts of any wind or string instrument.

Some of the birds belonged to species previously unseen by the group of friends. One bird gently bobbed up and down along with the rhythm of the ripples and garnered attention in its magnificent splendor. Its bright blue feathers faded into metallic green at the tips. Three long tail feathers that formed into a diamond shape at the tips fanned across the water. The feathers on the back of its head spiked out as if purposely formed a hairdo. Its long, thin beak gleamed in a magnificent yellow.

The friends stood in admiration of the view. The sparkling deep blue waters and the majestic birds in an array of colors entranced them in a splendor of calm, tranquil beauty.

"Vaylon, put me down at the shoreline if you would."

Carefully placed on the bank, Elendor began to remove himself from his harness. Jocia and Galain joined Vaylon in turning away to offer privacy from the awkward sight of the handicapped elf struggling to remove himself from his confines. He knew his friends intended to be polite by not looking, yet their avoidance left him feeling all the more uncomfortable. Once freed, Elendor rolled over to prop himself up on his half-arm. Dipping his hand into the lake, he formed a cup and brought the cool water to his mouth for a sip.

"How?" Jocia finally spoke.

Elendor looked at her, puzzled by her question. "Waterfalls empty into rivers, not lakes. How does the lake not overflow?"

During his last visit, Elendor pondered the same question and concluded, "I believe the lake empties into an underground river."

"I see!" Jocia exclaimed with wonderment. Elendor stared at the only thing he found more beautiful than the Hidden Falls, Jocia. He wished he could tell her how he felt. In the past, he tried to express his feelings but the reality of being a disabled elf kept him from revealing the truth. Even if he could tell her, even if she felt the same, he could never allow her to share in the shame of being an outcast.

"Where is Vaylon?" Galain asked.

The friends looked in every direction, flustered in a panic over their absent friend, but the mystery did not take long to solve. Further down the embankment, they spotted him slowly marching toward Nigereous Forest, his arms stiffly hanging at his sides.

# Dorian

Peeking out of the forge, Dorian saw a tall, slender man standing near the front door of the cottage. The man stood roughly six stones in height, a full head taller than Dorian, with a mop of curly blonde hair. His round ears identified him as human, even though his appearance resembled the pictures of the elves in Dorian's books. Mud covered his worn boots, and his loose, disheveled clothing indicated he did not belong to the king's guard. A green knapsack hung low over one shoulder due to the weight of its mysterious contents. Turning to face the forge, the man's face came into view. Dorian ducked to hide behind the forge wall, covering his mouth with both hands to prevent a yelp from escaping his lips. Bumping into a pair of tongs hanging from a hook, the tool crashed onto the floor with a ring that alerted the stranger to Dorian's presence.

"Hello?" Dorian heard the man say. The scuffing of

footsteps drew closer, a sound nearly drowned out by the heavy thumps of Dorian's heart in his ears. Biting his lip, he gathered his courage and burst out from the doorway, ready to face the imminent danger.

The suddenness of Dorian's actions startled the man as he entangled his feet and dropped onto the dirt with a thud. The stranger ran his hand through his hair and began to laugh a rather high-pitched chuckle for a man. A far departure from the accustomed baritone laughs his father guttered.

"By the gods, you scared me there! It's fortunate that my bladder was already empty!" His dark, thick eyebrows looked silly compared to his blonde hair. His brown eyes glittered with warmth and his smile consumed his face.

All his father's warnings flooded Dorian's mind, allowing fear to clutch his heart tighter than the white-knuckled grip he held with his sword. Resolving to keep his words steady to hide the terror, he gathered himself to address the man, aiming the tip of his sword toward him in a threatening posture. "Who are you? What brings you into the woods this late at night?"

"Whoa, whoa, I'm sorry, my name is Nathaniel, and I am just a little lo…" The man stared at Dorian. "Oh, you're a mul!"

"Don't call me that! I am a half-dwarf!"

Dorian furrowed his hairless brow. Hearing mul, the derogatory term-utilized to shame those of half-dwarven blood, allowed anger to mix with the trepidation coursing through his body.

"I'm sorry, I didn't mean to offend. I was just surprised. I have never met a mu...half-dwarf before."

"You still haven't answered my questions," Dorian demanded in a stern voice that took even him by surprise.

"My name is Nathaniel Liber. I was supposed to meet some friends in an old cabin in these woods, but I must have followed the directions wrong and got lost."

Dorian thought about the young man's response. He knew the cabin. In his youth, he played there countless times, but the decrepit shack laid over an hour-long walk away. With the sun rapidly giving way to the night, no amount of haste would let the man arrive there before the shade of night blanketed the land.

The sun permitted a safe existence in the woods of Dorian's home, but when the sun dipped below the horizon, safety gave way to danger. Umbra beasts, the nocturnal creatures that craved the taste of flesh, roamed the woods at night seeking unwitting prey. Light reflecting from the cottage, the forge, and the lit torches around the perimeter kept him safe, as the umbra beasts despised the light. He knew directing the man to his friends, meant sending him to his death.

"Do you know the cabin I am talking about and how to get there?"

"I do, but you can't go there now."

"Why not?"

"These woods are crawling with umbra beasts. If you try to go there now, you will die."

"Does that mean my friends are in danger?"

"If they stay inside and keep a fire going, they should be fine. The umbra beasts don't like the light."

"I'll have to take the risk. Please tell me how to get to them. I fear for their safety and must warn them."

Dorian considered giving Nathaniel the directions. He knew that if this young man were to venture into the woods at night, he would never make it to his friends alive, eliminating the only witness to Dorian's existence. He dwelled on the lessons his father taught about the wickedness of man, and the hatred all men bore for those of half-blooded ancestry. Intending on providing him the information he desired, Dorian's mouth snapped shut.

The tales in his favorite books came rushing into his mind like a tidal wave of guilt and shame. The stories told of chivalrous knights and heroes who always did the right thing, even to the detriment of their want and desires. As a child, Dorian idolized these heroes. The guilt of considering sending this innocent man to his death weighed on his soul.

"Sorry, you won't make it. You are going to have to stay here tonight." Dorian could not believe those words escaped from his mouth.

"But what about my friends?"

"Do any of them travel outside the city?"

"Yes, my friend Lukas lives near the edge of the city and ventures into these woods often. He's the one who found the old cabin."

"Then he is well aware of the umbra beasts, trust me, everyone, who travels these woods knows. He must be planning to spend the night in the cabin if he told you to meet him there so late."

Nathaniel paused in relief. The look turned to astonishment as he glanced at Dorian's sword. "Your sword! It has two runestones!"

Dorian felt a rush of embarrassment. The runestones,

the source of all magic and technology, granted weapons unique qualities. He read many stories of brave warriors using the power of the runestones. Garrett the Bold died during the Battle of the Rivers, but not before slaughtering a horde of orcs with his sword imbued with a fire runestone named *Dusk*. Warren of the Heartwoods single-handedly halted the Marshal's Rebellion in the Prasillo Province with his spear imbued with a wind runestone named *Doombringer*. His favorite hero of all, the dwarven warrior named Torbin the Wise, halted the advance of a thousand gnolls at the Hygard Summit with his earth runestone imbued ax named *Shatter*, which still adorns the wall of the great hall of Durrum.

These heroes all used the power of the runestones, but none used the power of two in unison. Dorian's father was adamant that imposing two runestones into a weapon was foolish and forbade him from the attempt. *The runestones represent the power of the Gods; they would never allow the union of their forces. Attempting such a thing is an affront to the Gods themselves, an insult that the Gods would not soon forgive.*

"That is amazing! Is one of those a darkness runestone?" Nathaniel approached to get a closer look.

Dorian took a step backward, raising the tip of the sword to separate him from Nathaniel, his eyes flashing the warning to go no further.

"Please, calm down. You have nothing to worry about with me." Nathaniel untied the drawstring at the top of his shirt. Pulling the shirt down, he revealed a green stone inlaid in the center of his chest.

Shocked at the revelation, Dorian lowered his sword. "A wind runestone? You're a mage! Only those of noble birth and soldiers enlisted in the king's guard hold the authority to utilize the runestones as mages."

"No, no, I am not a noble, nor am I a member of the king's guard. I illegally study magic, despite the consequences of doing so. I wouldn't normally tell someone I just met, but I don't think I have to worry about you turning me in with a sword like that."

Dorian felt unsure if Nathaniel's charisma or his own loneliness led to offering this young man a safe place to stay for the night, but whether or not his father would approve, he did not question. Regardless, a glimmer of happiness emerged through the doubt and fear at the thought of relieving his isolation.

"Let's go inside," Nathaniel suggested. "I'll answer

all your questions in there. I don't know about you, but I could use an escape from this cold!"

The two talked late into the night. Dorian told him all about his occupation as a weaponsmith with his father, and that Nathaniel was the first person he ever met. They talked about how his mother died during childbirth and all the stories about her that his father told him. Dorian's sword, a constant topic of conversation, seemed to peak Nathaniel's interest. For years, Dorian explained, he attempted to create a weapon that utilized two runestones, but much to his disappointment, activating the dual stones escaped his comprehension.

Nathaniel informed Dorian that he and his parents managed the royal library and that he marked the sixth generation to do so. He and his three friends practiced magic using the books snuck out from the royal library. Born without the advantage of noble blood, the friends learned the secrets of the runestones in defiance of the law. They taught themselves in an underground tunnel that once served as a draining system from the upper portion of the city. A narrow escape with a member of the king's guard almost finished their education, so they decided to find a new place to study.

Nathaniel pulled the books from his knapsack to

show Dorian. A musty odor emanated from each one, and old age deteriorated the frail bindings to the point that made Dorian believe they would soon turn to dust. The pages turned yellow long ago and the writing, written in a dialect not used in centuries, made for a difficult read. Ancient symbols appeared on the pages that Dorian recognized from the runestones around his home, like the symbol for flame on the fire table he used to cook his food, or the symbol for rain on the rain bath he used to shower.

Nathaniel enjoyed talking and rambled for hours about many things already known to Dorian. He spoke on how runestones, when imposed on weapons, give a warrior an advantage, allowing the bearer to cast low-level spells that could turn the tide of battle in an instant. He also explained how a mage imposes a runestone on their skin, allowing them to cast the highest level of spells.

Dorian could not remember a time filled with such enjoyment. Telling and listening to exciting stories. Laughing and enjoying time spent with another person besides his father. For the first time in his life, Dorian finally made a friend.

The next morning Dorian rose with the sun. He knew Nathaniel needed to find his friends. They would not be surprised he got lost, as this was the first time he left the city. They likely feared for his safety after his failure to show the previous night.

Dorian went to the icebox, powered by a water runestone, and removed some dried meats, celery, and carrots. The perfect meal for a traveler, or at least that is what his father told him. He woke his new friend and handed him a sack filled with the food. Dorian told Nathaniel how to get to the cabin and gave him some landmarks to help guide his way.

"Thank you for everything! I doubt I would still be alive if it were not for you! Why don't you come with me? I'm sure my friends would love to meet you! Plus, that way I won't get lost again."

"I can't. I have work to do, and my father will know if I slack on my chores. But he will be gone for at least a fortnight, so you can come back if you'd like."

"Okay, if I can, I'll come back tonight," Nathaniel reached out for a handshake.

# Brett

After the few hours of sleep that Brett could muster, he woke to the guards sliding trays of food into the cell. He assumed morning came, although he couldn't be sure due to his windowless accommodations. He darted to grab one of the trays, an urgent necessity he learned the night before. The guards slid one meal for every prisoner into the cell, and if an inmate was not quick enough, another prisoner would take two for his indulgence.

Brett grabbed a tray and went back to his corner. He consumed his slop of ground meat, peas, carrots, gravy of unknown origin, a slice of bread, and a cup of rust-colored water. After pulling the mold off the bread, he scooped up the food with it, and choked down the entire meal, only pausing to spit out the bits of bone within. He drank the water while pinching his nose to cover up the sulfur smell and spent the next two hours fighting to keep his meal down.

Brett heard his name called by the guard. "On your

feet, Shaw!"

Brett's expression fell blank. He enjoyed a good bar fight as much as the next scoundrel, but at his core, he was a thief, not a murderer. He felt his face getting hot. His nerves shook his hands and weakened his knees.

The guards opened the cell. "Get moving." They shoved him down the hall toward the large, impending double doors. Four guards escorted him, one on each side and two more walking behind with their spears brandished just in case he foolishly decided to turn and run.

When they arrived at the double doors, Brett noticed they were abnormally large, tall enough to fit Dak through with Brett standing on his head, and wide enough for a set of horse and carriages to enter side-by-side. The massive doors operated using a counterbalance pulley system to eliminate the need of an entire team of men to open and close them.

In a monotone voice, the same overweight guard from the night before instructed Brett on the rules of the arena. "When you enter the arena, you will see a white X on the ground. Step on the X and remain there until you hear the blast of the battle horn. Once you hear the blast, you may retrieve any weapon within the arena. You are hereby ordered to fight with your opponent to the death. If you win your battle, you are to immediately drop your weapons and wait for the guards to retrieve you. There are archers posted along the perimeter of the arena. If you do not drop your weapons, you will be shot. If you fight with the guards, you will be shot. If you attempt to escape or try to harm the crowd in any way, you will be shot. Do you understand?"

Brett tried to tell the guard where he could stick his rules, but could only utter a nod in agreeance.

"May the Gods have mercy and bestow victory upon you." The guard said in a voice that told Brett he meant none of those words.

Brett saw the arena for the first time. The circular shaped stone walls rose to double the height of the doors from which he emerged. Weapons hung on the arena walls of varying size, shape, and style. Loose, dry dirt served as flooring, and the white chalk X laid ten paces before him. The vast fighting area spanned wide enough to hold half the kingdom's populace, and the surrounding seats above the wall climbed toward the sky.

The deafening cheers of the blood-thirsty spectators drowned out Brett's nervous heavy breathing. At the top of the seating area, a velvet rope outlined a canopy-covered section with elegant accommodations. Ten empty chairs spanned the private observation deck with the center three trimmed in gold. Brett immediately recognized the reserved seating belonged to the king, queen, prince, and the representatives of the seven noble houses.

"I told you to move to the X!" The guard shouted, making a rapid shooing gesture with his hands. Brett took a couple of strides and assumed his position.

The doors across from him creaked open. A man sprinted from the gate, wildly screaming and cheering along with the crowd, causing veins to bulge from his neck. His unevenly cut hair grew long in random patches across his head and swung wildly as he twisted and turned. Wearing only pants and boots, the man's scars were displayed across his well-fit body of youth. He walked with confidence to his X, looked at Brett, then dragged the thumb of his clenched fist across his throat to announce his intention to Brett and the jubilant spectators.

Realizing the disadvantage of wearing a shirt for an opponent to grab onto, Brett removed his shirt and threw it to the ground revealing his own muscled and stout stature.

The crowd silenced as the nobles entered. Brett glanced at his opponent and saw him staring in the king's direction. He stood with his feet together and arms held firmly at his side. Assuming this was customary, Brett mimicked the man's stance to address the king.

The nobles lined up in front of their respective seats, and once the king sat, the rest followed suit. Bodies occupied each of the three seats, save three. Brett never cared much for following the politics of the noble houses, but everyone within the kingdom knew the status of the hierarchy. The empty seat to the king's right belonged to the queen who passed away some fifteen years ago. To his left, the unoccupied chair belonged to the prince, who currently traveled the kingdom to learn about the provinces he would one day rule. The final empty seat belonged to one of the noble houses, but Brett did not know which one, nor did he care.

The presence of the king demanded his attention. Brett never bothered attending any of the royal announcements, and therefore never laid eyes upon him before this moment. A gold crown adorned his head and his exquisite clothing sparkled in the midday sun. Gold and jewels wrapped around his fingers and neck in varying degrees of luster and color, each worth more than the common man's wildest dreams.

King Thomas raised his hand with his palm facing

the crowd. From the corner of his eye, Brett noticed his opponent's attention shifted from the king to Brett as he bounced on the balls of his feet with an intense look upon his face in anticipation of the upcoming battle. As soon as the king dropped his raised hand, a loud blast of a horn echoed within the arena walls.

The rowdy man dashed to the wall to retrieve a weapon. Peril rang like an alarm bell in Brett's head. Quickly scanning the walls for the closest armament, he dashed to retrieve a weapon to defend himself.

With a rusted short sword and splintered shield in front of him, Brett grabbed the shield. Before he could snatch the sword, the rapid pounding footsteps of his enemy forewarned of his rival's approach. Turning, while raising the shield, he peered over the edge to see the precarious situation. His opponent, now wielding a flail and shield, leaped into the air, bringing his weapon down to split Brett's skull.

Brett quickly knelt, bracing the shield to block the incoming attack. The impact jolted his arm as a spike penetrated the shield, raining splinters of wood across his face. Struggling to break his weapon free, the man violently yanked the handle, jerking Brett forward with each pull. In response, Brett swung his arm wide, ripping the weapon from the man's hand. For a moment, Brett felt proud of his quick thinking to relieve his opponent of the instrument of his demise. Raising the corners of his mouth, the fighter quickly wiped the cocky smile from Brett's face by ramming the shield into his nose. The dizzying blow dropped Brett to his hands and knees, forcing him to fight the urge to vomit as blood trickled down the back of his throat.

Tears filled his eyes, blurring his vision as the ground spun, reminding Brett of his many drunken nights in the local tavern. Droplets of blood fell from his nose and mouth, instantly soaking into the dirt that absorbed countless gallons of blood from centuries of battles. Using his tongue, he checked to make sure his teeth remained in place.

Brett wiped his eyes to clear away the tears. Turning to locate his opponent, he saw the man retrieve the rusty sword he intended to grab at the start of the match. The man released a primal scream as he raised the blade overhead, telegraphing his intention to split Brett into two halves. With no means of defense, Brett ducked and rolled away from his pursuer's overhand strike.

Shooting to his feet, Brett began to run in the direction of the nearest weapon. The pounding vibrations of his opponent's pursuit felt like miniature quakes, reverberating in his bones like tremors of fear. He began to run toward a mounted ax, but quickly changed direction when the glint of a familiar weapon gleamed further down the circular arena wall. A strap containing four throwing knives instilled a wave of confidence with the remembrance of the many knife-throwing contests he won in the past.

Grabbing the strap from the wall, Brett spun away, barely avoiding another vertical strike from his opponent. The clang of metal striking stone rang in another failed attempt to end his life.

Brett drew a knife, cocked back his arm and released the dagger with full force. Anticipating the throw, the foe raised and ducked behind his shield to protect his head, but Brett's target remained unhindered. The knife sunk deep into the man's thigh, allowing a cascade of blood to pour down his leg as he howled in pain. Brett reached for another dagger to end the fatal contest, but before he could reach it, the man yanked the knife from his leg and tossed it aside as his face twisted into a rage.

The wounded warrior began his pursuit once more, ignoring the gushing injury. Brett, startled by the ineffective attack, threw another of his knives, but in his panicked state, haphazardly released the dagger, missing his target by a wide margin. With his opponent bearing down upon him, Brett turned to run in an attempt to put distance between them, but his effort proved too slow.

Brett's adversary leaped onto his back, wrapping the sword around his head to slice his throat. Dropping the knife and leather strap, Brett grabbed the blade of the incoming sword with both hands, halting its deadly progress a finger's width from his neck. Deep wounds opened on Brett's hands, leaking streams of blood down his forearms to form crimson pools in the dirt. Brett screamed as searing pain ran from his hands and into his arms. Swinging his other arm around Brett's head, the man grabbed the blade of the sword and drove his knee into Brett's back. The dull blade of the rust-covered sword sliced through skin, leaving the bones in Brett's hands as the only shield from certain death. In a desperate counter move, Brett snapped his head backward with as much might as he could muster, striking the fighter's face hard with the back of his head.

Brett's opponent dropped his blade to plug the fountain of blood spurting from his now broken nose. Brett broke free and fell to the ground and rolled to gain distance between him and his adversary. With a fluid motion, Brett reached for the leather strap on the ground, which still held one knife and popped up in preparation to continue the death match.

Brett's enemy, with a blood smeared face, relaxed into a smile, bearing his bloody teeth. His shoulders shook with a laugh as he casually bent over and retrieved his sword. Brett blindly reached to pull the last knife from the strap only to discover the reason for the man's laughter. Brett grabbed the shirt he discarded earlier instead of the knife strap.

Dread filled Brett's entire being as the fighter twirled his sword and darted at him. The angry man swung his sword in a horizontal strike, but Brett ducked beneath the swing. As Brett stood, he pivoted. Bringing his shirt up, he wrapped it around his foe's throat and twisted it on the back of his neck, strangling him. The man dropped his sword and struggled, trying to get his fingers beneath the shirt, but the cloth was wrapped too tightly around his throat. Shifting his position, Brett stood off-center so that the choking man could not duplicate the head-butt move he had previously used. Not seeing where Brett stood, the imprisoned warrior thrashed his head in a desperate attempt to break free. The momentum of his failed attempt landed him on his back.

Brett stepped over the fallen brawler and grabbed the
dropped sword.

The man wiped blinding tears from his eyes. He
raised his hands in a futile attempt to block, but he couldn't
prevent Brett from plummeting the sword toward his
abdomen. The man released a terrified scream as Brett thrust
the sword down with all his remaining strength and plunged
it deep into the man's chest.

Brett heard a gurgling sound as his opponent's lungs
filled with blood. The dying man let out two short coughs,
spewing blood from his mouth like a fountain before his
body fell limp. Brett remained kneeling and closed his eyes.
His body ached in places he didn't know could ache as he
inhaled deep breaths to calm his excited nerves. Slowly, the
roar of the crowd returned to him, allowing him to realize he
had been deaf to their cheers since the battle began.

Brett opened his eyes to see the lifeless body of his
opponent before him. The glazed, unseeing eyes of the dead
man stared blankly into the sky. His mouth hung open in a
soundless scream as small trails of blood leaked from the
corners. Exhausted, Brett fell onto his side and then to his
back. Looking over at the man with the sword still planted
firmly in his chest, the name Max escaped his lips with the

sudden recollection of his opponent's name.

Hands grabbed Brett's arms and began dragging him until they propped his limp body against a stone wall. He struggled to keep his fluttering eyelids open as a man dressed in a long robe and turban came into view. Grabbing Brett's chin, he turned his head from left to right then yanked each of Brett's hands looking at them closely. The man disappeared from Brett's vision, and he heard a voice say, "Those hands are going to need stitches."

Brett felt hands on his arms again as they pulled him to his feet. Poked and shoved like a beast being provoked into a cage, the guards forced him into the tunnel from which he had arrived. His awareness began to return as he passed the cell where he slept the night before. He heard the raucous cheers of his fellow inmates, but their words were lost on him.

A guard shoved him inside a room through a door painted with a red cross. Brett looked around at his new surroundings. Locked cabinets lined the walls, and a padded table stood in the center of the room with splatters of dried blood strewn across it. The same man who examined him in the arena entered with two more guards in tow. "Get on the table and lie down," the man sternly demanded.

Brett, who despised being given orders, thought to disobey, but the fleeting idea vanished when the guards placed their hands on the handles of their swords. Two guards strapped down his legs, arms, and head, limiting his movement like a baited worm on a hook. Brett heard the jangling sounds of keys, chiming their one-note song on a key ring, followed by the clicking sounds of unlocking locks, which were like the sounds of music to a thief's ear. The man stood over him, crushing and stirring a mixture of unknown substances in a mortar and pestle. "This may sting a bit."

He felt a cold, damp-feeling gel being slathered across his hands. To say the concoction would "sting a bit," proved to be a gross exaggeration. The cool sensation of the substance quickly turned to agony, as though someone placed hot lava on his palms. Brett screamed at the top of his lungs. The pain from the initial cuts paled in comparison to the torture of this unknown material placed on his hands. Writhing against his restraints, he buckled and arched his back as a needle repeatedly stabbed at the wounds.

With the procedure completed, the man bandaged his hands and unstrapped Brett from the table. Instructed to sit up, Brett rose and stared at the bandages. He expected that some of the dexterity in his hands would never return. Dwelling on the importance of the full use of hands for a professional thief, he wondered if he would still have skills to steal if he somehow discovered a way to escape this hell. Brett desired gold and riches as much as anyone in his profession, but performing acts of thievery were never about the attainment of wealth. To him, the thrill, the adrenaline rush of doing an illegal act, the euphoric sensation of successful plunder, gave more satisfaction than any bag of loot. The awareness that he may never steal again weighed greater than a death sentence.

When led back to his cell, the escorts stopped Brett mid-journey. Twelve guards stood in the hall facing Razuul's cell. One of the guards unlocked his cell, pushed the door open, and quickly jumped back, brandishing his spear in terrified defense. Razuul emerged from his cell. The guards backed down the hallway in both directions, making sure to give the wild elf a wide berth. Six guards approached the double doors while the other six backed up toward Brett, never taking their eyes off Razuul.

Guards posted at the end of the hall opened the doors and escorted Razuul to the X in the arena. With the prisoner in position, the guards sprinted back through the doorway and slammed the doors behind them.

Brett returned to his cell, went to the corner, put his back against the wall and slid to the floor. Exhaustion settled across his body. The match and the excruciating pain that followed left him drained. He barely noticed the return of the foul stench as he scanned the occupants of his cell. The population decreased in his absence. Most notably, the ugly man, Skank, was missing. Another victim of this inhumane arena. Bringing his knees to his chest, he folded his arms atop and rested his head against the wall.

Dak greeted Brett, "You survived, mate!"

Before Brett could reply, the sounds of armored men echoed in the hall. A procession of guards escorted an unscathed Razuul back to his cell.

"Forty–nine," Dak claimed.

Brett's jaw dropped in amazement. In the time it took for him to walk into his cell and sit on the floor, Razuul vanquished his opponent.

"What kind of monster is he?"

# Clarissa

The light pouring in through stained glass windows cast a rainbow of colors on Clarissa as she sat at the head of the table. With alluring, delicate features and wavy, golden blonde hair, her visage stood as the paragon of youth and beauty. A thin tiara adorned her head that resembled interwoven golden vines, encircling a light runestone imposed in the middle of her forehead. Her sleeveless white robe, with intricately woven lace, demonstrated her access to the finest tailors, and the golden rope tied at her waist proved the vast wealth of her heritage. Her smooth ivory skin lacked a single blemish and her nails were polished to perfection. Picking up scroll after scroll laid out in front of her, she unfurled each one to read its contents.

Six chairs surrounded the table. In each chair, a person wearing gray, long-sleeved robes sat rummaging through the scrolls to study their contents.

"Your Holiness," said the man seated to her right,

speaking above the rolling and unrolling of parchment. "A decision must be made." The young man's tall and slender profile was evident even through his sitting position. His drawn cheeks and thin jaw gave him as much of a feminine appearance as his slicked-back blonde hair styled with precision. The gold pendant pinned to his chest took the shape of the sun and signified his unique position within the council.

"I realize this dear brother, but unfortunately, we must be thorough." She replied with an annoyance in her voice.

Clarissa wanted to scream. The sudden requirement for her to perform her duties ruined her plans for the afternoon. She had prepared to spend time riding horses with the stable master. It pleased her to spend time with him, and while she could never marry a lowborn, she could enjoy his well-muscled body, chiseled features, and witty charm.

For hours, she poured through the scrolls until her frustration reached its limit. "I've seen enough. Marshal Bartram is guilty!"

Rising to her feet, the man seated to her left raised his hand. "Your Holiness, I must advise against this course of action." The hunched man spoke with a withered voice.

"Lord Bentley Harken has denied the claim!"

"There are thirty accounts here that prove otherwise!" Clarissa stated, gesturing toward the scrolls in front of her.

"My lady, I…"

"Enough!" Clarissa interrupted the old man with a shout, grabbing the attention of everyone at the table. Realizing that her outburst betrayed her regal persona, she continued in a harsh whisper. "I am the High Priestess. The representative of the Holy Mother Matera. My judgments are both divine and absolute. Do not question me further, uncle."

The old man silently gazed at the scrolls on the table.

"Let us proceed." Clarissa gracefully walked to the ornately carved door and knocked three times.

Even through the thick oak door, she heard a man's voice announcing. "All rise in the presence of Her Holiness!"

The door swung open and she stepped into the large room. The white walls shimmered in the light pouring through the arched windows. The ceiling, supported by decorative white columns trimmed in gold, prominently displayed golden sun symbols in the center.

On either side of the door, two men wore white full-plate armor decorated in gold. Helmets hid the men's faces, leaving only a slit for them to see through. Oversized white shields, with the sun symbol at the center, were strapped to their arms, and a sword rested in a scabbard on their hip.

To her left, a stately white chair with an identical sun symbol carved at the top awaited her presence. A massive sun banner hung motionless on the wall behind it. In front of the chair stood a long ornate table bearing a gold sun embossed in the center.

Beyond the table, two groups of plain white chairs, separated by an aisle covered by a red carpet, awaited to seat an audience. Men and women stood silently in front of every chair in the room, and each person stared impatiently at the young woman.

Standing in front of the oak table, a man bound in shackles waited. His tidy clothing matched his maintained brown hair and beard.

Escorted by the guards, Clarissa walked to her chair. Before sitting, one of the guards announced to the crowd, "High Priestess Clarissa Bright presiding." Clarissa took her seat, and everyone in attendance sat except for the man in shackles.

Clarissa's chair looked abnormally large when occupied by her delicate frame, leaving ample space between her well-postured back and the plush velvet cushion. Placing both palms on the table, she fixed her gaze at the man before her.

"Marshal William Bartram, who serves under Lord Bentley Harken, of the province of Prasillo, you have been accused of conspiring the murder and subsequent burning of properties of Marshal Charles Paisley. What have you to say?"

"Your Holiness, these accusations are both ridiculous and false. It is true that Marshal Paisley and I were at odds, but this is all conjecture. Thieves went to Marshal Paisley's home, murdered his family and burned his home to the ground. I had nothing to do with it."

"And what about the witnesses on the record that saw you conniving with men of lesser character?"

"Jealousy, Your Holiness! There are those who wish to see me removed so that they can take my title as marshal."

"Over thirty accounts of eyewitnesses are all lies? Even the men who were captured, and admitted to carrying out the act, have claimed that it was you who had bid them to kill Marshal Paisley. They are liars as well?"

"That is correct, Your Holiness. Lord Bentley Harken backs my claim of innocence."

The crowd broke into a murmur at the mention of Lord Harken. Clarissa cared little for the man nicknamed "The Sea Snake," Lord Bentley Harken. The mere mention of his name made her blood boil. During her years of training under the tutelage of the previous high priestess, her mother, Clarissa had watched Lord Harken scream and yell at her mother many times over trivial disputes. It angered her further that the mention of Lord Harken, backing the claim of Marshal Bentley, swayed the crowd to think Marshal Bentley would be deemed innocent. She thought it undermined the authority of the high priestess and Clarissa would not allow it.

"After reviewing all facts and accounts, I Clarissa Bright, High Priestess of The Holy Mother Matera and Lord of the city of Sanctum, find you, Marshal William Bartram, guilty of the murder of Marshal Charles Paisley. You are hereby sentenced to death, to be carried out at sunset of the morrow."

The crowd burst into an uproar at the verdict. Marshal Bartram's face fell pale. Falling to his knees, he began shouting his contentions to the verdict, but the crowd's roar drowned out his pleas. Clarissa raised a single hand to silence the crowd, but the attendees paid no attention. The commotion only ceased when a man sitting in the front row abruptly stood to his feet, knocking his chair to the floor.

Roughly six stones tall, the man who brought the room to silence glowered at the high priestess. With a furrowed brow and heaving chest, his eyes burned with fury as he stared daggers at the high priestess. Clarissa, seeing the house sigil of a fish imposed upon a pair of crossed spears embossed on his chest, instantly recognized the man known as The Sea Snake, Bentley Harken. She prepared herself for a verbal assault from him, but to her surprise, he remained silent as he stormed out of the courtroom, slamming the doors behind him. The presence of Lord Harken in the crowd escaped her notice until that moment, but she did not care that he heard her verdict. To the contrary, she felt a sense of satisfaction to defy the wishes and authority of the Lord of Prasillo. It took a great deal of control to prevent her lips from curling into a smile.

Two guards entered the room to escort Marshal Bartram to his cell while Clarissa returned the chambers of the high priestess. The raucous clamoring of the courtroom continued as she exited. Some of the attendees threw insults while others demanded her removal from the High

Priesthood, but Clarissa paid them no attention. As the doors shut behind her, she could hear objects thrown by the crowd deflecting off the shields of her guards and the chamber doors.

Clarissa sat at the head of the table and waited for her council to join her. Doubt began to creep into her mind as she gazed off into space, watching the dust dance in the rays of light shining through the stained glass. Part of her dwelled on the ramifications of executing a man who held the backing of a man with the political influence of The Sea Snake. Her mind lingered on his reactions and the influence he held on the other great houses. His reputation as a man of great pride and cunning intellect garnered great respect, and his propensity for quick temperament and self-confidence earned him an amount of fear from the other noble houses uncommon to a lord. His influence could easily affect her relationships with other lords of the province, but her willingness to stand up to the man of such renown would serve as a reminder of her own conviction. She resolved that her verdict was both right and just.

The committee entered and the six members sat in their chairs and looked to the high priestess.

"Your Holiness," the old man began, "you have

made your bold decision, but I must advise you…"

"Now, uncle," Clarissa's brother interrupted, seeing disdain forming on his sister's face. "The decision has been made. As High Priestess, she cannot go back on her verdict. Therefore, there is no need to rehash previous arguments."

"Thank you, Aaron," Clarissa looked at her brother, relieved that someone supported her decision.

"Why the young refuse the wisdom of the old is beyond me." Clarissa's uncle remarked.

"Uncle Vincent," Clarissa calmly spoke, "the young refute the wisdom of the old because it is just that…old. The world does not remain the same. It evolves to fit the needs of the time. Traditions and customs become forgotten, replaced by new and more relevant ways. Old buildings are torn down to be replaced by new ones. The elderly perish to make way for the young.

"If I had allowed Marshal Bartram to escape justice because The Sea Snake wished it so, this court would have remained as it has in the eyes of the people, a puppet for the lords to use as they see fit. This court is not a tool for those in power to use as a means to retain power. I have already allowed that to happen once. I will not allow it again! This day, I have made a statement. The Court of the Holy Mother

Matera shall serve as the source of justice it was meant to be. Righteousness shall prevail through fact and impartial judgment, not the whims of the rich."

Clarissa's uncle remained silent as he pursed his lips and stared at the table.

"Your Holiness, how shall we proceed with the sentence?" Aaron inquired.

Clarissa confidently proclaimed, "The Holy Judgment Spell."

"Clarissa!" Her uncle shouted as he rose to his feet in shock. "You cannot be serious!"

"Uncle, you will address me properly, and I am quite serious. This man has committed murder."

"He is a marshal! He deserves his last rites in the ceremony of Tenebris! Even Marshal Paisley received his!"

"Marshal Paisley did not commit murder; he was murdered! The entire kingdom will know that the Court of Sanctum shall not be manipulated."

"But Your Holiness, death by the Judgment Spell is far too cruel. It wipes away all traces of a person's existence. It is the highest dishonor, and in doing this, you will spread that dishonor to Lord Harken!" Vincent protested.

"None of that matters. The only thing that matters is

doing our job, dissenting justice."

"Your judgments are both divine and absolute," Aaron interjected, hoping to put an end to the dispute. "Shall we adjourn, and gather for the sentence tomorrow in the afternoon?"

"No!" Clarissa responded as she remembered her plans for the next day. She had already missed her plans for this afternoon and would not deny her desires another day. "The execution will proceed at sunrise."

"But, Your Holiness! It is customary to allow twenty-four hours to grant the king time enough to consider a pardon!" Aaron pleaded.

"Aaron, in all the years with mother, or even grandmother as High Priestess, have you ever seen the king grant a pardon?"

With a shake of his head, Aaron agreed, "No."

"It is because the king cares little for these proceedings," Clarissa stated as she rose to her feet. "The sentence shall proceed as planned."

The council rose to their feet, and in unison proclaimed, "Your judgments are both divine and absolute."

Clarissa exited the chambers and returned to the courtroom, now empty except for the two armored men guarding their post. The Hall of Justice seemed hollow and grim compared to the commotion that inhabited the space just moments ago. Clarissa turned to each man, "Sir Kenneth, Sir Gabriel, you may escort me to my chambers now."

"Yes, Your Holiness."

The clanging sounds of Sir Kenneth and Sir Gabriel's metal boots striking the stone floor resounded during the wordless stroll, maids and servants bowed as she passed by.

That evening, after her chambermaids bathed and dressed her in her nightgown, Clarissa sat at her small oak table and waited for her dinner to be served. A servant entered her room with a plate of venison, steamed vegetables, and potatoes. She consumed half of her plate, remembering her mother's instruction that a highborn lady never finishes her meal.

She finished chewing her last bite when a knock came at her door. Knowing that Sir Kenneth and Sir Gabriel's presence outside her door guaranteed her safety, she pulled her door open wide to see her brother waiting to enter.

Clarissa sighed and turned, walking away from the

open door as Aaron entered. She sat on her bed waiting to hear the reason for his visit. "I hope you are not here in an attempt to dissuade my decision. You know I cannot do that."

"No, I know you cannot. I am here to let you know that Lord Harken wishes to speak with you. I believe he has learned the expedient nature of Marshal Bartram's sentence."

"Request denied."

"Your Holiness, Lord Harken only…"

"Request denied!" She repeated, emphasizing each word.

"Clarissa, look," her brother began, causing her eyes to widen with surprise. Many years passed since she last heard anyone speak to her without formalities. "I am speaking to you now as a Bright, and mostly as your big brother. I am so proud of you!"

Taken back by her brother's surprising statement, she found herself speechless. She expected Aaron to protest her decision and warn her of her course of action, but instead, his manner presented warmth and kindness.

"You are doing what mother never could. You are bringing true justice back to the court. I am glad you are not meeting with Lord Harken. He could only spew venomous words at this juncture. Show him that the Bright family will not be persuaded."

"Thank you, Aaron!" She stood and hugged her big brother. Fighting tears of joy, she felt elated to hear her brother act like a brother again. Since her mother's passing, and the consequent inheritance of the high priestess title, everyone treated her differently. She felt as though the title dictated her character more than the person who bore it. No one called her by her name any longer. All of the kingdom's constituents showed more concern for her comfort than how she felt. She longed for the everyday interaction between people that others took for granted, and the gentle words flowing from her brother's mouth rose her spirits to new heights.

"I am going to go tell him you denied his request." Aaron shot a warm smile at his sister before exiting.

That night, Clarissa went to bed happy, hoping that her brother's visits would become routine.

The next morning the chambermaids woke Clarissa. They dressed her in another white robe adorned with lace, this one bearing long sleeves to protect her from the chill of the morning air. They placed a hooded white traveling cloak over her shoulders and pulled satin gloves over her hands.

Clarissa sat in front of her mirror as her chambermaids bushed and styled her hair before donning the thin golden tiara on her head. With her morning ritual completed, she exited her chamber to greet her armed escorts.

Clarissa ventured to the courtyard with Sir Kenneth and Sir Gabriel in tow. Her robe left a trail behind her as she walked in the morning dew on the manicured grass. Approaching two wide-trunked trees, with snow-white leaves budding from their branches, a semi-circle group of people awaited her arrival. Marshal William Bartram, restrained between the trees with taut chains, fought and squirmed to break free of his bindings.

Clarissa stood before the crowd and looked at each face present attempting to locate the presence of Lord Harken. Realizing that The Sea Snake decided to forego the execution, she pressed her palms together in front of her, closed her eyes, knelt, and began her silent prayer.

Ignoring the profane obscenities and threats directed at her by Marshal Bartram, she waited for the sun to rise before proceeding with the deadly ritual. Marshal Bartram's screams turned to pleas for mercy as she approached him. Standing within reaching distance, she moved her right arm to draw out a runic symbol with her finger on the marshal's bare torso, took a step back, and closed her eyes. The runestone on her head began to glow, and a blinding white beam shot from the sky, bathing Marshal Bartram in light. The attendances cringed at his screams of agony and the overbearing radiance. Lasting no more than a few seconds, the light disappeared, and so did the marshal.

Clarissa opened her eyes. No evidence of the marshal's existence remained, except a pile of ash at the center of the circle burned into the grass. Feeling she accomplished her duty, the high priestess silently walked away with the guards in tow.

Returning to her room, Clarissa's chambermaids began getting her ready for the day. She had been looking forward to riding with the stable master, and her heart sang with excitement. The chambermaids pinned her hair up in a high bun, leaving two curls dangling from her temples. They laid out her riding gear, and slipped her into tall brown boots, white pants, a white blouse, and a brown leather vest. Before they finished lacing her pants, a loud, rapid knock beat against her door.

"Who is it?" Clarissa shouted, hoping that her brother returned for another visit.

"I have a message, Your Holiness!" An unfamiliar

voice sounded off.

"You may enter!"

A young boy entered, holding a rolled parchment.

"You may set it there." Clarissa pointed to her table.

Clarissa looked at the document and noticed the royal wax seal keeping it furled. The stamp of a heart adorned with a crown pressed into the wax proved that the message bore the seal of the king.

Her heart began to pound in her chest. "Get out," she whispered, but the chambermaids remained, completing their dressing ritual. Their persistence fueled Clarissa's rage until she shouted at the top of her lungs. "Get out!"

The chambermaids scurried out of the room like cockroaches escaping the light. Clarissa reached her shaking hand to retrieve the parchment. Slowly, as if the message would break if she opened it too quickly, she unfurled and read.

*Your Holiness, Clarissa Bright:*

*The king has decreed that Marshal William Bartram is hereby pardoned from his crimes and is to be set free henceforth.*

*Signed, His Royal Highness,*

*King Thomas Magicent*

Dread washed over Clarissa as she realized the severity of her crime. Treason.

# Elendor

---

"Vaylon!" Elendor shouted, but he did not seem to hear.

"Vaylon!" Jocia shouted, followed by Galain's plea. The friends yelled his name repeatedly, but Vaylon kept his slow pace, ignorant to his friend's cries.

Jocia and Galain burst into a sprint toward Vaylon, leaving their legless friend behind. Elendor formed a runic symbol with his finger to conjure the earth beneath Vaylon to rise in front of him and block his progress, but the wet, loose mud prevented his magic from gaining control.

Jocia and Galain caught up to Vaylon and shouted his name, waving their hands in front of his expressionless face. The two young elves attempted to halt Vaylon's advance. They pushed his chest and stomach, they pulled his belt and arms, but Vaylon trudged forward in a trance as an unseen force ensnared his mind.

Elendor felt panic rising within him. He cursed having disabilities more times than he could count, but with his friend heading straight into the heart of danger, his inability to help weighed heavy. Then an idea struck him. He would do the one thing he could do, manipulate plants. Drawing a runic symbol in the air, he reached out with his mind to the only vegetation near Vaylon, the gnarly trees of Nigereous Forest.

With his eyes closed, Elendor called out to the trees, mustering all of his magical strength. In response, a jolt of electricity coursed through his body. The trees repelled his call to action as if they possessed a sentience that refused his plea. Assuming he had miscast his spell, Elendor tried again, striking forth with his mind to force the trees to bend to his will. Magical energy poured from him, leaving him flush and drenched in sweat from the effort. He pushed through his fatigue using the full capacity of his mental strength until a snapping sound rung in his mind like a branch being ripped from a tree.

Elendor's body tensed. His muscles tightened and cramped in pain. It felt as though an invisible force bound his body, twisting and contorting it in awkward, agonizing positions. His back arched, his limbs jerked in angles of sharp spasms as terror overtook his senses. His vision blurred until darkness encircled his sight, leading Elendor to believe he was near unconsciousness.

Through the void, a hooded shadow figure emerged and began to walk toward Elendor. With each step the mysterious effigy jangled as if it dragged chains across stone flooring. The haunting visage closed in, bringing his cloaked head level with Elendor's eyes.

Two hands, covered by black gauntlets, pulled back the hood, revealing an untold terror that consumed Elendor's entire being. No head or facial features existed save for a pair of glowing blood red eyes with wisps of gray smoke rising and dissipating, like fire in a hearth. The eyes seemed to peer into his soul with an intense gaze full of malice and murderous intent. Elendor attempted to yell out for help, but fear froze his voice in his throat, colder than his chilled, shivering body.

A scream gushed from the mouthless face. The intensity and high pitch of the scream pierced the air and consumed all sound. Recoiling from the profound pain in his ears, Elendor squeezed his eyes shut, expecting the figure to end his life at any moment. Memories of his dear friends flashed as sorrow and regret filled his mind over the thought of never seeing them again. Drawing in a deep breath, he waited for the inevitable deathly release, but without warning, the assault ended and the apparition disappeared. Vanishing as suddenly as it arrived, it left nothing behind but a memory that Elendor would not soon forget.

Elendor forced his eyes open. His muscles no longer ached and no evidence of the horrifying vision remained. Not a single footprint was left imprinted into the surrounding sand, and no sign indicated that his friends bore witness to the terror. He saw that Vaylon still pursued Nigereous Forest with Jocia and Galain struggling to keep him from entering the dark place. Within the deepest recesses of his mind, Elendor felt confident that the hooded figure entranced Vaylon, enticing him to join the inescapable abyss of the forest. His mind raced for a solution to break Vaylon free from the hooded being's spell. Elendor attempted to scream for his friend in a final effort to break him free from the spell, but only a squeak escaped his parched throat. Panic consumed him as he scrambled to find a solution to prevent his friend's certain doom, but before an option could enter his mind, a blurred object swooped down from the sky and plucked Vaylon from the ground.

Elendor looked up to see his abducted friend hovering in the grasp of a griffon. Atop its back, Heece sat in his saddle as his steed flapped its mighty wings above the lake.

Jocia and Galain clambered in a hasty retreat to escape the shadow of the forest. Above, a small regiment of guards hovered on the backs of griffons, brandishing spears and notched bows and arrows in preparation for battle. The guards gazed down upon the delinquent young elves. Leading the unit, one figure grabbed Elendor's attention. Morace, the elf who held disdain for anyone who did not meet his standards of conduct, held a scowl, signaling the unavoidable punishment for the young arbormancer and his friends. Elendor hung his head in shame, but in his heart, their interference calmed his nerves. Their presence, especially that of Morace, meant retribution for their actions yet any sentence would be a welcome penalty to the alternative of losing his closest friend.

That evening Elendor and his friends were brought to the Grand Hall to face the consequences of disobeying the law. The immense structure served a variety of functions within Parvus Arbor, including celebrations, weddings, war meetings, and in this case, court hearings. Walls of interwoven branches rose from the flattened trunk of an ancient tree that converged at a peak many stones higher than the tree line. Between the interwoven branches, vines bloomed with wisteria in colors of purple, blue and pink. The floor of the hall spanned long and wide enough to fit the crowd of elves standing behind them in the congregation. In front, a single table grew from the trunk of the tree, and behind it, Elder Jalaana, whose resting face always seemed to bear a smile, sat waiting to perform her duty as Chief of the village.

At one thousand and fourteen years, Elder Jalaana's smooth skin hid her age well. Her long straight hair faded to white long before Elendor's birth; the only hint that revealed her ancient status. Standing to her left, Heece dressed in casual attire, putting aside the customary elven armor he usually wore. To her right, the next oldest elf in the village and next-in-line Elder of Parvus Arbor, Morace, stood bearing his usual miserable expression. The friends nervously stood side-by-side with Elendor in the harness on Vaylon's back as they awaited judgment.

"Let the meeting come to order!" Jalaana announced as a hush befell the crowd. "Well met to all."

"Well met, Elder," the congregation returned in unison.

"We are here to discuss the punishment of these four young ones as they have disobeyed the laws of Parvus Arbor.

Morace, please tell of the events that led to this hearing."
Jalaana spoke with a kindness that put Elendor at ease. A
relief that ended once Morace began his re-account of the
events in his usual harsh tone.

Morace told the tale, embellished with words such as
"disrespectful, careless, obviously, and unimaginable."

Mentioning that the young friends journeyed near
Nigereous Forest made the crowd gasp in disbelief. By the
time he finished, Elendor felt ashamed, a feeling he knew he
shared with his friends.

Morace attempted to place the blame of the ordeal on
Elendor, accusing him of corrupting the impressionable
Galain and Jocia to perform acts of rebellion against their
better judgment. Elendor wished he could refute the
accusations thrust upon him, but the thought of nearly losing
his friend to the madness of Nigereous Forest kept him
silent.

"I have heard the tale and will now listen to the
defense of the accused." Jalaana declared.

Galain, the first to muster enough bravery, spoke.
"Elder, Morace tells the truth. We did knowingly disobey the
laws. However, the blame does not solely rest on Elendor's
shoulders. He tried to discourage us from the journey, and

only accompanied us in fear for our safety." Galain bowed his head in shame. "The notion was mine. I deserve the harshest punishment."

Galain's proclamation shocked Elendor. While true that Elendor had not devised the plan to venture to Hidden Falls, he knew that Galain had not persuaded everyone to make the journey. It was Jocia who concocted the excursion and convinced the friends to accompany her. Glancing at Jocia, he saw her staring at Galain in disbelief of his false statement.

"Thank you for your honesty, Galain. I shall now pass judgment."

A hush fell over the crowd. A chorus of insects singing their nightly tunes echoed within the branch walls of the otherwise silent Grand Hall.

"Jocia and Vaylon."

"Yes, Elder?" The two responded in unison.

"You are hereby sentenced to one week of hard labor under the supervision of Sendri, the Beastmaster."

"Yes, Elder."

"Galain."

"Yes, Elder?"

"Because it was you who led the group on the

expedition, your punishment will be extended for a two-week period of time."

"Elendor."

"Yes, Elder?"

"Due to your disabilities, you shall be confined to your room for one week. The sentence for all four of you begins tomorrow."

"Elder! That is all?" Morace exclaimed, appalled by the lenient sentencing.

Jalaana looked at Morace with her looming smile still present on her face, "You disagree with my judgment?"

"Yes!"

The crowd uttered disbelief at Morace's response. His disrespectful, arrogant tone bordered on insolence.

"This one" Morace shouted, pointing at Vaylon, "is a half-elf! A fangrel left on our doorstep! We have no responsibility to care for him!"

Elendor felt the heat of shame radiating from Vaylon. He had witnessed many elves sling the derogatory term fangrel at his friend during their formative years. He had long ago lost track of the number of tears he had wiped from his friend's face due to his brethren's intolerance for Vaylon's half-elven heritage.

"Morace…" Jalaana interrupted, but Morace continued his rant.

"And this one," he spewed, pointing to Elendor, "this one should never have been allowed to live. If you would only follow the old ways, he would have been sacrificed on the day of his birth! A deformed elf? He is an abomination!"

"Morace, stop!" Jalaana shouted, the ever-present smile leaving her face for the first time. "You would excommunicate Vaylon because he is a half-blood? You would have me throw a child into the wilderness because of a heritage he cannot control? He is the only one who possesses the strength and stamina to carry Elendor, and he does so with pride. Furthermore, you would have me take the life of the only elf within Parvus Arbor with the gift of arbormancy. Does your pride take control of your common sense? Having an arbormancer is vital to the survival of our home! Just as with Vaylon, you would sacrifice a child over circumstances he cannot control! The only abomination in this room is you, Morace. I weep for my precious Parvus Arbor for when the day arrives that you are Elder. I pray that I live for another thousand years so that elf-kind never suffers under your rule!"

Morace, disgusted by Jalaana's tirade, stormed out of

the hall like a child throwing a tantrum, leaving the crowd in a murmur.

"Please, everyone, calm down. These proceedings have concluded. Please return to your homes and may Terram, the Goddess of Earth, watch over you all."

Elendor looked at his friends. "Let us take our leave. Morace's bitterness remains in the air, and I would rather not breathe it any longer than necessary."

That night Elendor contemplated the day's events. He fondly reflected on some of the adventures. The garden, the birds of the falls, and the joy of Jocia's smile warmed his heart. However, Vaylon's trance-like state overshadowed the happiness of the day. The mystery of why only he became entranced to enter Nigereous Forest puzzled him. Perhaps Vaylon's heritage played a role in the transfixion. Whatever the reason, the young arbormancer intended to discover the truth. Vaylon had no recollection of the event, making this a most curious predicament.

Elendor dwelled on the faceless man. In describing the feeling of the moment when the cloaked stranger appeared, unadulterated fear came to mind. Elendor felt sorrow and regret spanning millennia flow from the faceless man. He wanted to search for answers about the apparition in the library of Parvus Arbor, but no book remained within the city that he had not read. He would have remembered any mention of a faceless man that resided within Nigereous Forest. Interrupting Elendor's ruminations, his mother burst in through the door.

"My son," she exclaimed, dropping to her knees and hugging Elendor, "I am so sorry!"

"Mother, I am unharmed. Please do not fret."

"Fretting is something Morace will do. When I get my hands on that…"

"No, mother. Morace only spoke what many elves feel in Parvus Arbor."

"That is not true. The elves…"

"What? Need me for my arbormancy? They despise who I am. If it were not for my ability, it is likely that the elves would have left me as food for the forest beasts long ago. Vaylon's fate would have been worse if it were not for his strength to transport me. I am a cripple, a blemish on the beauty and perfection of the elven race."

"No Elendor, you are one of the Miracle Three, and you are my miracle. In thousands of years of history, three elves have never been born within the same year. You and your friends are all a blessing from the Gods."

"Thank you mother, but I must make plans. Elder Jalaana has surpassed millennia, and her time grows short. I must prepare for the inevitability that Morace shall be the next Elder. He has more supporters than you think, and they are all believers in the old traditions. When the day comes that he is named Elder, the best I can hope for is that I will be forced to leave with Vaylon."

"I shall never allow that to happen," Elendor's mother replied with a well of tears in her eyes.

"You will not have a choice."

Elendor dwelled on the fate of his mother. She had lived the past hundred years defending her disfigured son and never allowed him to feel like a burden to her. He knew she felt she would always protect him from the harsh reality of his predicament, but the day would come that she would have to face the inevitable truth.

"No matter what happens, you will always be my miracle." Elendor's mother followed with a gentle kiss to his forehead.

In the morning a vanguard came and took Elendor's books, leaving him with nothing but boredom. During the day Vaylon, accompanied by a Parvus Arbor Guard, brought food and water. This momentary interaction served as the only break from his mundane confinement. That night his mother burst through the door and interrupted his solitude. "Elendor!"

The sudden appearance of his mother startled Elendor. "Mother? You should not be here. If anyone sees..."

"None of that matters. I have terrible news. Elder Jalaana has passed. You must pack your things and leave post-haste. Morace is coming, and a contingent follows him!" A jittery panic consumed his mother.

Elendor knew this day would come eventually, but he assumed there was more time. The news of Jalaana's passing brought upon a series of trepidations that overwhelmed his mind. Attempting to figure out his first move, he barely finished his first thought when Vaylon burst through the doorway with the harness already strapped on his back. "Elendor..."

"I have already informed him, Vaylon," Elendor's mother began shoving clothes into a knapsack.

Vaylon ran over to Elendor, dropping the harness beside him. "Get in! We have to go now!"

Elendor climbed into the harness. "Mother, in that corner. My other bag, I must have that one too!"

The three began to make their escape when the approaching herd of elves blocked their path. Turning to run in the opposite direction, more elves drew upon them.

"Well! Well! Well!" Morace's voice boomed. "It seems as though your protector has passed abomination!"

"Morace, how dare you!" Elendor's mother shouted as she charged him. Before she could reach him, a guard grabbed her arms, twisted her around and held her in place.

Ignoring her screams and pleas, Morace pointed at Elendor and Vaylon and demanded, "Take them."

"No!" Jocia and Galain came barreling through the group to stop in front of their friends with their arms open wide. "We won't let you do this!" Jocia said with tears spilling from her eyes.

"Child," Morace began in a low tone. "You do not understand now, but one day you will. That...thing cannot be allowed in Parvus Arbor. It is a disgrace to all elf-kind." Turning his attention to a nearby guard, he gave the order. "Move them."

Two guards tried to apprehend Jocia and Galain until another voice impeded their progress. "Don't take another step." Heece maneuvered through the crowd until he came face-to-face with Morace. "You have no authority here."

"What do you mean? Jalaana has passed, and I am next-in-line to become Elder."

"'Become' being the operative word. The ceremony has not taken place, and until it does, Jalaana's orders still stand."

"The ceremony is just a formality!" Morace spat incredulously.

"Yet still a part of 'the old ways,' as you insistently point out every occasion. Are you saying that 'the old ways' only apply when it is convenient for you?"

Morace's expression displayed evident frustration. The words Heece spoke were accurate, and to go against his own words would crush the political standing he held with the elves that supported him.

"So be it," he admitted, "but what reassurance do I have that Jalaana's orders will be followed and this thing will remain confined to his room?"

"I shall personally stand guard to ensure he does not depart."

Morace spoke with agitation. "If that abomination leaves, Heece, I shall hold you personally responsible."

Heece smiled at Morace as he watched him leave. Once the gathering dispersed, Vaylon returned Elendor to his room and retreated to his own.

The sleepless night remained waxed with doubts and fears. Elendor pondered his options, trying to discover an escape from the inevitable judgment that would soon be cast upon him. Whether Morace planned excommunication or execution, he did not know, but he assumed it would be the latter. Breaking his deep trance, a whisper through his open window caught him by surprise.

"Elendor."

"Jocia!" he responded excitedly with more volume than he meant to use.

"Shhh." She responded with her finger in front of her lips. "Vaylon is coming to get you. We must leave immediately."

"What?" Elendor returned in the same hushed tone. His door creaked open and Vaylon tiptoed in with the harness on his back. Placing the restraint in front of Elendor, he signaled. "Get in."

Softly, his door opened again and Jocia and Galain slipped into his room. "What's going on? Where's Heece?" He whispered to his friends.

"We don't have time for that," Galain hushed. "Just get in, we shall tell you when we are clear of the city."

The group traveled north toward the edge of the city where three horses packed with saddlebags awaited them. After placing their belongings into the bags, they rode from Parvus Arbor as fast as they could.

When they were far enough away, and he could not see any signs of pursuit, Elendor began asking his questions to his friends. "What is going on? Where was Heece? How did you all get out?"

Jocia responded, "I was sitting in my room when Heece came to my window and told me to gather my belongings. He told me to get Galain, Vaylon, and you. He said to head to the northern city entrance where he had provisions ready for a journey."

"Heece did all of that? What of the repercussions when Morace discovers our absence?"

"I had the same concerns. He told me to let him worry about that, and that this was the only way to get you and Vaylon out alive."

"So Morace did plan execution. What of you and Galain? The two of you were not in danger. Do you not wish to stay within the safety of the city?"

"Are you mad?" Galain demanded. "Do you believe we would allow the two of you to go on an adventure without us? Besides, what would you do without us? You need us, and you know it!"

"Where shall we go?" Jocia wondered.

Elendor responded confidently, "I have the perfect destination in mind."

# Marius

"Marius, Lord Hardwood summons you to his chambers." A woman said as she opened the door of a small room made of stone.

Marius raised his hand to signal the woman to wait. Three men sat at the same table, waiting for Marius to make his move. A sly smile crept across Marius's face as he laid five cards on the table. The three men groaned as they slammed their cards down in frustration and watched as the victor gathered the small pile of silver coins piled in the center.

"Well, men, sorry to take all your money and run, but you heard the lady." Marius addressed the embittered men as he gathered his belongings and left.

"Do you know what he wants this time?" Marius and the woman walked briskly down the stone hallway.

"I never know what that man's intentions are."

Marius, the high commander of the guard in Baxis,

remained as the only soldier within the city who held the distinct privilege of serving under two different lords. Seven years had passed since the Baxis Marshal's Rebellion occurred, where Eric Hardwood took the title from Lord Roman Drake. The seat of power had been handed from a madman to demon when the uprising ended. The newly appointed lord executed every member of the Baxis Guard who had remained loyal to Drake, except Marius, whose fame and reputation was too valuable to discard.

At a glance, nothing remarkable stood out about him, but his speed, quickness with a blade, and agility were well known throughout the kingdom. He never wore armor, due to the detriment it would provide for his mobility. Instead, his attire matched that of the common citizens, allowing him to blend in as an average person to those unfamiliar with his renown. His only distinguishing features, copper skin, and hair black as onyx, separated him from the fair complected citizens of Baxis.

"What took you so damned long?" Lord Hardwood demanded as Marius entered the chambers.

"Just needed to finish up a task. I came as soon as I could, my Lord." Marius replied with a bow and a hint of sarcasm in his voice.

"I don't care what tasks you have. When your Lord calls for you, you drop what you are doing and answer the call!" Lord Hardwood replied with a shout.

Eric Hardwood was an obese man when he acquired his seat of power, but these days, he resembled more a blob than a man. His thin hair was slicked back in a failed attempt to hide the ever-widening bald spot. Where his neck should have been, a pocket of fat jutted out further than his hidden chin.

The lord put every effort into his appearance except diet and exercise. He wore clothes made from the best cotton and silk, and each shirt he owned displayed his family crest of a red chimera across the chest. Marius often wondered how expensive the lord's clothes must cost due to the amount of material required to produce them. He decorated himself in as much jewelry as his portly frame could handle, and flashed his extravagant baubles to any visiting marshal or lord. Although his ornamentation gave the appearance of a man of wealth, rumors abound that the Baxis vault ran dry with his insatiable appetites.

Lord Hardwood's chambers were among the most massive rooms in the ancient castle of Baxis, and one of the few places with windows not covered by stone and mortar.

Many of the windows throughout the castle had been removed due to destruction from battles long forgotten, or damage from the harsh weather of the province. The inviting scents of the fire in the hearth would have filled the room, if not for the powerful stench wafting from an overfilled chamber pot sitting in the corner where flies hovered in delight.

Lord Hardwood rarely left the comfort of his colossal four-poster bed, as evidenced by the condition of his bedding. The yellow stained sheets, originally woven in vibrant white fabric, were nearly translucent from excessive use. A permanent indent from his corpulent physique sunk into the mattress, releasing a musky odor that could only be removed by setting it ablaze. The lord's wife had not entered this room in over a year, and Marius needn't wonder why.

"I apologize, my Lord," Marius said with another bow. "How may I be of assistance?"

"I have a mission of great importance, Marius." Lord Hardwood grunted as he rose from his bed. Marius could see a thin layer of sweat on the lord's forehead as he heaved and wheezed from the effort of lifting his beastly body. "I have received word that my cousin, Marshal Marcus Bane's wife has recently borne him a son. I want you to prepare a small regiment to visit him."

"That is wonderful, my Lord! You are an uncle once again. Shall I also prepare a coach so that you may accompany the regiment to meet your newly born nephew?"

"That won't be necessary. I want you to dispose of the baby."

Marius's eyes widened in horror as he struggled to comprehend the directive. He knew Lord Hardwood as a selfish and unpleasant man, but an order to kill a newborn child exceeded even his loathsome nature.

Marius turned to his lord in hopes that he would soon admit to a failed attempt at humor. "M-my Lord, are you sure that…?"

"Do not question my orders, High Commander! The province of Baxis cannot afford another rebellion. This is why the law had been passed. Any marshal within the province is permitted to have only one son. This boy could very well grow up, realize that he will never be marshal or lord, and stage a rebellion of his own to take the seat of his older brother or worse, my son. Marshal Bane has broken the law. I will not hold him accountable for laying with his wife, but the boy cannot be allowed to live. Marshal Bane may choose to execute his first-born son in the baby's stead, but I doubt he will. The eldest son is merely five years old."

"I doubt he will choose either! The marshal will not allow someone to enter his manor and kill his child! Marshal Bane is a simple man. You have nothing to fear from his offspring."

"Whether or not the marshal allows you to fulfill my order is inconsequential. You shall bring a regiment of men with you to ensure the task is completed. It may be true that Marshal Bane is simple-minded, but there is no guarantee that his child will be the same. The province cannot risk war."

"You're asking me to enter into a bloodbath! The marshal will order his men to defend his child at all costs, and we will be forced to eliminate them all. More than a hundred men will die due to future uncertainty!"

"Watch your tone, Commander! My order is final. You will leave in the morning to execute your duty!"

"And if I refuse? Perhaps I would rather die than kill a child." Marius proclaimed, walking up to Lord Hardwood, bringing his face close enough to the lord's own so that the round man could witness the intensity in his eyes.

"If you disobey my orders," Hardwood began in a harsh, foul-breathed whisper, "it is not death you should fear.

You have no wife or children for me to threaten, so I will threaten that which you hold most dear. I will have both your arms and legs removed from your body, but you will not die. I will have you stitched up so that you may live the rest of your life as a helpless invalid, incapable of walking, feeding yourself, or even wiping your own ass. I will make sure you eat and drink water even if I have to force tubes into your gullet to ensure you suffer for years on end in helplessness. Your mind will slowly slip into madness as you wither away."

Marius stared in anger, his gaze fixed on the leader's eyes as he searched for any sign that Lord Hardwood's words were under pretenses, but he saw none. He knew the fat man meant every word and that he possessed the means to accomplish such a dastardly task. Marius grabbed the handle of his dagger. He wanted to slash Lord Hardwood's flabby throat, but killing Lord Hardwood would be the death sentence for himself and the province. The empty lordship would fall onto the young Caelius Hardwood who required many years of training before he could carry out his duties with success. The other marshals of the province would likely start a war to gain the vacant lord's seat. The war-torn province of Baxis could not survive another battle that would further ravage the land. "Yes, sir!" Marius responded with venom in his voice.

"Oh, and Commander, I'm going to have to insist that you execute the child in sight of the regiment. Just to ensure that the deed is done."

Marius left the room in silence. Lord Hardwood's dry, coarse laughter echoed through the thick chamber door.

That night, as Marius lay in his bed devising a method of escaping the lord's dubious plan, a knock at the door broke his reverie. Richard, the first-born son of the stable master of Baxis, beamed from ear to ear as he awaited permission to enter. "I'm sorry Richard, but I'm in no mood for any company this evening."

"What's the matter?" Richard asked, putting his hand on Marius's cheek. His hand, rough from years of manual labor, felt warm and coursed a pleasant sensation throughout Marius's body. Changing his mind about allowing Richard in, he sat on his bed as Richard entered the room.

"I spoke with our Lord earlier and he assigned a task that I am far from pleased with."

"What does that fat old boar want you to do?" Richard pulled up a chair to sit and listen. He sat wide-eyed, with his hands covering his mouth in disbelief, as Marius told him the entirety of the events.

"By the Gods! Just when I thought that man couldn't be any more foul!" Richard remarked.

"I don't know what I am going to do! How could I live with myself if I killed that innocent child?"

Richard sat next to Marius and put his arm around him to offer comfort. "You're Marius the Swift! The legendary warrior of Baxis. If there is anyone who can figure out how to get out of this mess, it is you."

"Marius the Swift. You know I hate that name."

Richard touched Marius on the cheek, gently turned his head and kissed him. "I know you can figure this out." Marius stared into Richard's russet eyes. The love he felt for him gave him joy, and feeling the same affection returned, brought a smile to each man.

Marius and Richard spent the rest of the night in each other's embrace. The ominous foreboding Marius felt kept his dreams at bay. He contemplated every possible scenario, and when the morning came, his restless mind devised a plan.

Marius revealed his intentions to Richard. He did not want to involve his love in a scheme that created such risk, but for his plans to succeed, he needed to have faith in someone. He could think of no one who held a higher level of trust than Richard did. Marius looked out of his door in all directions. Feeling assured that no lurkers would spot Richard leaving, Marius gave him a kiss goodbye and resumed his morning activities.

The time came to prepare for the trip to Tarkan. Marius found himself hoarse from barking orders to the regiment of troops he selected to make the excursion. They had prepared for travel to numerous destinations throughout the kingdom, yet the soldiers still acted as if it was their first journey. His position demanded that he deal with half-witted soldiers with no more sense than a moth flying into a flame. The task always left him frustrated.

Adding to the long list of planning for departure, the horse and carriage, usually reserved for Lord Hardwood, sat ready for travel amongst the regiment. Some of the men asked the reason for bringing the lord's empty coach, but Marius dismissed each question with a reply about Lord Hardwood's eccentricities. He heard the idle rumblings between the troops. Some assumed they prepared the ride in case the lord changed his mind at the last moment. Others guessed that Marius intended on bringing the Bane family back to Baxis in celebration of the newborn child. He heard some say that the lord just wanted to make a pretentious display by showing off the expensive cart. Every excuse he heard could have been the truth, but none of it was. Marius desired to have the carriage brought along as an end to his means.

Seeing a large troop of soldiers approaching the town would raise the suspicion, but witnessing an escort of soldiers bringing Lord Hardwood to see his newly born nephew would be well within the realm of believability. Lord Hardwood wouldn't be in the carriage, but only appearances mattered for this deception to work. Far too many men made up the regiment to be an escort of an ordinary lord of the province, but for the insecure and paranoid Eric Hardwood, the size of the entourage would seem reasonable.

With the first part of Marius's plan in motion, he felt confident that he would gain entry to the town without incident. The second part of the strategy, however, did not hold the possibility of execution without bloodshed.

Marius led the battalion to their destination. The town of Tarkan was the nearest town within the province, making for a swift journey. As expected, the trip proceeded without issue all the way to the open wooden gates of Tarkan.

"Who do you escort?" The gate guard inquired when Marius approached.

"Lord Eric Hardwood has come to meet his newly arrived nephew."

The guard admired the extravagantly carved carriage. Marius knew the guard's responsibilities required him to inspect the coach, but Lord Hardwood's reputation would precede him. His tendency for spewing venom on anyone that dared disrupt him would give the guard pause in his duties.

The guard approached the coach. Marius blocked his advance with a gentle hand to the man's chest. "By all means, inspect the carriage, but Lord Hardwood is asleep, and I wouldn't want to be the one to wake him."

The guard contorted his face as he considered the situation and stepped out of the path of the procession. "Proceed."

Marius followed the only stone road with his regiment close in tow. The town sustained its existence by relying on the nearby Fleming River. Rare fish, considered a delicacy to the nobles of the kingdom, swam in the clear waters. The port dwelled in one of the only places where the flow did not run harsh and rapid. Not a single farm or crop grew within the town's land, as the sediment-filled soil allowed for little vegetation to thrive. The townsfolk, mostly anglers, traders, and keepers of small livestock, lived slightly above poverty. Despite this, the local's joyful demeanor relayed a placated existence.

Each citizen presented a smile to the passing entourage. Some waved a friendly gesture, while others vocalized their pleasure to witness the members of the Baxis guard, gracing their presence to the tiny hamlet. As the procession made its way through the town, the shadow of guilt loomed over Marius, knowing that he would soon bring tragedy to the kind inhabitants.

Marshal Bane greeted the Baxis Commander at the manor entrance. "Well, if it isn't Marius the Swift! I am so happy to see you. Is that my cousin?" He trotted toward the carriage to greet his family member, but Marius halted his pursuit.

"I wouldn't do that. Lord Hardwood fell asleep during the ride, and you know how he is about having his slumber disturbed. It's best to let him rest a bit more."

"I understand. Are Junia and the children with him?"

"I'm afraid it is only Lord Hardwood. Lady Junia said that the girls are feeling a bit under-the-weather, and preferred to keep watch over them, but she sends her regards and congratulations."

"Ah! Such a kind soul that Junia Hardwood. I should make a trip to see her soon. Come in, Marius. It's been too long since we spoke."

Marius followed Marcus into the manor. The marshal began to ramble about the baby as he escorted Marius to meet the child. He talked about the trials and tribulations of having a newborn: the sleepless nights, the feeding, and the burping. He even went as far as describing the color and consistency of what they found in the diapers. The chubby marshal stood a stone shorter than Marius, yet outweighed him by a wide margin. His hair had left the top of his head early, and his bulbous nose matched the roundness of his face. His sage green eyes showed kindness, putting Marius at ease, even in this uncomfortable circumstance.

The smiling face of the marshal's wife greeted Marius as she nursed the newborn child while their first-born son played with a set of wooden knights beside them.

"You remember my wife, Dulcia. And this is Julius." Marshal Bane leaned over and kissed the top of the baby's head.

Not able to take any more of the happiness that

enriched the room, Marius decided to tell the marshal the real reason for his visit. "Marshal Bane, I have deceived you."

"W-what do you mean Marius?"

"Lord Hardwood is not here to meet your new son. He is not even here. The carriage is empty."

"By the Gods! Then why are you here?"

"Lord Hardwood sent me here to kill your son. But…"

"What? No! Guards!" The marshal shouted.

"But wai…"

"Guards!" The marshal shouted again.

"If you'd just…"

"Guards!" Three guards burst into the room brandishing spears and shields.

Marius's plan went completely awry. He intended to tell the marshal that he would not kill his son and that he devised a deception that would allow his son to survive, but he underestimated the protective nature of parents.

The marshal's shout reached beyond the manor walls. Marius held little faith that his men had enough intelligence to react accordingly. His second-in-command, the only person privy to Marius's true intentions, hopefully, instructed the squadron to surround the manor to prevent any more of the marshal's guards from entering.

The three guards began thrusting their spears at Marius as Marshal Bane shouted instructions and obscenities. Marius avoided each attempt at his life. With his far superior skill, the high commander of the Baxis Guard could end the lives of his attackers, but his goal of avoiding as much bloodshed as possible remained as his staunch objective. Ducking and dodging, Marius began to come up with a new, possibly even riskier plan.

Marius drew his dagger and one-by-one used the handle to knock the guards unconscious.

"Marshal Marcus Bane." Marius began as the family embraced each other, sobbing with fear. "Under the authority of Lord Eric Hardwood I…"

"I invoke the Right of Challenge!" Marshal Bane interrupted.

"What? No, I…"

The marshal darted over to the window, threw it open, and repeated himself for the whole town to hear. "I invoke the Right of Challenge!" He shouted, bringing another of Marius's plans to fall to pieces.

Invoking the Right of Challenge, the right entitled to

all marshals, allowed a challenge to any decision made by a lord of province. The Right of Challenge pitted a champion of the marshal's choosing against the lord's champion. The winner of the contest would be considered blessed by the gods, thereby reversing or confirming the decision that the lord set forth.

Since Marius joined the Baxis army, he knew of only one other time a marshal issued the Right of Challenge. Seven years ago, the then Marshal Eric Hardwood invoked the Right of Challenge on a law set forth by Lord Roman Drake. The legislation would have further increased the already heavy taxes of the province, forcing thousands more into poverty. The new tariff caused many of the marshals to lose faith in their lord, and the region teetered on rebellion long before the imposition, but Lord Drake made a fatal error. A marshal's authority is slight, and taking away power from greedy men is an assured way to force a reaction. Lord Drake denied the Right of Challenge, enraging the other marshals, and allowing Eric Hardwood to gain their trust. Soon thereafter, the rebellion ensued, killing thousands and leaving the land decimated.

"Marshal Bane, you don't understand."

"Oh, I understand perfectly." The kindness in the

marshal's eyes turned to rage. "You come into my home, and threaten the life of my child! How could you do this Marius? Orders be damned! I thought we were friends!"

The marshal's words cut Marius like a knife. Marius did consider Marcus Bane a friend, and as the gods as his witness, he would not kill this man's son, nor would he accept the consequence of living life as an invalid. Two times, he devised a plan, and twice they failed. He needed a third plan, and he needed one fast.

# Dorian

The next day, after Nathaniel's unexpected visit, Dorian completed his daily duties as usual and cleaned up in the evening. He put away his tools and checked the feed for the horses. While filling the water trough, he heard a faint voice in the distance.

"Dorian!" The voice unmistakably belonged to Nathaniel. Turning in a circle, he strained to hear from which direction the shouts originated.

"Dorian!" He heard again, this time realizing that the voice came from the east. Dorian followed Nathaniel's voice, listening to his shouts grow louder with each passing call. Finally, he saw him. Nathaniel's arm waived in the air to get Dorian's attention. A smile glossed across his face at the sight of his new friend, but it did not last long.

Three other figures walked along with Nathaniel. Still too far away to get details, he could only make out their general appearance.

One of them, a man with a similar build to Nathaniel, strode alongside a squat man walking with an unsteady gait. The last figure bore a frame far different from the other two. Bobbing from side to side with each step, the dainty figure's long, dark brown hair waved like leaves in the wind from within its tied-back confines. This one's body reminded Dorian of an hourglass, and seemed just as fragile yet beautiful in its curvaceous form. He guessed this person to be a female, although he had never seen one before, other than the portrait of his mother hanging on the wall of the cottage.

Dorian felt a chill overcome him. Having just met the first person he could call a friend, he felt uneasy about meeting anyone new. He cautiously approached the group, gripping the handle of the sheathed sword brandished on his hip. Never having met people, Dorian absorbed every fascinating, diverse detail of the individuals before him.

Coming face-to-face with his friend, Dorian saw Nathaniel's smile. "Let me introduce you to my friends. This is Lukas Maynard."

"Hey," Lukas dismissively waved. A slender man with a grumpy look that reminded Dorian of his father, he stood about half a head taller than him. His thick, wavy, hair seemed closer to black than brown. His thin, pointy nose matched his long, gaunt face, and his narrow lips drooped slightly, giving him an almost sad look. Like Nathaniel, facial hair began to emerge across the lower portion of his face, signaling his approach to manhood. His brown eyes glossed over, and seemed to reflect a weariness, perhaps due to the dark circles beneath them.

"This is Elijah Sartor,"

"Nice to meet you." Elijah extended his hand for a shake. Just barely taller than Dorian, his features and demeanor stood in stark contrast to those of Lukas. His skin possessed a darker tone, reminding Dorian of the copper metal he worked with on occasion. His thin hair shifted in the breeze like a million strands of spider's silk. The shape of his head reminded Dorian of an acorn, and his flat nose expanded wider than that of his friends. A big smile spanned across his face, and his narrow, brown eyes nearly shut when he smiled, exuding warmth and kindness.

"And this is Margaret Hagen," Nathaniel said.

"Nice to meet you. Thank you for keeping Nathaniel from being eaten last night," she said, reaching out for a handshake. Her melodic voice held a pitch that reminded him of the woodland birds of his home, a pleasant surprise to

Dorian. Dark hair framed her thin, oval-shaped head which resembled the shape of a grape resting upon a narrow stem. Her nose seemed slightly large for her face, and her plump lips glistened more than the males of the group. Her bright white teeth shimmered when she smiled and her green eyes danced with friendliness.

"I'm sorry for bringing a group of strangers to your home," Nathaniel chimed in, "but after the other night, I thought you might like to meet them. Besides, I told them all about your sword, and they are dying to see it. Is that it on your hip?"

"No, this is just another sword I made. No runestones on this one." Dorian felt heat rise in his face. Discussing his secret project embarrassed him.

"Can we move this meeting to your forge so you can show them?" Nathaniel asked excitedly.

Dorian thought to have one friend seemed like something he could explain to a furious father, but a group of four passed defiance. His father's warnings echoed in his head. For a moment, he thought to deny the request, but seclusion and loneliness cannot fulfill a heart that desires companionship and adventure. He knew he should turn the travelers away, but "aye, of course," blurted out instead.

Dorian asked them to wait in front of the forge while he went to his hiding spot to retrieve the sword. Upon returning, Nathaniel gazed upon it with wonderment as he passed it to Lukas.

Lukas looked at the sword as if he were disinterested. Reaching toward the blade with a finger extended, Dorian knew he intended to test its edge. "I advise against that! It's sharper than most blades."

Margaret took the sword. "I have never seen anything like it!" She remarked, taking a curious look before passing it to Elijah.

"Wow, I wish I had a sword like this!" exclaimed Elijah as he stared at it.

"For what purpose? Cutting thread at your father's clothier?" Lukas joked, leading the group to chuckle.

"Dorian," Nathaniel began, "I must admit that seeing the sword isn't the only reason I brought my friends here. Ever since I left your home, I haven't been able to get your sword from my mind. I searched the library trying to find a book that would tell me how to make two runestones work simultaneously. I even looked in the back section of the library where only my family and the king's closest advisors are permitted entrance. It took some effort, but I believe I may have found the answer."

Nathaniel reached into his knapsack and removed an ancient book with bindings made of frayed rope. The thin, wooden cover appeared to have once been painted red, but age faded the hue to pink. Etched into the surface, the book's title featured strange symbols of an unrecognizable language. "I believe this book holds the secret to making that sword work the way you intended it."

Astonishment struck Dorian like a hammer driving in a nail with a single swing. He had tried and failed to get the two runestones to work together for so long that he no longer believed it possible. With renewed hope, he felt the rush of excitement as he flipped through the yellowed pages.

"This book is written in another language. What makes you think the secret is in here?" Dorian asked.

"I've come across quite a few books written in this language. I think it is kymarian." Nathaniel guessed.

"Kymarian? The language of the ancient race? I thought no one knew anything about them." Dorian's interest piqued.

"Most of our studies have been devoted to deciphering Kymarian," Margaret explained. "We have spent more time translating than learning how to cast spells."

Elijah continued. "We've had some assistance with books meant to guide in deciphering the text, but even they provide little help because they are printed in an ancient dialect. The key is to figure out the pattern. We are still learning, and there are words we remain unsure of, but we think we are near mastering the language

"You are all mages?" Dorian asked.

"We are still apprentices, but yes. All of us have runestones embedded in our skin. I chose the earth runestone." Margaret lifted her shirt to reveal an earth runestone where her naval would be.

"I chose water." Elijah lifted his shirt to reveal the water runestone on his chest.

"I chose fire, but I work with my shirt off a lot, so I had to attach it to a more hidden spot, and I am not showing you," Lukas said while pointing in the direction of his posterior. Lukas's explanation brought laughter from everyone.

"From what I can discern," Nathaniel began, eager to return to the matter at hand, "the method for combining the power of the runestones involves layering and combining the relative runic symbols of each element. There are six different kinds of runestones: water, wind, earth, fire, light, and darkness. These runestones have their own set of runic symbols and represent the power of six of the seven gods. These runic symbols allow a user to cast spells. If a symbol is carved into a runestone, that stone will only cast that particular spell. This is the same principle as the symbol representing cold on a water runestone to cool an icebox. Same goes for the symbol for flame on a fire runestone attached to the fire table you use for cooking.

"The size of the runestone and the size of the symbol carved upon it determines the size of the spell. Every time you touch the runestone, you are giving a bit of your energy to cast a spell. In everyday household items, the amount of energy you dispel is too small for you to notice. If a mage imbues a runestone on their skin, they do not carve a symbol into the runestone, but rather draw the symbol in the air to cast the spell. This allows the user to cast a variety of spells. The larger they trace out the symbol, the larger the spell will be. It requires a considerable amount of your energy to accomplish the feat. If a sorcerer isn't careful, they can use all of their energy and pass out, or possibly die. Learning how to balance this and memorizing the runic symbols is why it takes so long for a mage to be expertly efficient in casting."

"It's also why we fail at it so often," Lukas interjected with disappointment.

Nathaniel hadn't told Dorian anything he didn't already know, but he still listened carefully to his lesson.

"I believe this book shows how to layer and combine symbols from different runic sets to cast spells more powerful than anyone has ever seen." Nathaniel spoke as he stared at the book.

"It is likely the reason no one has ever seen a mage with more than one runestone. The danger could be immense. The amount of energy required to cast spells of this magnitude is beyond comprehension. One mistake and you run the risk of putting too much of one element into the spell. Even if you succeed, you would likely use every ounce of energy you have, and possibly perish in the process." Elijah directed his serious reply to Dorian.

"Either way, the results would be disastrous for the caster," Margaret added with intensity in her voice.

"But," Nathaniel continued, "if you were to cast from an item, say a sword, instead of your own body, the size of the spells would be limited. That would reduce the risk to the caster."

"I see. So how do you figure out which symbols to

combine?" Dorian was most curious.

"I spent all day today trying to figure that out," Nathaniel replied with enthusiasm. "If a warrior wants his weapon with a fire runestone to light a flame, he merely draws out the symbol for fire. If a warrior wants his weapon with an earth runestone, to smash his adversary's weapon, he merely draws out the symbol for earth. Think of the name of the runestone as an activation spell. If you layer and combine these activation symbols along the vertical plane, the theory is that you will have activated and connected the power of the two runestones. In your case, fire and darkness.

"Theory?" Dorian asked with concern.

"We haven't exactly had an opportunity to test it out. So, yes, at this point it is just a theory." Lukas added.

"What do you think? Do you want to try it out?" Nathaniel addressed Dorian.

All eyes laid upon him in anticipation of his reply. The prospect of his sword actually working filled him with excitement. The accomplishment of a dream many years in the making brought upon a giddiness in Dorian. After looking at each one of the friends, he finally agreed. "Let's do it!"

Nathaniel and his friends burst out in a cheer. Even

Lukas, who to this point seemed disinterested in everything, let out a gleeful hurrah.

The group walked into the forge where the lanterns along the walls kept everything well lit. The smell of recently extinguished embers permeated the air. Nathaniel reached into his knapsack, brought out several pieces of tracing parchment and a shaped stick of coal used for writing. He opened the ancient book and rummaged through the pages until he found the right page. Placing the parchment over the design, he traced the symbol for fire. Opening to another page, he traced the symbol for darkness. Layering the two pieces of paper, he added a third piece on top. Lukas and Margaret held torches to provide sufficient light for seeing through the parchment. After completion, Nathaniel proudly held up the newly formed symbol.

"Now what?" Dorian asked.

"Now is your part," Nathaniel replied. "I am going to hold up this paper. You are going to hold your sword in one hand and use the other hand to trace out this symbol."

"Trace the symbol on the parchment? That's all?" Dorian asked, feeling as though the process seemed far too simple.

"Yes," replied Margaret. "It's a common practice

technique used by all apprentices. It sounds easy, but a true mage cannot exactly tell an opponent to wait a moment while they fetch a piece of parchment so they can cast a spell. The symbols must be memorized to the exact size and shape and must be ready to use in an instant."

"Okay, let's give it a shot!" Nathaniel said, holding up the paper. "I'll guide you."

Dorian traced out the symbol. When finished, he checked the sword. Nothing happened, leading to the familiar feeling of disappointment.

"I guess it didn't work." Dorian no sooner uttered, when the sword began to vibrate in his hand. He looked at the weapon and saw both runestones glowing. Dorian felt a mixture of excitement and terror. He could feel the power of the stones permeating his arm.

Green flame burst from the sword. The heat from the blaze felt like an inferno. Turning his head, Dorian held the sword as far away from himself as his stretched arm would allow. The group gasped and took a step back, watching in amazement.

"It worked!" Uttered an exuberant Elijah.

Suddenly, the sword began to shake. Dorian struggled to maintain his grip. A black shadow crept up the blade until the weapon became cloaked in a swathe of pitch darkness.

Without warning, the weapon erupted in an explosion of light. The intense illumination blinded the group, forcing them to close their eyes and turn their heads. Dorian, squinting from the sudden blast, could hear the panicked horses in the stables. The booming surge of light frightened the neighing stallions as they kicked and struggled to free themselves from their restraints.

Calm returned to the forge in an instant. Dorian opened his eyes, looked to his hand, and saw that he now only held the hilt of his sword. The blade crumbled, leaving a pile of ash on the floor.

He looked to Nathaniel in bewilderment. "What happened?"

"I don't know. We must have done something wrong." Nathaniel spoke in a disappointed tone.

Dorian thought for a moment. "Yes, but we also did something right. You saw it. The sword had a green flame! It turned black! That shows that both runestones were working in unison! We need to try again. We can get this right. I know it now more than ever!"

"You're right, Dorian!" Nathaniel interjected. "We'll

keep researching the books. Now we know that it is possible, and that is all we need! We are going to be the first people in history to combine the power of the runestones!"

Dorian spent the remainder of the evening enjoying his new friend's company. They talked and laughed throughout the night while finishing what little ale remained in the barrel outside his home. Early in the morning, the friends departed with a promise to meet up again the next night.

# Jonas

Jonas strapped on his armor. His hair struggled to maintain its natural black color as the gray slowly took over. Even with the several small scars on his face, and a crooked nose from having been broken too many times, most considered him a handsome man. His black armor shined with a coal-like luster. The shoulder guards resembled skulls with curved spikes protruding from the mouths and the metal of his gauntlets took the shape of bones surrounding his forearms. The buckle of his belt mirrored a skull, whereas above his armored boots, a smaller version of his shoulder guards served as knee protectors. A cape hung to his ankles and a darkness runestone imbued on his chest shimmered through the hole at the center of his breastplate.

Finished with adorning his armor, Jonas entered the quaint living quarters. An old woman sat in the center of the room on a rocking chair, staring blankly into space while a child of no more than five years sat on the floor playing with a doll made of straw. To his left, a woman with dark hair pulled into a bun prepared a morning meal in the small kitchen.

"Father!" The child exclaimed as she ran to Jonas and hugged his waist.

"Careful of the spikes, Sofia," he cautioned as he returned the hug by carefully placing both hands on her back.

"I know," Sofia replied and gave her father one more squeeze before returning to play with her doll.

"Good morning, Jonas!" His wife called from the kitchen. "Breakfast will be ready in a minute."

"Good morning, Marie. I am running late. Going to have to skip breakfast this morning, I'm sure they are waiting for me right now."

Jonas walked over to the old woman. Looking into her eyes, he saw nothing but a blank, expressionless gaze. "Good morning, mom," Jonas gently whispered, kissing her forehead as he wiped a small amount of drool from her chin.

Walking to Marie, he embraced her. "Any change this morning?" Jonas turned to look at his mother.

"None. I'm sorry, Jonas."

"I hate seeing her like this. Is the doctor coming to see her today?"

"He said he would be by this afternoon to check on her. Your helmet and sword are on the table. Do you think you will see King Thomas today?"

"I don't know. If I do, I will speak to him." Jonas replied, knowing the purpose of her inquiry.

"Okay. Is there anything, in particular, you'd like to have for dinner?"

"Whatever you'd like. I'm sure whatever you prepare will be delicious." He kissed his wife and added one final embrace. "I'll see you tonight."

Jonas exited his home and immediately stood in the palace courtyard. A thin veil of dust covered the area as armored men kicked up clouds of dirt. Some dueled each other to hone their swordsmanship while others practiced throwing spears at straw dummies. Some fired arrows into targets, some jogged the perimeter to keep in shape. When the men saw Jonas, they ceased their activities and took formation.

The soldiers lined up in ranks. A single soldier stood out in front, guiding the men into position through shouts and gestures. Ten blocks of men lined up shoulder to shoulder. Each block consisted of ten rows of ten men, roughly half of the men enlisted in the king's guard, not including the Bannermen who bore allegiance to the seven lords of the kingdom.

The soldiers wore identical half-plate armor and stood rigid with their arms straight at their sides. A red, crowned heart decorated the front and back of their breastplates and helmets. The man guiding them into place wore armor identical to the rest of the men with the addition of a yellow pair of crossed swords painted on the shoulder guards, signaling that he bore the rank of colonel.

Jonas approached the colonel from behind. After guiding a few stray soldiers into place, the colonel spun on his heels and placed his fist over his heart in a salute. Jonas returned in kind.

"Good morning, Colonel. Anything to report?"

"Good morning, High Commander. All troops present and accounted for. Nothing to report."

"Good. Any promotions to consider?" Jonas asked.

"No promotions, sir, but we have a new recruit, and I felt that you might find him…interesting."

"Interesting, huh? Very well. Bring him forward."

"Yates! Private Yates! Step forward!"

Jonas watched a young man jog down the aisle between the blocks of men. He saluted hard against his breastplate after approaching the colonel. Posturing himself to attention, the young man shouted, "Colonel! Private Yates reporting!"

Private Yates measured a little shorter than Jonas. His disheveled and unevenly cut dirty blonde hair gave him a raggedy appearance, and his mismatched and loose fitting armor only added to his slovenly appearance. Whether clean-shaven or too young to grow a full beard, Jonas couldn't tell, but the high commander thought he appeared too young to be an enlisted member of the king's guard, yet his build represented that of a man in his prime.

A staff with long curved blades at each end, unlike any Jonas had previously seen, was clutched in the new recruit's hand. Ragged bandages, covered in stains of dirt and blood, spanned the length of the shaft, providing evidence of years' worth of arduous practice hours with the weapon. A piece of copper wrapped around the center kept the two halves together, and the blades looked worn yet well cared for with nicks, scratches, and dents covering the rustless, shiny metal.

The colonel turned to Jonas and said with a smile, "Enthusiastic, isn't he?"

"What is your full name, Private Yates?" Jonas

asked, approaching him.

"Private William Yates, High Commander, sir!" He replied with a loud shout while fixing his gaze blankly forward.

"Where are you from, Yates?"

"High Commander! A small town called Granja in the province of Villam, High Commander, sir!" William provided with an even louder shout that caused Jonas to cringe a bit.

"Yes, High Commander." He responded at a lesser volume.

"Granja? Isn't that a farming town? Are you a farmer?"

"I come from a family of farmers, but joining the king's guard has always been my intention, High Commander, sir."

"How old are you Private?"

"Eighteen, High Commander."

"That weapon, where did you get it?"

"I made it myself, High Commander, sir!" William began shouting again.

"Made it yourself? It's not exactly regulation."

"Shall I turn it in for a regulation weapon, High

Commander, sir?"

"I haven't decided yet. How about you spar with me so that I can make a determination?"

"Sir?" William asked, shifting his eyes to look at Jonas for the first time.

"You heard me."

"High Commander! The blades of this weapon are sharpened. I do not have a sparring weapon."

"I didn't ask if you had a sparring weapon, Private. I want you to use that one." Jonas said, drawing his sword, a massive blade that dragged on the ground when sheathed on his hip.

William reacted by twirling his weapon in both hands and moving to a fighting stance.

"Fall out and bring it in!" The colonel shouted. The troops formed a circle around Jonas and William, as the two men rounded each other.

The soldiers cheered and chatted amongst themselves. Jonas beamed a smile as the thrill of battle flashed across his face. To his surprise, William's expression did not show an ounce of fear.

Jonas rushed in for the first strike with an overhand swing, knocking the young man's weapon sideways. William quickly swung the opposite side of the staff toward the commander's head, but Jonas leaned back to dodge. Jonas returned with a series of strikes that, to most, seemed unnaturally fast for a man to swing with a sword of that size, but William successfully met each stroke with his blade.

"Nice reflexes, son, now let's see how you handle this!"

Jonas darted in with another overhand strike. William aimed to knock the swing away, but Jonas halted the attack short, forcing William to miss the parry. Jonas followed up with a horizontal swing, forcing the soldier to duck. With William's head low, Jonas lifted his knee to strike the young man in the chin, making sure he tucked his leg far enough to ensure the spike on his armor did not puncture William's skull. Private Yates fell hard onto his back and swiftly spun to his feet, returning to a fighting stance.

The crowd cheered. Jonas could not tell if they were cheering for him, or William, who already lasted longer than soldiers of higher rank endured in the past.

"You're going to have to do better than that if you want to keep using that weapon, Private!" Jonas jeered twirling his massive sword.

"Yes, sir!" William replied with a shout as he darted

in for the attack, surprising Jonas with a bold initiative.

The young private spun his weapon around, attempting to land a blow on the high commander, but Jonas skillfully blocked each strike. William tried a feint of his own, but Jonas, being the far more experienced warrior, predicted the move, and drove his elbow into William's chest.

"Done already?" Jonas taunted as William clutched his chest, knowing the blow would produce a substantial bruise.

Sweat dripped from the warriors' heads. Jonas's heavy breathing seemed shallow compared to William's panting, a result of facing a far superior foe.

In a surprise move, William took two steps back, dropped his weapon, and began to take off his armor. Jonas watched in amusement. With the suit removed, William picked up his weapon and twisted the shaft in opposite directions, revealing the purpose of the copper fitting at the center. The staff separated with a small chain connecting the two halves, leaving both sections to resemble sickles.

William spun the weapon around his body with the grace and ease of an experienced warrior with many years of practice with the unorthodox blade. Finished with the demonstration, William held the two halves in each hand and crouched down to prepare for another attack.

"Now that, I did not see coming," Jonas stated with a smile as he raised his sword. "Well, let's see what that thing can do."

"With pleasure, sir!" William leaped into the air and swung his weapon with a twirl, producing a swooshing sound to momentarily linger in the air. Jonas knocked away the initial attack with his sword, but William followed the advance with a series of broad swinging and rapid attacks that left Jonas reeling in defense. Spinning the weapon between his hands with lightning speed and unexpected force, the flurry of attacks forced Jonas to retreat. Fatigue began to wane the effectiveness of William's assault. Jonas, seeing the opportunity, took advantage by swinging his sword horizontally, but William leaned back and landed a back handspring in avoidance.

Whipping his weapon in a circle, William launched the bladed tip at Jonas's head. Jonas raised his sword to block, but William yanked the weapon back before the strike could make contact. Following up, William swung the saber in an arc at Jonas, forcing him to dodge, but his reaction proved too late. The sickle grazed Jonas's breastplate leaving a small scratch on his sable armor.

The crowd fell silent. No one had ever lasted this long against Jonas, let alone touch him. Jonas's face fell deadpan as he narrowed his eyes at William. Jonas now knew that he must take this match seriously, something he had not done in many years.

Jonas stepped forward and began his assault. Each swing brought down with the full force of his considerable might. Pressing his advance, Jonas forced William to recoil, leaving him no room for a counter-strike. Dodging and ducking proved to be his only means of defense, as each deflection sent the private reeling. The speed and power of Jonas's attacks proved too much for the young soldier as Jonas raised his sword overhead and forcefully brought it down. William crossed the two halves of his weapon and raised them to catch Jonas's blow, but the overwhelming strength outmatched the young warrior. Jonas's sword crashed through the young man's weapon, splintered the shaft into pieces, and knocked William onto his back. Jonas placed his foot on his opponent's chest and hovered the tip of his sword above the defeated soldier's face.

William's face turned pale with terror as he stared back at the high commander's demonic look. Suddenly,

153

Jonas shifted his face into a broad smile as he offered his hand to William and pulled him to his feet.

"Now that…was fun!" Jonas exclaimed as the crowd erupted with applause. Without a doubt, Jonas knew who the crowd cheered for now. The troop poured admiration on the young man who, despite all odds, stood up to the fearsome high commander.

Jonas waved for the colonel to approach. "I want you to take this young man to the weaponsmith and tell him to recreate his weapon to his exact specification under my authorization."

"Yes, High Commander." Jonas could barely hear the colonel over the rapture of the crowd.

"You have a real future here, Private!" Jonas boasted to William. "I look forward to us having a rematch."

"Yes, High Commander. Thank you, sir." William responded excitedly.

While the crowd gathered around William in celebration, Jonas departed to attend his meeting in the Commander's Council, a room where the first through fifth division commanders met with the high commander to receive the orders of the day.

Walking through the courtyard, he heard the praise

being poured upon the young soldier. The regiment had forgotten to give Jonas the customary salute before he departed. Other high-ranking officials would have been insulted by the lack of respect, but not Jonas. Only joy sprang from his heart and the anticipation of witnessing the young man's bright future within the king's guard brought a smile onto his face.

# Razuul

Razuul sat in his cell. The thunderous roar of the crowd echoed down the hallway in anticipation of his upcoming match. They chanted his name at ear-splitting levels, hoping to entice the famous arena fighter into making an appearance, but he cared little for the crowd's desires. The opportunity to remove himself from his horrid living conditions awaited. His singular focus to escape the living hell of the last seventy years could now bear the fruit of freedom.

The identity of the king's champion, Razuul's final opponent in these atrocious fighting pits, remained a mystery. He lost count of the number of opponents he defeated to get this far, but it did not matter. Only whoever he met beyond the doors mattered, the final obstacle blocking him from joining the outside world.

He wished he could pray to the god that his wild elf brethren prayed to, but which god that was he could no longer recollect. Wild elf customs, traditions, and way of life fully escaped Razuul's memory. The imprisonment that he knew he did not deserve further fueled his rage. The only evidence of his heritage that remained were the tattoos near his left eye, on his shoulder and calf. They served as a constant reminder of his proud ancestry. He knew that he received these tattoos in his youth for accomplishments earned within his tribe, but he no longer remembered what he had done to deserve them, nor the meaning behind each marking. For seventy years, a short period for the long-lived elves, he dedicated every waking moment to concentrate on survival, purging his mind of all thoughts other than contempt and hatred.

"There he is! The only fighter to ever face the king's champion in the arena. I just had to come see you one more time old friend!"

Razuul lifted his head to see the familiar grin of a madman. Adam Garrison, one of the members of the team nicknamed, the Three Heads of Cerberus, laughed his high-pitched, maniacal cackle. Known throughout the kingdom as the elite group of fighters serving under the high commander of the king's guard, the Three Heads of Cerberus' reputation reached even the ears of those imprisoned. Adam Garrison embodied the brutal repute earned by the unyielding warriors. His dark brown hair hung in a long ponytail that dangled near the small of his back. He stood roughly as high as Razuul's chin but rarely stood still long enough for anyone to gauge his stature. His wide eyes always held a murderous look, leaving anyone else uncomfortable in his presence. His black half-plate armor, trimmed in red interwoven designs, reflected the dim light of the dungeon hall. A sword rested in its scabbard on his left hip, revealing the handle of the blade, which bore a silver dog's head with purple amethyst eyes.

Razuul sneered. He wished he could reach through the bars and break every bone in this man's body. The past few years taught him better than to try. He had attempted to assault his foe through the bars of his prison cell, but Razuul proved no match for Adam's speed and reflexes.

Razuul despised no one as much as Adam Garrison. For nearly a decade Garrison visited Razuul to harass and degrade him. He relished Razuul's misery. He would spit in Razuul's food and urinate between the bars of his cell for amusement. No one earned Razuul's hatred as much as Adam Garrison, and the thought of killing him drew a smile on the wild elf's face.

"How about you come in here so we can have a proper send-off." Razuul taunted.

"Oh, I would, but I'd hate to spoil the fun we are about to have in the arena."

"You are the king's champion? If you're the best this kingdom has to offer, an army of ants should be enough to topple it." Razuul mocked with a half-crooked smile. If the king selected this vile human as his champion, his day would be even better than he anticipated. Razuul wondered which method he would use to kill him. Perhaps pulling his tongue out through his throat or widening his expansive smile with the blade of a sword. The possibilities seemed endless!

"Oh, I didn't say that. The king's champion is even scarier than me!"

"Then who is it? The High Commander?"

"Now, now, I wouldn't want to spoil the surprise! Where's the fun in that?" Adam boasted, bringing his face dangerously close to the bars of the cell. "I just came here to see my ol' pal one…last…time!"

"I don't know. Maybe we will see each other on the outside! I wonder how that meeting would end." Razuul remarked, thinking he might risk returning to the arena just to kill this man.

"Oh! You still believe you're going to get out today? Now that's funny! Sorry, my friend, but you stand no chance!"

"We'll see about that!"

"Yes, we will!" Adam walked away while his evil laugh echoed down the empty corridor.

Razuul sat on his cot, contemplating the identity of his opponent. He assumed the high commander of the king's guard, Jonas Werner, would be the king's choice. The high commander never set foot in the arena, but his fierce reputation spread to every corner of the kingdom. Jonas Werner, considered the greatest warrior in the empire, possessed legendary sword skills and vast magical abilities. If the king wanted Razuul dead, he thought, no candidate stood a better chance to complete the task.

"Hey, Razuul!" A voice from outside the cell called. "Over here!"

Razuul looked into the cell across the hall and saw a stoutly built man leaning against the bars. He looked in prime condition for a prisoner, making a worthy opponent for any fighter. Razuul thought it would take double the amount of time it usually took to kill this man, two seconds.

The other prisoners in the man's cell retreated to the

perimeter walls as they stared at the man who dared to speak to Razuul. Typically, he would have ignored or threatened the man talking to him, but the day's circumstance placed him in a particularly good mood. Even though Adam Garrison managed to stir his rage, Razuul felt confident that today he would walk as a free man.

"Who's talking to me? Do you have a death wish?"

"My name's Brett, and you can threaten me all you like, but today is the day you can earn your freedom, so I doubt you'll have an opportunity to kill me."

"What do you want human?"

"Nothing. Just wondering, what will you do if you get out?"

"You mean when I get out."

"Apologies, when you get out."

"I am going to find my people."

"Your wild elf tribe? How do you know they are still alive?" Brett slid to the floor to take a seat near the bars.

"How do you know I'm not going to kill you for asking me that question?" Razuul replied in annoyance, rising from the cot to walk to the bars of his cell. "If you think those prison bars will save you, you are dead wrong!"

"Whoa, you sure are touchy," Brett shifted his body

to sit criss-cross, facing Razuul. "You know, on the outside, if you kill someone just for asking you a question, you'll end up right back here."

"I'm never coming back here. I'd rather die. Why do you even care?"

"I don't. Just thought I would have a conversation with the first person to free himself from the arena. I don't care what that idiot Adam Garrison says. I believe you are getting out of here today. Besides, having a conversation with the infamous Razuul might be the last interesting thing I do, because I know I am not making it out of here alive. I'm a thief, not a fighter."

Razuul thought for a moment and realized that he spoke with a man who had come to terms with his fate. Terms he could never accept. For the first time, a human earned a small amount of respect. Fighting his urge to kill any prisoner that dared speak to him, he decided to tell his story for the first time since his incarceration.

"I know they are alive because I saw them. Slavers took me when I was still very young. After being thrown into a cage, I saw my people fighting as the cart took me away. I did not see how it ended because I was gone before the battle ended. I am sure of one thing though, my people were winning! I've thought about it a thousand times. There weren't enough of the slavers left alive to win that battle. I am sure they survived!"

"Good, good. I hope you find them. I also hope that the king's champion is that asshole High Commander so that you can kill that bastard."

"You know him?"

"Yeah, I know him. He came from the same place as me, Tenebris. He's the type of man that would rather push someone down instead of helping them up. When he looks at you, you feel like he's thinking of ways to kill you. I bet he's the reason I'm in here without receiving a trial, that prick."

The creaking sounds of the massive double doors opening interrupted the conversation. Two guards walked past the cells carrying a body on a stretcher covered by a blood-soaked sheet. Razuul knew that the guards would arrive shortly to escort him to his final match.

As expected, a cavalcade of guards arrived at Razuul's cell, but something seemed different. The guards didn't look as terrified or nervous as usual. One of the guards stood with his spear upright as another one opened the cell. Razuul guessed that the guards must have known that Razuul wouldn't risk his chance at freedom.

Razuul exited his cell and began, what he believed, his final descent down the familiar hall. He heard Brett wish good luck and responded with a nod of his head. It amused him that on this, his last day as a prisoner, he held a conversation that didn't end in death threats. Even though the chat was short, he took it as a good omen for positive things to come.

The guards escorted Razuul to the X in the arena. As the guards ran away, he heard one of them shout, "See you later, asshole!"

Razuul closed his eyes and basked in the rays of the sun. Feeling the light's warmth had always been his favorite part of these contests, a brief interlude of tranquility in an otherwise bleak existence. Today he would ensure that no one ever took the sun away from him again. Opening his eyes, he looked down at his shirtless body. Countless battles left scars scattered across his bronze skin. The origin of the wounds faded from his memory long ago, yet he felt pride for the story they told. He thought of them as replacements for the tribal tattoos he should have received by his age, for the wild elves were a race of proud warriors.

The crowd poured their excitement into the arena. The screeching pierced Razuul's elfish ears like a thousand needles. Looking at the bloodstained walls, he noticed a difference to the typical layout. None of the weapons that normally hung on the arena walls were present, and no one laid out the chalk X for his opponent. His mind raced to figure out what deranged game played in the king's mind.

The crowd grew silent when the king stood. Razuul knew the proper tradition of standing at attention in reverence to the king, but he refused to give the man responsible for his incarceration any respect. The king approached a metal podium where a wind runestone, attached to a copper funnel, stood before him. Placing a finger on the runestone, the king spoke into the device, amplifying his voice. "Welcome to the final match of the evening!"

The crowd erupted in cheers. Razuul heard the king's voice for the first time. None of his previous matches preceded with an announcement, leaving him to assume that the special circumstances of the contest prompted the king to address the crowd. The king waited for a moment before raising his hand to bring a hush back to the crowd. "For this match, the city of Sanctum has generously provided the aid of the paladins, who currently cast a Barrier Spell around the arena walls."

Razuul looked at the top of the arena walls. In place of the usual archers, several heavily armored men surrounded the perimeter. With hands raised, a white glow emanated from their chest pieces. The air distorted around the men, like the vapors rising from a flame, but Razzul couldn't see any other sign of a barrier. He looked at the king, confused by the sudden changes.

"Today, we shall bear witness as the wild elf, Razuul, fights in his fiftieth contest against a champion of my choosing. This is the first time anyone has defeated forty-nine opponents in the history of the arena. To mark this auspicious occasion, I have instructed the guards to remove all weapons from the arena walls. The fighters shall utilize only what the Gods gave them, and if the Gods deem Razuul worthy, he will earn his freedom this day through victory."

The crowd roared, heightening Razuul's anticipation. The king raised his hand to finish his announcement. "I give to you, my champion!" The king gestured toward the doors.

The opposing doors began to creak open, but before they could reveal Razuul's opponent, a dragon burst through the opening. The doors smashed into pieces, leaving jagged splinters of wood hanging from the hinges.

Razuul's eyes widened in shock as the dragon let out

a deep, guttural roar to the sky, loud enough to drown out the gasps and screams of the astonished crowd.

Razuul instantly realized the king's game. Removing the weapons to "use only what the Gods gave them" put the wild elf at an insurmountable disadvantage.

The enormous dragon sneered at Razuul with the look of a starving, crazed beast. Its head spanned the length of Razuul's body, with small spikes of bone protruding across its face. Green saliva leaked between rows of long, jagged teeth, releasing puffs of smokes as the acrid slime dripped onto the dirt of the arena floor, sizzling like grease in a hot skillet. Two horns jutted backward from the top of the dragon's head, and a row of curved spikes fell in a perfect row down the creature's back, from the base of its skull to the tip of its long whipping tail. Daylight highlighted tinges of green across its otherwise black, scaly hide like the reflective surface of murky pond water. Four sturdy legs supported webbed toes embellished with brown, crusty talons. Pinned to the dragon's torso, a pair of wings bound by thick rope protruded from behind its shoulders.

The dragon reared its head, and with a snort, shot a streaming jet of flame. Instinctively, Razuul dove to avoid the flames, leaving the firey breath to crash into the wall.

Glancing to where the attack landed, Razuul saw the circle of black embers on the stone and knew it could have been his demise. The dragon charged as the lone warrior scrambled to his feet. With an arm's length of distance between Razuul and the stampeding beast, it snapped its jaw but bit only air as Razuul sidestepped the attack. Without thought, the undefeated warrior cocked his arm and punched the dragon's face with all his might.

The dragon seemed unfazed by the strike, and Razuul knew his folly well. Blood dripped to the ground, the causality of putting a fist to the pointed bone. Razuul turned to flee the beast's follow-up attack, but the winged lizard's quick reflexes prevented escape. Whipping the side of its head, the force of the blow tossed Razuul into the air and sent him crashing into the arena wall.

Razuul's head swam as he lay in the dirt, feeling the warm sensation of blood pouring down his face from a broken nose. Regaining his senses, he craned his neck to locate his beastly opponent, only to see the treacherous danger of his situation. The dragon's body swelled as far as the constricting ropes would allow, drawing another deep breath to spew more jets of flame. Razuul clambered to his feet and dove away from the flaming attack, but his dulled senses from the wall strike slowed his reaction. The fire bathed his legs below the knee in scorching heat, peeling the skin and leaving charred hunks of tissue where bronze flesh was a moment ago.

Intense pain seared in his legs as Razuul struggled to regain posture. Forcing himself to his feet, he glanced at the ruin of his legs before turning his attention back to the dragon. Rumbling a deep growl, the dragon crept toward him with his head low and legs crouched. The earth vibrated with each step. Its upper lip trembled in a sneer, flashing the fangs within its maw. Taking him by surprise, the beast launched into the air to pounce.

Razuul darted, grimacing from the pain in his legs. The attack missed Razuul, producing a rumbling thud that quaked the ground. Bracing himself, he expected another strike from the dragon's head, but the beast whipped its tail into Razuul's side instead, sending him flying once again.

After his body stopped rolling and scraping against the gravel, it took all of Razuul's effort to stand. With diminished strength, the prideful elven warrior devised a plan and grabbed two handfuls of dirt as he rose.

The snarling dragon approached its prey. Razuul swayed like a blade of grass in the wind. The dragon cautiously gained on the disillusioned combatant, bringing its long snout before Razuul's face, close enough for him to smell the dragon's rancid breath. Sniffing and tilting his head from back and forth, while staring into Razuul's eyes, the dragon looked confused by the wild elf's inaction to the threat presented. The dragon let loose a guttural roar, blowing Razuul's hair back like a windstorm and drenching him in foamy, hot saliva. With a fearless, blank expression, the dazed elf remained motionless. The dragon, confident that Razuul had given up the fight, opened its mouth to make a meal out of the stationary warrior. Just before the fire-breathing monster could rip him in two, Razuul pitched the two handfuls of dirt into the dragon's eyes.

The dragon squeezed its eyes closed, violently throwing its head from side to side, leaving strands of spittle spewing in all directions. Razuul stepped away from the convulsing dragon and waited for his opportunity. The beast shuttered its eyelids to clear its vision and roared in frustration. Seizing the moment of temporary blindness, Razuul jumped onto the dragon's back. Wrapping his arms around the beast's neck, he leaned back and squeezed, choking the dragon with surging energy.

The dragon fought back like a bucking bronco, but

Razuul refused to release the mighty creature. The dragon's spikes drove into Razuul's body as he brought his legs around the dragon's neck, hooked his feet together, and added his leg strength to the stranglehold.

The dragon began to panic. Smoke billowed from its mouth and nostrils. Its wings struggled to break free from the binding ropes. The determined warrior's arms and legs bled, rubbed raw against the razor-rough hide. Razuul leaned his head back, howling a primal roar as he poured his waning strength into the grip. Before his attack could yield results, he felt the beast shift, and he knew the dragon's intent. The dragon dropped to its side to roll and crush the wild elf with its tonnage. Before he could be flattened, Razuul released his grasp and jumped from harm's way.

The dragon struggled to its feet and wavered like a drunken soldier. Razuul glanced at his body, his bronze skin disappeared beneath the layer of blood and filth that covered him. He felt woozy, and staggered for a moment, barely keeping his mind from falling into unconsciousness. Looking back at the scaly serpent, he saw it rear back as it drew in air to release another inferno from its gullet. The attack would have found its mark, but before throwing the flame, powerful energy enveloped Razuul, heightening his awareness.

Calm tranquility cloaked Razuul. Colors became brighter and more vibrant. The foul scents within the amphitheater flooded his nose with distinguishable and overwhelming odors. Sound left his ears except for the rasp of his labored breathing. The warm spring breeze tingled on his skin like a thousand feathers gently brushing against him. Razuul could feel the presence of every living thing in the arena, including the tiny life force of the scurrying ants, as they carried the dropped crumbs from the crowd to their queen. He felt the blood thirsty essence of each person in the audience. In particular, the life force of the king stood out to Razuul, like a beacon, full of malice and contempt.

Time crawled. The crowd moved in slow motion. The inhale of the dragon appeared to take an eternity, allowing Razuul to contemplate whether this change came from some strange magic, or from somewhere within himself.

Flames rolled from the dragon's mouth at a snail's pace. An amber glow, like embers from a smoldering fire, radiated from the dragon's chest. A soundless alarm rang inside Razuul's mind, drawing his focus to the winged serpent's gleaming chest. He knew the glow marked a weakness in the dragon's hide, a vulnerable chink in the beast's scaly armor that he could exploit if he reached the dragon before it finished spewing its deadly flame.

Razuul sprinted, avoiding the firey blast. He could feel the intensity of the flames as he closed in on the light that burned inside the dragon's chest. Mustering every ounce of strength, Razuul cocked back his arm and drove his fist, elbow deep, into the dragon's chest. He clutched the pulsating organ gyrating inside the ruptured breast. Blood splattered Razuul, drenching him in the hot crimson liquid as he yanked his arm from the crater in the monster's torso.

Looking at the bloody mass in his hand, Razuul spiked the dragon's pumping and spurting heart to the ground. Its eyes crept shut as the mammoth body toppled on its side, releasing a puff of slow-moving dust from the earth.

Within an instant, Razuul's senses returned to normal. Time began to move at its normal pace again. Colors returned to their usual vibrancy. The odors of the arena restored to their original pungent mixture. His hearing returned, although the crowd's utter silence made it difficult to be sure. Staring at the lifeless dragon, the edges of his vision grew black, shrinking his field of sight until the enclosing circle of darkness shrouded his view.

# Elendor

The half-moon floated in the clear night sky like a ship in a shimmering sea of stars. The four friends sat around a small fire, attempting to keep the frigid evening air at bay. Elendor clutched his one good hand on the inside of his travel cloak to keep the cold from his shivering bare skin. The biting chill in the air stung on his nose, cheeks, and the tips of his ears. He scurried his legless body across the ground to bring himself closer to the fire.

Jocia helped Elendor to wipe his runny nose. He despised having to rely on his friends for the most mundane of everyday actions, but he appreciated those who never complained about assisting.

Galain spoke above the crackle of the fire. "You must tell us our destination. We have been traveling for days without any clues as to where this journey ends. I believe it is time for you to relinquish the answer to this mystery, Elendor."

"The answer is the same as it has been every night Galain, it is a surprise," Elendor replied with a sly smile.

"Can't you at least tell us when we will get there?" Vaylon asked, shivering.

"Please Vaylon, cease these contractions. The word is cannot." Elendor corrected. "And to answer your question, we shall arrive in the afternoon of the morrow."

"If our destination draws that near, could you not provide a clue? Please?" Jocia asked in sweet tones that made Elendor's stomach flutter with butterflies.

Elendor's soft spot for Jocia's sweet voice always crumbled his resolve, and he felt as though she knew it. He stared at the fire for a moment before resigning to provide the answer that wore on the minds of his friends. "Very well, I shall give the information you desire; however, you must ensure that you remain calm, and keep your minds open."

The friends held gleeful expressions as they nodded their heads in agreeance. Elendor knew their smiles would extinguish by uttering the single word, "Tenebris."

As predicted, Jocia, Galain, and Vaylon's faces fell blank. "The City of the Dead?" Galain questioned.

"A horrible title given by an ignorant populace to incite fear of what is misunderstood. The citizens of Tenebris worship Morthem, the God of Death. This does not mean that they are evil; rather they are…different."

"Surely this is understood, Elendor," Jocia informed. "The history of the provinces was taught to us at a young age. Tenebris is the location of the Gates of Transet. The nobles of the kingdom bring their dead there to receive the Last Rites for safe passage into the afterlife. It is considered a holy city with a rich cultural heritage. The concern is that the residents practice necromancy! They consider death to be an honor! A stark contrast to the values and beliefs of the elves."

"It is rumored that the creation of chimeras is permissible there! To combine severed portions of animals with the goal of creating an unnatural beast is an insult to the laws of Terram, the Goddess of Nature!" Galain insisted with disgust in his voice.

"I heard skeletons and zombies roam freely within the city walls," Vaylon added.

"I am quite sure those rumors are exaggerations, and I have read that the creation of chimeras is no longer a lawful act." Elendor kept his gaze fixed on the fire, unwilling to look at their faces for fear that they would sense his uncertainty.

176

"What could you possibly hope to achieve by visiting that place?" Jocia asked with genuine concern.

Elendor knew he could no longer hide the goal of this journey. He hoped he could keep the secret until they were nearly upon their destination. To cure his friend's curiosity, he decided to reveal his objective. Looking at Vaylon, he pointed to his knapsack. "Could you hand me that please?"

After receiving the pack, Elendor withdrew a thick piece of refined wood in the shape of a left arm, cut off where the elbow would typically be. Polished to a glossy sheen, the arm reflected the flickering light of the campfire. The five fingers curled slightly, as if grabbing an invisible sphere. The lines carved into the joints and palm gave it the appearance of a natural born appendage. Elendor held up the prosthetic arm and said, "This is the reason I wish to reach Tenebris."

"I don't, I mean…I do not understand." Vaylon stated in confusion.

Galain understood Elendor's intentions. Jumping to his feet, he shot a look of disdain at Elendor. "He intends to attach that to himself! The amount of our laws you are attempting to break is unfathomable, this is…"

"What Galain? An abomination? I know the laws of

the forest! 'Be one with nature, not merely a part of it.' I have heard it for the entirety of my existence. It is why I grew this in secret on the floor of my room without involving any of you. I knew that you would not understand, but circumstances have changed. The elves, my own people, have exiled me from the only place I have ever called home. For what? The deformations of my birth? What control did I have over my development within the womb? Now I face more uncertainty than ever, but there is one thing I am sure of: the laws of Parvus Arbor no longer apply to me. They are for those who reside within the safety of the treetops, and I am no longer a welcome citizen of that place. All I desire is to do the things everyone else does, like walk, or wipe my own face! Is that so wrong?"

"But why Tenebris? I thought you could already control plants?" Vaylon asked.

"My ability only applies to plants that are living. The moment this was removed from the tree, my magic no longer held any sway over it. The necromancers of Tenebris can control the dead. If I can acquire the knowledge of how they accomplish such a feat, I may be able to combine their necromancy with my arbormancy."

"Have you created legs as well?" Jocia asked. The

178

dejected look on her face threatened to tear Elendor's heart in two.

Reaching back into his knapsack, he pulled out two wooden legs as smooth, polished, and detailed as the arm.

"I'm impressed, Elendor. I think it is great that you want to walk. I hope this works!" Vaylon expressed with delight.

"I think you meant 'I am' impressed, Vaylon. I am surprised that you find this agreeable. How do you intend to remain so big and strong if you no longer have to carry me around anymore?" Elendor joked.

"I understand, Elendor. The ways of the elves are no longer our ways. We are our own elves now, free to make our own choices and our own decisions." Jocia stated, taking Galain's hand. "We shall support you in this and assist you however we can."

Elendor felt that his heart would soon burst with jealousy upon seeing Jocia take Galain's hand, but he refused to allow his emotions to get the better of him. Shooting a fake smile, he gave his friends a nod to show his silent gratitude.

Galain stared at the fire as he contemplated the unexpected information. "You are correct, Jocia. The ways of Parvus Arbor no longer apply. If they cannot accept our friend, then they cannot accept us. We shall assist you in any way we can, Elendor. I cannot wait to see you walk for the first time."

"Thank you, my friends. I am deeply sorry that I have placed my burdens upon you. I know this has been difficult, being ripped from our homes, having to sleep without a roof over our heads. Perhaps after we arrive in Tenebris, and get my new legs and arm to function, we can return to Parvus Arbor and demonstrate the folly of their beliefs. I am not some monster to be hated and cast out. We can show everyone, even that old grump Morace, that we can evolve and accept everyone for who they are."

"Do you not believe that everyone will be offended when they see you walking about on wooden legs?" Galain asked.

"At first, yes. However, when I show them that I can be a productive member of society, perhaps I can convince them that I had no other choice. My absence should soon provide them with clarity. My arbormancy provides many necessary functions within the city. It will take time, but I believe I can make them see."

The friends embraced one another. Elendor knew

they felt the same as he did. They longed to return to their home. He could feel the joy brought to their hearts upon hearing his intentions. Bundling up near the fire, they drifted off to sleep, dreaming fondly of their eventual return home.

The next morning, the young elves packed up to resume their journey. Traveling until the sun rose to its apex, they arrived at an entrance to a swamp. The dirt path before them twisted and turned throughout the trees, concealing its destination. Barely wide enough for two horses to walk side-by-side, the overgrown tree branches formed a natural tunnel. The pathway felt confined, as if the decrepit foliage underpass threatened to enclose them in a prison of moss and knurled branches. On either side of the trail, the murky water hid its contents as tiny pockets of air burst at the surface from the invisible creatures that thrived in the foul swamp. Black-trunked trees covered in moss and vines rose from the turbid water. Reeds with cattails danced in the breeze. A chorus of frogs and insects filled the swamp in song with a medley of high-pitched screeches and low toned croaks. The smell of rot and decay turned the advantages of the elven bloodline into a curse, as Elendor's heightened sense of smell forced him to hold his breath to keep his breakfast down.

The group urged their mounts forward, much to the dismay of the trembling horses. Vaylon led the pack followed by Jocia. Galain trailed the procession, keeping his eyes sharp and bow with arrow in hand, ready to intercept any enemy they might encounter. Elendor remained on alert, expecting a creature to leap from the water at any moment. Swarms of mosquitoes and gnats constantly buzzed in their faces and bit at their skin as they cautiously proceeded down the eerie path.

The nervous silence remained until the group encountered a fork in the road. "Which way?" Vaylon queried, looking over his shoulder to Elendor.

"I do not know!" Elendor nervously exclaimed. "I have studied the terrain a thousand times, I memorized how to get here years ago, it is how we got this far without a map, but I have never seen a fork in the path to Tenebris! At least not on any map in Parvus Arbor."

"It's the path to the right." Came an unfamiliar feminine voice from behind, putting everyone on high alert. As they turned to find its source, Galain raised his bow and drew back the string to the ready position. Jocia and Elendor raised their hands to cast a spell if the need arose, while Vaylon fumbled to pull a dagger from his belt. What they saw made them collectively gag and fight the urge to vomit.

Standing before them, a horse-like-abomination, saddled with a young girl on its back, loomed like a statue of grotesque hideousness. Black hair covered its head and neck except where patches of rotted skin hung, revealing red and blackened muscle tissue and bone fragments of its spine and skull. A portion of its upper lip was missing, exposing the monstrosity's rotting teeth. From its mouth, a tar-like substance oozed, hanging in loose strands from the bare bone of its chin. Its glossed eyes lacked any sign that the creature sustained life, and only scattered patches of mane remained on the decomposing hide. The neck, sewn to the body of a brown horse, appeared disproportionate to the creature's body, which bared sections of its rib cage as ropes of entrails swung loosely from its side. One front leg seemed to be from the same horse as the body, evidenced by the lack of stitches, while the other shorter and white furred leg caused the creature to lean awkwardly. Its twisted spine sloped down in the hind, revealing two feline legs of separate breeds. The tan fur of the left leg appeared to belong to a lion while the orange and black striped right identified a tiger origin. The long, hairless tail, belonging to an unidentifiable beast, whipped around its body in spasms.

The girl sitting atop its contorted back, a tiny human that appeared short and thin for her species, looked to be in the later years of youth. Her black, disheveled hair looked in need of washing many days ago, as did her filthy, yet pretty face. The runestone representing darkness embedded in the center of her forehead revealed her noble birth, as only those of high social standing were permitted to display runestones so prominently. Her sapphire blue eyes shone as brightly as her smile. A black hooded travel cloak draped across her shoulders exposed a dirty purple blouse beneath. Holes littered her pants and mud-covered her mismatched footwear, one tightened by a single strap near her knee, the other laced at mid-calf.

"W-what is that thing?" Jocia pointed.

The girl looked behind herself and then looked back at the group with a confused look on her face. "What is what thing?"

"Th-that h-horse…the thing you are sitting on!" Galain said nervously while still aiming his arrow.

"Oh! This is my horse. I named her Bunny! Isn't she cute?" The girl exclaimed, embracing the neck of the undead beast.

"Who are you?" Galain demanded.

"Oh, I forget my manners. It's hard to remember politeness when you're so rude to me. I'm sorry, my name is Lena Richter." She said with a smile and cheery voice.

"Rude? How are we rude?" Galain asked sternly.

"Well, you are pointing an arrow at me, and your friends are prepared to cast a spell. Is this acceptable behavior for meeting someone where you come from?"

Realizing the truth of Lena's words, the friends lowered their arms while keeping their uneasy gaze glued to Bunny.

"No, it is not. We apologize for our rudeness. My name is Elendor; this is Vaylon, Jocia, and Galain of Parvus Arbor. We are here to meet the Lord of Tenebris. Can you help us?"

"Oh, my!" Lena responded while looking at Vaylon. "The head growing out of your back talks!"

"I'm not-, he's not-, ugh, I am a tri-pelagic. He is carrying me. I am not growing out of his back!"

"Oh! That makes more sense!" The girl responded excitedly. "I thought maybe he was growing a new person."

"Why would you think…never mind, can you help us please?" Elendor asked.

"To meet Uncle Stefan? Sure! Come along. I'll show

you the way!"

"Uncle?" Elendor, Jocia, and Galain repeated. Lena snapped the tattered reigns and trotted ahead of the group. Dumbfounded by the lopsided gait of the unnatural mount, Elendor found himself staring at the bizarre sight while wondering how she kept from falling off. Lena followed the curve of the path and disappeared from view. Breaking their bewilderment, the group urged their horses forward to catch up to their guide.

The open gates of Tenebris sprawled out before them with a barricade wall extending beyond the reaches of sight on either side. Roughly twenty stones high and constructed of vertically stacked tree trunks, the defensive walls looked in desperate need of repair. In some places, rot and decomposition left gaping holes. In others, entire sections of the barrier bent in half, leaving the tops to rest in the marsh.

Black banners emblazoned with the white profile of a dog's head swayed in the breeze on either side of the lowered portcullis. Stationed in front of the gate, two armored skeleton guards, brandishing a spear and a shield on each arm, stood still as statues. At the top of the battlements, two more skeletons watched for intruders with drawn bows and arrows aimed at the gate's entrance.

Lena dismounted and gave the undead steed a gentle pat before the creature dissipated into a cloud of black smoke. "You can tie your horses there. They aren't allowed in the city." Lena pointed to several hitching rails in front of troughs filled with water. "I'll get the guard to allow you to enter, but wait for me to tell you it's safe. These skeletons will attack anyone who comes too close."

"Hey, Sebastian!" Lena called out. A crashing sound came from the top of the battlements as a portly black-robed man appeared. Rubbing his eyes, as if waking from slumber, he looked below to see who called his name.

"Oh, Lady Lena! Good afternoon!"

"Good afternoon, Sebastian! We have visitors!"

"Visitors? I don't have anyone on the list for the day!"

"They aren't here to schedule rites; they want to see Uncle Stefan!"

"Really? Yes, My Lady, hold on!" The man drew a runic symbol with his finger, persuading the four skeleton guards to lower their weapons. A moment later, the portcullis raised, releasing high-pitched screeching noises from the infrequently oiled gears of its operating mechanism.

"Alright follow me, but just so you know, you might

get some stares. We don't get many visitors here, and most people have never seen a person growing out of another person's back."

"I am not growing out of anyone's back!" Elendor refuted with frustration.

Lena shrugged her shoulders, turned and skipped merrily through the entrance as the four visitors followed. When the friends emerged from the gateway, they paused for a moment to take in the sight.

Like Parvus Arbor, each building utilized wood as construction material, although hammer and nail built these instead of arbormancy. The old, weathered buildings, stacked close to one another, featured the same dog's head banner at the entrance of each structure. The worn, uneven cobblestone streets showed their age and served as a hazardous walkway to anyone not paying close attention to each step. The decomposing odors of the swamp mingled with the city's scents of coal, wood, and meat, and left a burning sensation in Elendor's nose.

To the elven travelers who had never ventured outside their home city, the inhabitants of Tenebris proved to be the most shocking sight of all, in that, nothing seemed strange about them. No zombies or chimeras roamed the streets. The citizens performed no rituals, ceremonies, or acts of moral depravity. They were just regular people. Some dressed in black robes, some dressed in tunics and pants, and even some women wore lovely dresses. They all seemed to carry on in usual everyday activities of shopping, selling, building, and cleaning.

As they walked, the people in the streets stopped their activities to stare at them, making Elendor uncomfortable. His life as a deformed elf allowed him to grow accustomed to awkward stares, but he could not imagine how the gallant Galain and beautiful Jocia felt. Glancing at his companions, he saw Galain clutching at the dagger sheathed to his belt, while Jocia shot darting looks in every direction. Vaylon strutted through town, oblivious to the onlookers.

Lena skipped far ahead and turned back to wave them forward. She fidgeted with her clothes and spun in place impatiently waiting for them to catch up to her. When they did, an expansive building came into view.

Another wall of tree trunks surrounded the building which Elendor equated to be Tenebris's version of the Grand Hall. They traveled through the winding streets, all the while, hearing the whispers and seeing the wide-eyed stares of the citizens until they arrived at the defensive wall surrounding the massive structure. In the center of the wall, a series of interwoven, pointed bone fragments blocked the gateway, preventing any unwanted visitors from entering.

Above the wall, Elendor saw an elevated edifice with steps as wide as the massive building. In the center of the steps, a smooth wooden ramp, wide enough for a horse and carriage, divided the entrance into two sections. The building, the only structure within the city constructed of red stone and mortar, felt intimidating to the young elf. Four towers loomed at each corner, and a tower twice the height and width of the others sat in the center. The numerous stained glass windows, evenly spaced throughout the building, gave the structure a beautiful, yet eerie appearance. A set of enormous double doors, emblazoned with the same dog's head that decorated the city, permitted entrance to those brave enough to venture into the mysterious cathedral.

Lena, with her face full of excitement, exclaimed, "This is the fun part. You probably didn't know this, but I, am a necromancer!"

The friends looked at Lena, dumbfounded by her declaration "Yes, Lady Lena. The piecemeal, undead horse enlightened us of that detail." Jocia responded, trying her best to avoid sounding rude.

"Oh, right! I forgot about Bunny. Anyway, only a necromancer of the High Order of Tenebris is allowed to enter unescorted, and I know the Lord of Tenebris!"

Elendor responded for the group. "That was apparent when you called him Uncle Stefan."

"Oh, right! Well, anyway, here we go!" Lena turned toward the bone gate. Drawing out a runic symbol in the direction of the gate, the bone blockade sunk into the dirt as tendrils of black smoke rose from the ground. The companions took a step back in awe as they watched the bones disappear. Unfazed by the spectacle, Lena skipped through the gate and shouted, "Follow me" over her shoulder as she hopped, skipped and twirled her way up the stairs.

They climbed the seemingly endless set of stairs. Elendor could tell, as they approached the summit, that each step threatened to rob his friends of all their remaining strength. By the time they reached the top, they all panted and rubbed their legs, save for Elendor and Lena, who seemed unaffected by the climb. Opening the creaking door, Lena resumed her merry skipping as she entered the lobby.

The nervous visitors followed into the cavernous room dimly lit by lanterns. Rows of pews sat vacant, ready to seat hundreds of people. Stained glass windows allowed the filtered sunlight to peek through, leaving a rainbow hue to lay across the dog's head banners lined on opposing walls.

Beyond the pews, four stairs led to a platform where a long wooden altar stood. Recently extinguished candles smoldered atop long metal stands. Of all these new and intriguing sights for Elendor to absorb, the wall beyond the altar drew his attention.

As they traversed the path between the seats, Elendor realized that what he thought to be wall proved to be a gate that spanned to the ceiling. The doors, made of mahogany and trimmed with silver, mesmerized Elendor and his friends. Two circular pull handles were fixed onto each door, and an intricately designed silver runic symbol decorated the center. Carvings of beings with the feathered wings of a bird and the leathery wings of a bat enhanced the doors in a montage of chaotic beauty. The figures were engaged in scenes of violence, torment, cheer, and passion. Each depiction conveyed a different emotion and captivated Elendor in its disturbing artistry.

Entranced by their surroundings, the travelers jumped when Lena called out, waving her arm in the air. "Over here!"

"Uncle Stefan, some people are here to see you, and one of them is not growing out of the other's back!" She spoke loud enough that her words echoed off the ceiling.

Elendor and friends followed Lena into an office. A man seated behind a desk rose to greet them. The thin man stood a stone taller than Vaylon. Snow white hair receded to form two peaks pointing to the back of his head. His shimmering black robe extended from the top of his neck to the floor and reflected the dim candlelight like moonlight off the ocean's waves. A white cloth hung from his silver belt, bearing an embroidered dog's head symbol at the bottom.

Slumped in a chair in the corner of the room, a man with long brown dreadlocks paid the visitors no mind as he picked at the dirt beneath his fingernails. Dark bags hung beneath his coal colored eyes and thick stubble spread across his unshaven face. Dirt covered his torn tunic and shredded pants. For a moment, Elendor felt a chill run the length of his spine when he locked eyes with the man. His gaze felt unnatural and threatening; an aura radiated from the stranger that warned Elendor to keep his distance, like a soundless growl from a cornered dog.

"Well met, master elves!" The jovial white-haired man greeted in the traditional elven way as he walked around to the front of his desk. "The scheduling of the Last Rites is performed by the minister."

Lena looked around the room with an expression of confusion before pointing to the group of friends questioning, "Elves? Them?"

"Yes, Lena, they are elves. Now please go wash up, and change from those dirty clothes. The heir to the House of Richter should not be seen in such disarray."

Lena stuck out her tongue at her uncle and skipped out of the room humming a tune.

"She is the heir to Tenebris?" Elendor asked.

"Yes, that is correct. I am Lord Regent Richter. I hold this position until she reaches the age to become lord. By the looks on your faces, I can tell that you understand my plight. Her father, my older brother, was the Lord of Tenebris. Fortunately for him, he was allowed to pass into the afterlife at an early age, even for humans. I have tried my best, but she is...unique, even for one who holds sway over the dead. The man in the corner there is my bodyguard, Alexander Lupus."

The man in the corner acknowledged their existence with a carefree glance before returning to pick dirt from his fingernails.

"Well met, Lord Regent Richter. My name is Elendor. These are my companions, Jocia, Galain, and Vaylon. We have come to address a different matter than the scheduling of Last Rites."

"I thought it strange for elves to be here for rites. It was my understanding that elves possess their own customs for those who have passed."

"That is correct, we do. My friends and I have come here to request access to your library."

"Our library? That is an odd request. What would an earth mage need for books on necromancy?"

"As you can see, I am missing portions of my left arm and legs..."

"Let me stop you there. Yes, necromancers who have lost a limb can attach an arm or a leg from the dead to replace it, but this only works through the power of the darkness runestone."

"Galain, would you hand me my knapsack please." Elendor pulled out the wooden arm, presenting it to Stefan. "I am trying to attach this instead of a limb from the dead."

"I see. That is interesting. Do you hold sway over plant life?"

"I do."

"A rare talent indeed, but I..." Stefan stopped mid-sentence. A man burst through the doors panting and covered in sweat.

"Lord Regent Richter, we are under attack!"

"Attack? By who?"

"Centaurs!"

"Centaurs?" Stefan shouted with skepticism. "We will have to continue our conversation at a later date."

Grabbing an obsidian staff leaning against his desk, Stefan rushed from the room with Alexander close behind.

# Dorian

The past five nights for Dorian had been a far departure from his usual routine. During the day his regimen remained, but once the evening came, instead of working on his secret sword, he anxiously awaited his friend's arrival. Each night the friends brought new and exciting things for him. They brought different food to taste and new beverages for him to sample. His friends were filled with delight in telling enchanting tales, opening the door to a new world of intrigue. One night, they brought a flagon of wine, giving Dorian his first taste of the sweet liquid. He knew of the fermented drink from his books, but his father condemned the beverage as swill reserved for elves and highborn snobs. Dorian thought the drink too sweet for his taste, but found it amusing to watch Margaret over-indulge with the alcohol and make a fool of herself while hanging onto Lukas the whole night.

While they dedicated a portion of their nightly

routine to merriment and laughter, a majority of their time went to practicing magic. Dorian held no interest in imbuing a runestone onto his own skin, but the idea of magic and learning its mysteries intrigued him. He watched his friends practice repeatedly. It seemed they failed more than they succeeded, except for Nathaniel, who seemed unusually adept. The most significant debacle happened when Elijah attempted to cast an Ice Blast Spell but incorrectly drew out the runic symbol, resulting in a small explosion of frost and ice that threw him back into a tree. He remained unconscious for nearly an hour.

Deep into his routine, sweat glistened across Dorian's body from the arduous chores. The clear sky brought warmth, and the cool breeze kept the heat bearable. The perfect weather conditions made tasks a little easier on an exhausted body operating on roughly four hours of sleep every night for a week. Hard at work in the forge, Dorian's ears perked to the sounds of hoof beats and crunching gravel of wagon wheels outside. He rushed to see his father coming down the path with a smile on his face that would have been hidden by his unkempt beard if it weren't for his cheeks rising almost enough to shut his eyes.

The sight of his father coming home with his

disheveled look from nights of being in a drunken stupor was
anything but new to Dorian, but plenty of other things about
what he saw shocked him. Instead of the two small horses
his father left with, four enormous horses trotted down the
trail. In place of their usual two-wheeled cart, a vast four-
wheel cart bounced along the rocky path, jolting his father up
and down in its rhythmic stride.

"Dorian!" His father called with anxious excitement.
"You are not going to believe what I got this time!"

"A new cart and horses?"

"No, my boy, that's not what I meant at all." Thane
dismounted from the cart.

Dorian figured the burlap tarp covering the contents
of the wagon hid several barrels of dwarven ale, for only the
stout malt could paint his father's face with such a wide grin.
Thane snapped the cloth back sharply and exclaimed,
"Hygard steel!"

Dorian stood in awe. He heard his father tell many
tales of Hygard steel borne from the dwarven mountains of
Hygard, but the rarity of the special metal kept him from
ever gazing upon it. In his books nearly every hero used a
weapon made of the legendary material. Since the day he
picked up a hammer he dreamt of working Hygard steel into

weapons that would become a part of history. After years of his father's search for the fabled metal without success, all hope vanished that he would have a chance to fulfill his dream. Yet, right in front of him, neatly stacked rectangular bars of Hygard steel gleamed in the afternoon sunlight.

The legendary Hygard steel emerged from myth to reality, leaving Dorian exuberant that a dream from childhood had come alive. According to his father, thousands of weaponsmiths would live their life without laying eyes upon the fabled material. Yet, the gods saw fit to allow a humble half-dwarf to not only see the metal, but to work it into weapons that bore a chance to live in infamy.

Dorian's excitement stole his words. The illustrious bars shimmered in the bright color of silver with a tinge of blue throughout. Reaching out to touch the steel, another revelation surprised the young weaponsmith. "It's cold." Dorian looked at his father in confusion. The steel sat in the back of the cart for at least six hours, and even though a tarp protected the bars from the sun's rays, the midday heat should have made the bars nearly hot enough to cook a meal upon them.

Thane laughed his unmistakable laugh. "I figured that'd spook ya. Ever wonder why the furnace has eight fire runestones, yet we never use more than two? It's because you don't need more than two when smelting ordinary steel. Hygard steel requires far more heat, even though it's much softer than regular steel when it's in its raw form. But once you heat it, it becomes nigh unbreakable with an edge that never needs to be sharpened."

Dorian couldn't contain his glee. The anticipation of working with the legendary steel raised his spirits to new heights. He grabbed a bar and pulled to begin unloading it, but the material did not budge.

Thane bellowed a hearty laugh. "Did I forget to mention that it's also a lot heavier than regular steel? It will take both of us to unload it piece by piece, but that's a problem for later. Grab the rest of the supplies. I skipped breakfast, and I'm starving!"

Dorian began to unload the supplies when a thought occurred to him. "Father, how much did this cost?"

"Bah, don't you worry about that."

"Father, seriously, how much?"

"It was cheap, all things considered."

"What does that mean? How cheap is cheap?"

"Dorian, I am your father and…"

"Father, please!"

"Ten thousand!" Thane finally admitted.

"Ten thousand gold pieces? How did you even afford that? Plus, the new cart and the horses? There's no way you had that much money!"

"I took out a loan."

"A loan? Last time you did that, armed men were showing up here every day for two weeks! I had to stay in a tent, wet and starving until you paid them back, and we had to eat scraps for nearly a month until we got our finances back up. We even had to put down two of our horses!" Dorian shouted.

"I know all that Dorian! Do you think I'd forget?" Thane shouted in return.

"I don't know! Did you?"

"Of course not! You are my son and I never want to put you through that again. I know you are worried, but this time is different, I promise."

"But father, there's enough steel here to make maybe forty weapons, fifty if we stretch it out. Your weapons sell at fifty gold pieces per weapon. That's two thousand, five hundred. We'll still be way behind!"

"I understand your concern, but you're wrong on two accounts. I do not intend on making weapons purely from this steel. If you make a Hygard steel alloy by mixing in common steel, there's easily enough here to make over two hundred weapons. Second, a Hygard steel weapon sells at a much higher rate than regular steel. I can get three hundred gold pieces for every weapon I make, even if it isn't a pure Hygard steel weapon. No one makes a weapon from pure Hygard steel anyway. It's too heavy!"

Dorian relaxed. To his father's credit, the math did add up, but one problem remained with his father's plan. "At three hundred gold pieces per weapon, can anyone even afford to pay for these weapons?"

"I am Thane Kinsman! Master dwarf weaponsmith. People from far and wide come to buy my weapons because no one can match the quality of my wares!"

Dorian couldn't help but laugh at hearing his father's favorite phrase again.

"Don't worry lad, it will be different this time, I guarantee it. Now, let's go inside and eat before I wither away." Thane said, patting his rotund belly.

As they ate, Thane explained how to work the Hygard steel to Dorian while adding in the tales of his drunken adventures during his departure. The pair finished their meal and went outside to unload the steel. It took longer than expected due to the weight of the material, but with the task completed, Thane decided they had done enough for the day.

During dinner, Thane began to quiz his son. "So how was everything while I was gone? Did you get everything done that you were supposed to?"

Dorian's heart jumped. With all of the excitement over the new supplies, he forgot his friends would assuredly show up again this evening. "Aye, as expected."

Dorian struggled to hide his trepidation as ripples of fear travelled through his body. The repercussions of his rule-breaking scared him, but far less than his father's reaction to discovering his friends.

One other time in his life, during Dorian's youth, a stranger had accidentally shown up at their cottage. Dorian was playing outside when the wanderer spotted him. It was the first time in his life Dorian heard the term "mul." Dorian watched as his father spun into a rage and smashed the man's skull with his smith's hammer. After dragging the man's corpse deep into the woods with a shovel in hand, it took many hours before Thane returned, covered in dirt and soot.

A plan developed in Dorian's mind. Grabbing his father's empty mug, he held up the container and asked,

"Ready for another?"

Thane raised an eyebrow to his son. Dorian condoned his father's indulgence in ale, so offering to fetch more seemed rather unusual. With a shrug of his shoulders and a nod of his head, Thane accepted his son's offer of a refill.

Dorian knew his father well. The old dwarf would still be tired from his trip, and an extra pint or two of ale would send him to an early bed.

His plan worked. After filling his father's mug one more time, Thane yawned, stretched his arms, and went to bed. The sun nearly set when Dorian heard the familiar sound of his father's snores echoing within the cottage. Being as quiet as he could, Dorian crept outside to intercept his friends. The moment he creaked the door closed, he saw his friends, chatting and laughing as they came up the path. Dorian rushed out to halt their advance, holding his pointer finger to his lips. Once upon them, he whispered to his friends of his father's return and the peril it brought them. With a hushed voice, he told them to make their way to the old cabin as fast as they could before the sun set.

"How will we know when it's safe to return?" Nathaniel asked.

"When my father leaves again, I will put a leather

bandanna on the table in the old cabin. That will be the signal that it is safe to return."

The friends agreed to the plan and shook his hand goodbye except for Margaret, who gave him a warm embrace, taking Dorian by surprise.

Dorian felt a confusing mixture of emotions. He would not see his friends for at least a week. He had grown fond of their company, and the thought of their absence saddened him. They, too, seemed dejected about the news. Their dispirited reaction warmed his heart, making him feel like a true member of their group.

For the next two weeks, Dorian and Thane worked tirelessly. They crafted swords, axes, and spears in various shapes with the Hygard steel. Dorian accidentally made the mistake of allowing the metal to cool too much before returning the metal to the intense heat of the kiln. The alloy hardened before he could finish pounding it into the desired shape. Thane ensured that Dorian understood his mistake by yelling every profanity he knew and throwing every tool he came across into the forge walls.

By the end of the two weeks, they made enough weapons to bring to the city with half of their Hygard steel still in stock. Proud of the work they had done, Dorian wished he could see the people's faces when they saw Thane's new wares.

"Father, I think I should accompany you this time. If the wrong people discover that you have Hygard steel weapons in your cart, you will undoubtedly face confrontation by men with more greed in their heart than sense in their brains." For the first time, Dorian requested under pretenses. Accompanying his father to the city may have been a desire in the past, but now things changed. He missed the company of his friends, and each passing day proved to enhance his loneliness, leaving a void in his life that his father could not fill. To avoid any suspicions, he made the ritualistic request.

"Aye, it's a risk, but don't worry, I've got it covered," Thane replied pointing down the trail. Dorian followed his father's gesture to see four cloaked figures riding horseback, heading in their direction.

"Father!" Dorian exclaimed. Turning in circles in search of a place to hide, he found no reprieve from the approaching strangers. He began to run into the forge when his father grabbed him by the arm to halt his progress.

"Not to worry, son. I trust these people with both our lives. They are my closest friends. Besides, they already know about you."

"Friends?" The shock of Thane's proclamation nearly knocked Dorian from his feet. In all of his father's many stories, he never mentioned any friends. Dorian believed his father to be an untrusting old dwarf who would not share the secret of his son's existence with anyone.

The four travelers approached and drew back the hoods of their cloaks, revealing their faces. Each of the mysterious visitors appeared to be human and at an advanced age for their race.

"Son, I'd like to introduce you to my friends," Thane said as they dismounted to greet him. First, a man with white hair and a hairline that retreated toward the back of his head approached. "This is Sir Eldritch Kane."

"Enough with the sir stuff, Thane, I'm retired. Nice to finally meet you, Dorian." His baritone voice exhumed a fluent eloquence. As he shook Dorian's hand, deep wrinkles formed at the corners of his eyes when he smiled.

"This is Edward Whiteman." Edward stood with a regal posture, keeping his chin held high. "So very pleased to meet you."

"This is Mary Comey." The woman Thane introduced stood roughly the same height as Dorian. Her thick white hair, fixed into a bun at the back of her head, did little to hide the wrinkles around her eyes and mouth.

"It's Whiteman now Thane, not Comey." Her voice, more baritone and raspier than the melodic tones of the only other female he heard speak, retained feminine qualities. She gazed at him with a melancholy sadness beneath the tears welling in her eyes. "Oh Dorian, I have heard so much about you. You look so much like your mother!"

"M-my mother? Father, she knew..."

Thane cut off Dorian's question quickly. "Last but not least, this is Kurtis Bright." The last man walked up and grabbed Dorian by the shoulders. His long, silver hair, resembled the color of steel. "I can't believe it took this long to meet you!" Kurtis hugged Dorian tightly. Releasing the awkward embrace, he took another proud, long look at Dorian.

Thane mounted the cart and began to direct the horses to leave. "Don't forget to do your chores! I will be back in a few days."

"Father, what...? How...?" Was the only things Dorian could utter in bewilderment, as he watched the group prepare to leave.

"I'll tell you all about it when I get back," his father

called as he snapped the reins to depart.

Dorian remained standing in the middle trail for an unknown length of time. His mind raced, replaying the events that transpired over the past few weeks. Discovering the existence of his father's friends shook the very foundation of who he believed his father to be. The man he knew as a grumpy, old hermit who avoided personal relationships, transformed into someone who held deep caring for a group of people that he comfortable enough to share his secrets. Those friends seemed to know Dorian's mother, proving the longevity of his father's relationship with these people and the bonds he must share with them.

Adding to the disruption of his mundane existence, Dorian found friends, voiding his loneliness and solitude. He desired to be part of something more than just a partnership between him and his father. He could not imagine a life without them, even though the budding friendships were relatively new.

Dorian broke his mystified state and returned home to retrieve his bandanna. As he walked through the woods, he used this time of peaceful tranquility to decide how he would handle the rest of his day. The anticipation of reuniting with his friends threatened to drive him into insanity. He could not wait to tell his friends about everything that happened. By the time he arrived at the old cabin, he made his decision.

Dorian decided to slack off on performing his father's assigned tasks and fulfill selfish desires instead. He would forge a new sword and embed both the dark and the fire runestones. Using techniques and physical attributes handed down by the dwarven half of his ancestry, he intended on focusing every amount of skill and talent he possessed into creating a blade of perfection. Not a single blemish, nick or deformation would be acceptable. In a typical day, he could forge two or three blades in the time allotted, but for his blade, precision and attention to detail would need to prevail.

He couldn't help but feel betrayed by his father. The mystery of why his father never told him about the people he called friends nagged at him. The woman telling him he looked like his mother replayed in his thoughts in an inescapable loop. Questions overflowed in his mind like emptying a gallon of water into a pint-sized cup.

Returning to the forge, Dorian began the process of smelting steel, utilizing the technique of creating the Hygard steel alloy his father taught him. Half of the reserve of the metal remained in the forge, and his father's habit of losing track of the amount of material they possessed would, for the first time, work to Dorian's advantage.

Every step he took stood in defiance of his father's teachings, including the mixing ration of Hygard steel with ordinary steel. Intending on increasing weight and durability, he added nearly twice the amount of Hygard steel to the concoction. For a human, the added weight would make the sword impractical for use, but for one of dwarven ancestry, the extra heft only contributed to its destructive capability.

Dorian worked throughout the day forging his sword, skipping breakfast and lunch to attend to his masterpiece. His determination to create a blade unrivaled by any other weapon in history provided the only sustenance he needed. With this new mix of Hygard steel, his nervousness soared. Fearing the possibility of allowing the blade to cool too much, he reheated the blade far earlier than usual. With the sun nearly set, he removed the finished product from the cooling water and marveled at his creation. The edge seemed fine enough to split a hair in two. A theory Dorian would have tested if a single hair grew from his body. The alloy of the metal reflected a deeper hue of blue than the previous weapons he created. He tested the weight of the blade with an arcing swing; the sword felt more like an extension of his body than a weapon in his hand. After a few more swings that cut through the air with a whistling sound, Dorian put down his masterpiece and relinquished to his growing hunger pains.

Thinking that his friends could be there at any moment, he rushed inside to eat. After scarfing down his ill-prepared meal, Dorian returned to the forge, grabbed his new sword, and began polishing the blade. To his dismay, the sun soon dipped below the tree line, leaving him to believe that Nathaniel and the rest would not be visiting this evening.

Dorian roamed around the property lighting the outdoor torches that kept the nocturnal creatures away. He lit the final torch when a rustling from the woods caught his attention.

Shuffling leaves and snapping branches resounded as if a pack of creatures trounced through the woods in terror. Thumping sounds accompanied indiscernible voices.

Dorian trembled with anxiety as he cautiously approached the woods to locate the source of the commotion. The possibility of the disturbance being his friends allowed him to push down the fear and investigate. Gripping his sword in one hand, Dorian grabbed a torch with the other and crept toward the darkness.

Through the space between the trees, he spotted his friends fleeing at full sprint. Dodging trees, ducking under low branches and jumping over raised roots, they glanced over their shoulders to see the hulking outline of a beast that perused them. The figure didn't bother ducking or jumping. Obstacles shattered as it barreled along unhindered by the wooden foliage. The popping and snapping noises became louder as the creature swiftly gained ground on its prey.

Dorian identified what gave his friends chase as an umbra beast. The only creature that dwelled in these woods with the monstrous size and vicious bloodlust to pursue humans with the sole intention of making a meal out of them. Without hesitation, Dorian broke into a full sprint to save his friends, despite the dangerous adversary at their heels.

Dorian saw Margaret trip and fall to the ground. Clawing to get away, she screeched as she attempted to get back to her feet, but terror and panic disrupted her coordination. She stumbled again before turning her attention back to her aggressor. The dread of the situation stole her voice as the beast reared up on its hind legs and let loose a high-pitched growl, as if it thanked the gods for the meal.

The beast began its downward pounce as Margaret let loose a blood-curdling scream that echoed throughout the woods. Before the monster delivered its deadly blow, Dorian leapt at the creature with his sword aimed to cleave the monster's skull in two. He brought his sword down with all of his might, but the beast caught sight of the attack and intercepted the strike with two tusks jutting from its jaw.

Dorian quickly recovered and shuffled himself in-between Margaret and the umbra beast. Frantically waving the torch toward the creature, he gazed at the hulking monstrosity as it returned to a four-legged posture.

Two beady eyes loomed above the short snout of its enormous round head. Its mouth spanned wide enough to fit Dorian inside, shoulder to shoulder. Jagged teeth, resembling a thousand needles stacked side-by-side, leaked pools of frothy drool. Two arm-length tusks jutted from its jaw. Long quills in different sizes protruded at the top of its hunched back and down its spine. Its forelegs, much longer and thicker than its haunches, bore four long, curled toes with curved claws much like the talons of a tree hanging sloth. Sparse, black fur covered the beast's visage, revealing the pink flesh beneath.

The beast let loose another piercing roar as it shook its head back and forth. Rapidly blinking its light-sensitive eyes, the animal reeled away from the torchlight and retreated with reluctance.

Dorian jabbed the torch at the creature to force the monster to flee, making sure to keep a safe distance from the dangerous tusks in front of him. The beast, too hungry to allow its meal to escape, jolted forward and slammed its tusk into the torch, knocking the flame from Dorian's hand. Twisting and turning through the air, the torch landed several stones away and extinguished on the forest floor, leaving Dorian without his only advantage against the nocturnal nightmare.

Without the torchlight Dorian knew the umbra beast held a significant advantage, but he refused to back down. Courage he did not know he possessed kept his fear at bay. Assuming his friends made it a safe distance by now, he resolved to face the threat before him to guarantee their escape.

The beast lunged, snapping its head in an upward motion to gore its meal, but Dorian's quick reflexes and years of training allowed him to sidestep the strike and counter with a sword swing aimed at the beast's head. The creature's reflexes proved sharp too, as it whipped its head, slamming its tusk into Dorian's side before the sword could make a skull-shattering strike. With Dorian knocked to the ground, the beast rose to its hind legs to pounce.

Dorian raised his sword in anticipation of the beast's attack. Before the monster could bring its crushing weight down, two blasts erupted from the beast's back. The first explosion lit the night with lightning, and the second flashed with an eruption of fire. Dorian recognized Nathaniel and Lukas's intervention, casting spells from their respective runestones, and saving him from certain death. The beast wailed a high-pitched growl as it dropped to its forelegs and twisted its stout neck to locate the origin of the assault.

Dorian, seeing his opportunity, scrambled to his feet, and brought his sword down upon the beast. The beast turned to defend itself, but its reaction proved too slow. Dorian's sword cleaved through flesh and bone, removing the beast's head from its shoulders.

Blood sprayed Dorian from head to toe. Wiping the gore from his face, he examined the beast's dismembered body. Its head sat a short distance from its grotesque abdomen, and the beast's innards spilled from the neck into a puddle of blood. Putrid smells rose in waifs. The revulsion made Dorian's stomach turn and filled the area with a warm, moist air of vile revulsion.

Gagging from the stench, he began to step away from the carcass when Margaret collided with him in a warm embrace. He could hear her whimper as she buried her head into his shoulder. Returning the hug, he looked up to see his friends approaching to join them. Cautiously, Lukas and Elijah curtailed the dead body of the umbra beast, while Nathaniel confidently walked past with a beaming grin.

"Thank you." Margaret released Dorian to look him in the eye as tears streamed down her face.

"Dorian!" Nathaniel announced, "You are amazing! You saved our lives!"

"Well, you and Lukas saved mine, so…"

"No, we blasted that beast with everything we had and couldn't even break its hide. You took its head clean off!" Nathaniel responded, looking at Dorian's sword. "You re-made the sword! How did…"

"Can we talk more at the house?" Dorian interrupted. "It's still dangerous out here, and that smell is enough to make a skunk jealous."

The friends returned to the safety of the cottage. Dorian excused himself to wash the entrails off. Margaret, covered in the same viscera from embracing Dorian, asked if she could do the same after he finished.

Upon his return, the young men barraged Dorian with compliments over the slaying of the beast. He attempted to hide the glee he felt from their adoration, but the broad smile on his face revealed his feelings.

"I hope you don't mind, but I have been looking at your sword," Nathaniel said, handing the sword to Dorian. "I have never seen metal with this luster, nor felt a blade this heavy. How did you accomplish such a task?"

With all the excitement from the umbra beast attack, Dorian forgot about the fabled metal. "It's made of Hygard steel!"

The young men burst into laughter. "Hygard steel?" Elijah looked with disbelief.

"That stuff isn't real! It was only made up for children's stories!" Lukas added.

"No, it isn't. There is still a large supply in the forge." Dorian boasted.

Skepticism plastered across the young men's faces. "Are you sure that's Hygard steel?" Elijah questioned.

"Of course!" Dorian responded with a nod of his head.

"How is it possible?" Lukas asked.

"None of that matters," Nathaniel spoke up before Dorian could answer. "In the stories, that metal links with the runestones better than regular steel. We should try the spell again!"

"Aye, that was my intent. It's why I used the same sword handle from before, but…"

"But what? This is amazing! You have a hero sword in your hands! We have to try it!" Nathaniel was jubilant.

"No!" Margaret insisted, emerging from the washroom, wearing clothes too big for her tiny frame. "I want to try the sword again as much as anyone, but after going through all of that, I need a drink!"

With a cheer of agreement they spent rest of the evening drinking wine the friends brought along with many pints of Thane's ale. Dorian told his friends about the Hygard steel his father obtained through less than reputable means, and regaled the tale of meeting with his father's mysterious friends. Their names escaped his memory, but the memory of the woman mentioning his mother repeated numerous times in his mind.

They told Dorian about the failed attempt to discover a new and faster path to get to his house. A route Nathaniel insisted on taking even after the vehement disagreement conveyed by the more experienced woods explorer, Lukas. After a teasing, Nathaniel promised he would not attempt to find a new path to Dorian's home. A useless promise, as the friends agreed never to follow his lead again.

That night, the drunken friends went to their usual sleeping spots, except for Lukas, who joined Margaret in the master bedroom. Drifting into slumber, Dorian could hear Margaret's moans through walls. He knew she twisted her ankle during the unbra beast's attack, but her wailing proved the injury was far worse than he imagined. He thought to check on her well-being, but figured Lukas would console her ailment better than he could.

The next day, instead of leaving early in the morning, they stayed at Dorian's house nursing hangovers. Nathaniel and Elijah spent most of the day reading while Lukas and Margaret drifted in and out of sleep in each other's arms. Dorian spent the day completing every chore that didn't include swinging a hammer, knowing what the sound of metal striking metal would do to his head.

In the evening they decided to practice getting the runestones to work in unison on Dorian's sword. As they walked to the forge, Nathaniel explained to Dorian how they would do things differently this time.

"After looking through the books with Elijah, I think I know what went wrong last time." Nathaniel began, holding up a piece of paper with a runic symbol traced on it. "I drew arrows on the symbol that shows the exact direction in which to trace your finger. I believe that last time I had you trace the symbol in the wrong direction. I think it would be best if you practiced tracing the symbol a few times without the sword to make sure you can draw the symbol fluidly and consistently."

Dorian did as Nathaniel instructed, following the arrows drawn on the paper while Nathaniel watched and corrected where Dorian's technique could use improvement. After practicing several times, they felt satisfied that Dorian could perform the motions without mistake. Grabbing his sword, Dorian listened to Nathaniel's further instructions.

"While you trace the symbol, I want you to envision a circle. Imagine that one-half of the circle is a flickering flame in colors of red, orange, and yellow. The other half should appear pitch black."

"Lukas, Margaret, Elijah, I want you to place one hand on Dorian's back. Envision the same image while allowing your energy to flow into Dorian."

"Let me to clean the blade first. The blood from the umbra beast is still on the blade," Dorian recommended. As he wiped away the dried blood from the blade, his nervous hands shook at the prospect of repeating the same mistake from before. The image of his previous blade crumbling into a pile of dust flashed in his mind, causing him to make the highly irregular mistake of allowing the rag to slip from his calloused hand. As the edge of the blade dragged across his hand, opening a short gash in his palm, a yelp inadvertently escaped Dorian's mouth as his blood ran down the Hygard steel.

"Are you alright?" Margaret asked with a concerned look.

"Aye, just a shallow wound. Just let me clean off the blood before we continue."

"If the spell doesn't work, it won't matter. Disintegrated metal requires little polishing," Nathaniel pointed out.

Dorian gave a nod of his head to signal his readiness to proceed. He concentrated on Nathaniel's suggested image. The spherical shape came to life in his mind. A planet consumed in the intense flames of the sun on one half, while the blackest void of nothingness overcame the other. Dorian lifted his finger and began to trace the symbol in the exact pattern he practiced with Nathaniel. The others placed a hand on his back and released their current of energy.

The sword began to vibrate. Waves of warmth traveled throughout Dorian's body like the roaring tide of the ocean. Before he could describe the sensation to his friends, black flame, the color of shadows, crept up the blade.

Dorian extended the sword away from his body, expecting a repeat of the flash of light. Instead, a shockwave burst from the sword, blasting the group into the walls of the forge. Momentarily dazed, Dorian gathered himself to his feet. Looking around the room, he saw his friends slowly rising, holding various parts of their sore bodies from the unexpected explosion.

The friends gathered around the sword to inspect the outcome. Nathaniel picked up the weapon and examined both sides of the blade. The blade appeared undamaged. "At least we didn't disintegrate the blade this time."

"Maybe if we…" Dorian gripped the sword. As soon as his fingers wrapped around the handle, shadow flames erupted, bathing the steel in extraordinary fire.

The friends stood in awe. Keeping his gaze fixated on the leaping blaze, Elijah broke the silence. "Does everyone else notice that? About the flames?"

"Of course! Hard to miss a black fire!" Lukas responded in a sarcastic tone.

"By the Gods! The flames give off no light!" Nathaniel interjected.

Hovering the palm of his hand near the flame, Elijah declared, "There is no heat either."

"What happens if you touch the flames?" Margaret slowly moved her pointer finger toward the blade. Grabbing her wrist before she could make contact, Nathaniel cautioned against her course of action.

"Let's test that on something that isn't flesh and bone."

They left the forge in search of an object for the experiment. Lukas pointed out a young tree. "How about this tree?"

"Seems as good as any, but maybe we should clear the ground around it to make sure we don't burn down my home." Dorian kicked at dead leaves around the base of the tree to make his point.

They raked leaves and pine needles surrounding the area until only dirt remained. Dorian thrust his sword, accidentally plunging the blade into the trunk. From the tree's wound, a wave of embers crawled outward like a ripple in a pond, until it reached the tip if every branch. Dorian yanked the sword from the trunk while everyone stared, mesmerized by the unexpected outcome. Margaret reached out to touch the tree. As soon as her finger made contact, the tree crumbled into a pile of ash.

The swirling vapors chocked the group as they waved their hands in front of their faces to clear the air. Nathaniel spoke through his coughing. "Congratulations Dorian! You now have the most powerful sword ever created!

# Marius

The realization of the flaw in his plans dawned on him like the blinding rays of the rising sun on the horizon. The issue lay not with Marius's plans themselves. The involvement of the Bane family became the hindrance. Love for a child is a powerful emotion and the Banes loved their son too much to listen to Marius's words, so he simplified his scheme to proceed without providing the Bane family the knowledge of his deceit.

"Very well, Marshal Bane, as is your right." Marius began, sheathing his dagger as he spoke. "You will be provided one hour to choose your champion. I shall fill the role of champion for Lord Eric Hardwood. Please choose the location of the contest for the Right of Challenge."

The marshal searched his mind for an appropriate answer. His face lit up like the sudden burst of flame on an oiled torch, signaling his realization of the perfect place. "The town's center. It is large enough for two men to duel and it can hold a vast crowd. A crowd that will watch your lifeless body fall!"

"Very well," Marius responded in a tone void of emotion.

Marius told his men what happened inside the manor, rekindling horrific memories of the bloody events from seven years ago.

Within the hour, a crowd filled the town's center. Marius stood near the edge of the inner circle in front of his men. Before the contest began, his second-in-command approached and whispered in his ear, "All set." Marius replied with a single nod of his head.

The assembly burst to life when a large man, Marshal Bane, and a procession of town guards, pushed their way through the crowd and entered the circle. The man leading the pack flexed and screamed, basking in the adulation of the on-lookers. Strutting across the inner circle, he enticed the mob to join him in his merriment by pumping his fist in the air. Slashing and stabbing scars covering his shirtless abdomen, proving his experience in combat, and the rust covering his double-sided battle-ax indicated age and neglectful care.

His screaming stopped as he entered the center of the circle and approached his opponent. "You're going to die today, Marius the Swift!"

Marius, who cared little for boasting, gave him a crooked smile. "We shall see."

The man resumed his unruly screaming as he raised his ax and fist in the air. Marshal Bane stood in the center, bearing a confident smile as he clapped for his physically superior champion.

A soldier entered the circle and raised his hands to quiet the crowd. Marius could hear the whispers of the attendees chatting about their champion's inevitable victory.

"Marshal Marcus Bane has invoked his Right to Challenge, disputing the ruling set forth by Lord Eric Hardwood. Each official has chosen a champion who will fight to the death to determine whom the Gods favor in this dispute. Combatants, please approach." The soldier announced.

The fighters moved to the center of the circle attempting to intimidate each other with their stern, focused eyes. The soldier projected his voice to ensure the combatants understood the rules of the match. "When I drop my hand, the two of you will fight to the death without the interference from outside parties. You may use any single weapon of choice. Please present your weapon."

The man kept his gaze fixed on Marius as he raised his ax to display to the soldier. Marius, also leaving his stone-faced gaze upon the man, reached to his belt, removed his dagger from its sheath and presented it to the soldier.

The man released a guttural laugh. "You think you can beat me with that little thing? I use toothpicks larger than that to clean my teeth!" The crowd burst into mocking laughter at the man's words. Marius's face remained statuesque, unfazed by the ridicule.

The officiating soldier raised his hand. Both men stepped back and set their fighting postures. With cocky confidence, the man juggled his ax between his hands while bouncing eagerly on the balls of his feet. In contrast, Marius stood flat-footed with his free hand extended, and the other gripping his dagger with the base of the blade at the bottom of his fist. Dropping his arm sharply, the soldier began the match.

Marshal Bane's champion roared and sprinted at Marius with his ax overhead. Bringing his ax down with force, the man attempted to end the contest with a decisive blow, but he soon learned the basis of the high commander's nickname. Marius swiftly sidestepped the attack and ran the edge of his blade across his opponent's forearm, opening a gash that ran a stream of blood down his arm. Raising his ax for another strike, the man prepared to continue the attack, but Marius turned and approached his soldiers, sheathing his dagger as he walked.

"Where are you going? Giving up already?" The man questioned with a shout and a hearty laugh that traveled through the crowd like an infection.

Marius turned his head. "I'm not giving up. The battle is over. I cut you."

"This fight is to the death! You think this little cut is going to stop me?" The man lifted his ax with his wounded arm until the strength in his arm failed, prompting his ax to fall to the ground. Looking to his shriveling arm, the man's face glossed over in terror. "What's going on? What did you do?"

"You were quick to mock my blade, and in your arrogance, you never noticed the darkness runestone embedded in the hilt. The spell, known as Decay, is what currently saps your strength. Your body is rotting. Soon you will be no more than dust."

The man's face turned to abject fear. His mouth widened in an attempt to scream, but gurgling sounds escaped from his throat instead. His skin yellowed and tightened around his bones, resembling old, dry leather. Wrinkles formed on his face, giving the appearance of a man well beyond his years, and his cheeks sunk, revealing the shape of his skull through the skin. Bones creaked and popped as his limbs contorted in awkward positions. His lips curled away from his teeth like a peeling orange, and his eyes rolled back, dropping deep into their sockets. Crumbling to the ground, the man perished, leaving a dry husk of what was, moments ago, a proud warrior.

Silence rippled through the attending town's people. The mid-afternoon choir of birds and cicadas rang through the otherwise quiet town. Marshal Bane crumbled to his knees and sobbed with the realization that the life of his newborn son would soon be forfeit.

Marius looked at one of his soldiers and nodded his head in the direction of the manor. The soldier returned with the marshal's newborn son in his bassinet. Placing the child at Marius's feet, the soldier slammed his fist to his chest before returning to his position.

Marius dropped to his knees and raised his dagger high over his head. The baby lay silently sleeping as Marius drove the blade into the bassinet. Removing the blade with a jerk, crimson droplets fell into the bassinet from the blood-soaked knife. Marius peered into the newborn child's bed, the baby looked like a sleeping angel despite the dead piglet laying beside him, stabbed in its belly.

Marius lifted the blanket to cover the baby and the dead animal. Placing the bassinet before the sobbing marshal, a stream of blood leaked into the dirt.

Marius knelt and grabbed the marshal by the back of his neck, bringing his ear close. He waited for one of his soldiers to announce the end of the contest before whispering instructions. "Do not move. Continue to sob into your hands and do not react no matter what I say now. Your son is alive and well."

The marshal looked into the bloody bassinet, but Marius quickly jerked his head. "You cannot move, I said. Listen to me. The baby has been given a mild sedative to ensure he does not wake and reveal the truth behind the ruse. It will not harm him, and he should come to within the hour. You must take your son somewhere. Give him to someone you know and trust to raise him properly, and keep your visits with him short and few. This is his only chance of survival. If Lord Hardwood discovers my deceit, he will have all of our heads on pikes, including your son's. Make sure you have a beautiful funeral for an empty baby's casket, and never speak of these events with anyone other than your wife. She must realize the danger she will present if she decides to tell the truth to anyone. Do you understand?"

Marshal Marcus Bane froze in place, whimpering fake cries while trying to glance at his sleeping son. Whispering a muffled word of thanks, he pushed Marius away from him to keep up the appearance of grief.

Marius stood and walked toward his men as he wiped the pig's blood from his dagger. Giving a sullen command to mount up, he and the soldiers packed up for their journey home.

On the return expedition, the second-in-command rode his horse up next to Marius. Leaving his face-covering helmet on, he quietly asked Marius, "Do you think it's going to work?"

"I hope so, Richard. Either this works, or you, me and the entire Bane family can only pray to face something as mild as the hangman's noose."

# Brett

Brett laid on a tattered cot, barely awake after a few hours of sleep. After moving to his new cell, he finally managed to sleep on a bed instead of the cold stone floor. The cell he now stayed in once belonged to the most celebrated arena fighter in history, Razuul. Two days ago, Razuul ripped the heart out of a dragon with his bare hands, earning the freedom Brett desired.

His new accommodations were much less crowded, but the sounds of dripping water, snoring, smells of human waste and body odors stunted his ability to achieve a full night's sleep. Shifting on his course bedding, his mind raced with the inevitability of his next death match.

His previous match left a burning in his hands that pained him less than the memory of taking the life of his opponent. The bandages, stained with blood and dirt, needed changing days ago, and the bruise on his face still ached. His injuries served as a reminder of his mortality, and the unlikely chance of survival in, what his fellow prisoners referred to as, the Death Game.

A conversation with a fellow prisoner lingered in his mind. The man told him that the guards usually allotted prisoners the time needed to make a full recovery before forcing them back into the fighting pits, but cautioned that it depended on the number of healthy prisoners available at the time. Only a few days remained until the next match, and Brett knew if he were forced to fight again in his current condition, his chances for survival were low at best.

Brett closed his eyes to escape into the world of dreams, where his harsh reality did not exist. Staring into the darkness of his mind, the familiar sounds of keys jangling grabbed his attention. Three guards opened the door to his cell.

"On your feet, Shaw!" One of the guards demanded.

"Well, good morning fellas. Are you here to escort me to breakfast in the garden?" Brett mocked.

"I said on your feet!" The frustrated guard repeated, raising his fist.

Brett rose to his feet. "Will Miss Fancy Pants be joining us for crumpets?"

"Still want to be a smart ass, huh?"

"Well, I…" Interrupting the comment, the guard threw a punch into Brett's stomach, buckling him over in pain. Before he could return upright, the other guards began shackling his wrists and ankles. With his bonds fully applied, Brett raised his wrists and joked, "Do you think Miss Fancy Pants will enjoy my new jewelry?"

"Keep it up, Shaw! We were told to deliver you, but no one said you had to be in good shape." The guard forced a thick burlap sack over Brett's head and pulled the drawstring tight around his throat, leaving Brett blind and barely able to breathe.

Pushed and shoved repeatedly, Brett shuffled his feet to an unknown destination. He thought to ask where they were going, but he knew that pressing the issue would only deliver more beatings. The putrid smell of his cell began to fade away as he walked, soon he felt the warm rays of the sun against his skin.

His senses informed him of his new surroundings. The feel of cobblestone through his worn boots, the faint murmur of conversations seeping through the hood on his head, and the musty air lingering with horse manure meant he stood where he desired to be since his incarceration: the bustling city of Regiis.

A hard shove came from behind, jolting him forward until he collided with a horizontal plank of wood. "Climb!" Came the order from behind him. On his hands and knees, a swift kick struck his ribs, knocking him onto his back. The blow forced the wind out of his lungs, leaving an ache that burned with each breath he took. "Sit up," came the next humiliating order, making Brett feel like an abused dog. Two sets of hands grabbed his arms and slid him until his back struck a half-wall.

Sweat dripped down Brett's' face. The morning sun beat upon the burlap sack, baking his head. Brett tried to loosen the drawstring to get air until a guard smashed his hand with a solid object, warning him not to continue that course of action.

Readying himself to unleash a flurry of taunts toward his captors, a jolt of the platform he sat upon knocked him from his seated position. The guards returned him upright, and the gentle rocking informed him that he sat upon a cart.

The cart shook back and forth, as it made its way down the bumpy road. The undertones of people talking in the streets came from every direction. Bakers preparing their morning bread filled the air with mouthwatering aromas. Smoky hearths burning in the forges sounded the beginning of the blacksmiths day.

They traveled for an hour. Brett's yearning for freedom rose as conversations echoed from every direction. He struggled to hear the catting to gain a clue to his location, but the surrounding sounds made each voice indiscernible. When the cart stopped, a pair of hands grabbed his ankles and yanked him to the edge of the cart. "Stand up, Shaw!"

Brett heard the wagon leave as the guards pushed him forward. He walked until his foot struck something firm, making him trip on a set of stairs. The guards lifted him and kept their hands beneath Brett's arms to prevent him from falling again. The journey continued up the stairs until the guards halted him, and the creak of a door reverberated.

The sun's warmth disappeared as he entered the enclave of this mysterious destination. The rattle of Brett's chains echoed as the escorts led him forward. Welcoming fragrances of rose water and sage mingled with smoldering fires. They turned in various directions as they proceeded in the cooling shade of the building. Before long, the guards stopped him again.

The scrape of another door opening hinted the nearing of their destination. Blinding light assaulted Brett's eyes when the guards yanked the hood from his head.

Squinting to adjust to the brightness, his vision cleared to reveal a scenario he never felt possible.

Light from the fireplace danced across the polished granite walls. The sun's rays beamed through peaked windows onto a large oval-shaped table in the center of the room. On top of the table, a sheet of glass covered an intricately detailed map of the kingdom. Eight chairs surrounded the table and at the head of the table sat a man Brett thought he would never meet.

Brett looked at the King of Preclarium. Aged well within his sixth decade, he seemed as fit and spry as a young man. A prism of light shone in all directions from his jewel-encrusted crown. His golden-sleeved black shirt, fastened with crest-embossed buttons of gold, glistened nearly as much as the gem-laced heart pendant that hung to the center of his chest.

The king sipped from a golden chalice. Ignoring Brett's presence, he silently rose, walked to the window, clasped his hands behind his back, and gazed at his bustling subjects below.

Brett did not know the proper royal etiquette. Assuming the king awaited Brett to speak, he began to address the king, but before he could speak, King Thomas raised an extended finger to symbolize silence. The awkward silence continued until the door crashed open.

A pair of guards dragged a shirtless man into the room. Shackles bound his ankles and wrists, and bruises covered the man's body. Upon seeing the king's visage, the man began to panic and struggle against his restraints. One of the guards reacted by throwing a punch into his gut, buckling him over with a grunt and shoving him onto the floor. The guards then struck their fists to their chests in customary salute and silently exited.

The shackled man rose to his feet, his chains rattling as he stood. His body trembled, his eyes darted across the room, and his lower jaw vibrated as if standing in the cold. His sunken stomach revealed his ribcage through the skin, signaling his malnourished state. A branding scar, shaped in an unrecognizable symbol, was seared onto his hairless chest.

The king remained at the window, seemingly oblivious to his audience. The shirtless man began to speak, "Your Grace, I…" but the king raised his hand to silence the man.

The king approached the prisoner. When he spoke, his voice exuded deliberate confidence, proclaiming his noble lineage.

"Captain James Turner. Do you remember the assignment you were given before your arrest?"

"Yes, Your Grace."

"And what was that assignment?"

"Your Grace, circumstances were out of..."

Cutting Turner's statement short, the king reprimanded, "I did not ask for excuses. I asked what the assignment was."

"To quell the skirmish between Marshal Paisley and Marshal Bartram."

"And how did that assignment turn out?"

"Marshal Paisley was murdered by a band of men hired by Marshal Bartram."

"What actions did you take to ensure that this outcome would not happen? I warn you before you answer, do not lie to me!" The king turned away from the man and began to pace with his hands folded behind him.

"Your Grace, I did everything within my power. I..." Screaming in agonizing pain, he fell to the floor as the branded symbol on his chest began to glow red. When the glowing on his chest dulled, the screaming ceased, leaving the man panting and covered in sweat.

Brett remained motionless as he stared at the tortured man. The origin of the man's suffering puzzled him. No runestone glowed from beneath the king's clothes, nor had the king raised a hand to cast a spell.

"You must think I am a terrible king, Captain Turner."

"N-no, Y-Your Grace! I-I…" The man screamed as he rolled onto his back. Brett could see the brand glowing again as the man writhed on the floor.

"Oh, but you do think I am a terrible king, Captain Turner because only a terrible king would not know what happens within his kingdom. Marshal Bartram paid you a large sum of money for you to not interfere with the men who attacked Marshal Paisley, directly disobeying orders that were handed down from your king."

"Your Grace, I would never…" The torment returned. The man clutched at his chest as his body shot from a fetal position to straight and back again.

The shriek continued as the king spoke. "Yes, I know. You think it is impossible for me to know this information. Only you and Marshal Bartram knew of this arrangement, and the High Priestess of Sanctum executed Marshal Bartram. No one should know of your deceit, but I am a good king, and I do know everything that occurs within my kingdom." The king crossed the room to stand over the Captain.

The glowing ceased, and the man lay flat on his back, gasping labored breaths. No physical signs appeared on the man's body that illustrated the torment he received other than the copious amount of sweat that covered his skin.

"Now, Captain Turner, I will allow you one reprieve to admonish the shame that has befallen you. I want you to look at this man here…" the king pointed at Brett, "and tell him if you would rather suffer through the same torment you have just received for three more minutes, or suffer a swift death."

The man lifted his sweat-drenched head in a quivering struggle and looked at Brett. "I-I would r-rather die!"

The glow and screams returned. Captain Turner's body shook in a seizure as the glowing on his chest intensified. His cries became gurgles as blood filled his lungs and spouted from his mouth. Brett wanted to look away, but the grotesque scene captivated his attention. The man's eyes melted into his skull, and his skin slid from his bones to the floor. The smell of burnt hair and flesh filled the air. Brett stared at the puddled remains of the man while fighting the urge to vomit.

"Guards!" The king called out. Several guards hurried in carrying a large metal bowl filled with red-hot embers with a pole protruding from the glowing coals. Four guards rushed Brett, tackled him onto his back and pinned him down. He struggled against his attackers, but the guards overwhelmed his fleeting strength and tore his shirt off, exposing his bare chest. Brett fought to break free as a guard handed the glowing rod to the king.

Plunging the red-hot iron onto Brett's chest, the king seared his skin. Screams of agony mixed with the sizzling of scorched flesh. The king removed the brand and gave a waving gesture, signaling the guards to release their grip.

"Now, Mr. Shaw," the king began. "I apologize for having to brand you, and for forcing you to witness that messy business with Captain Turner, but it was necessary. However, you may rejoice, as I have selected you for an extraordinary mission."

"Mission?" Brett clutched his burning chest.

"Yes, Mr. Shaw. I want you to follow the recently released prisoner, Razuul. You will be given a handsome sum of money to help and support Razuul with anything he chooses to do. Every night you will report to me any and all of his activities, including acquaintances he may have made. Your reports will be delivered in secret, and you will never allow Razuul to know that you are following him on my orders."

"Follow Razuul? Why me...Your Grace?"

"That's simple, Mr. Shaw. You are the only person in over seventy years to have a conversation with the wild elf that didn't result in a severe beating or death."

"B-but, Your Grace...that only happened because he was about to fight his final fight! I am sure he would have killed me had it been any other day!"

"Do not diminish your capacity for resourcefulness and charm, Mr. Shaw. I am sure I have chosen the right man for this task. Unless you would rather return to the arena?"

"N-no, Your Grace. Thank you for choosing me." Brett realized the opportunity before him. "How shall I keep in contact with you if he decides to travel? Messenger bird?"

"Outstanding question, Mr. Shaw. I am even more assured that I have chosen the right man for the job." The king reached into a white pouch hanging from his belt and removed a small leather bracelet. A jade-green wind stone embedded in the center of the bracelet glimmered in the light.

"This bracelet offers direct communication with me. Touch the stone and speak into it. It is connected by magic to another stone that is kept in my chambers. Even if I am not there to hear it, your message will be stored in the stone until I can retrieve it."

"I have never heard of anything like this!" Brett accepted the bracelet from the king.

"Certain spells and magical methods are reserved for the exclusive use of the royal line, such as the spell now branded to your chest."

Brett looked at the king and clutched the blistering brand on his chest. Captain Turner's demise would forever remain in his memory.

"Speaking of which…" the king said as the brand on Brett's chest began to glow. Brett screamed and fell to his knees in excruciating pain. The intense suffering resonating throughout his body felt as though a giant twisted his body like a damp rag. Just as he began to wish for death to release him from his agony, the pain ceased. It lasted for no more than a second, but the intensity of the anguish implanted into his memory.

The king bent over, bringing his face close to Brett's

as he spoke sternly. "Remember this pain, Mr. Shaw. Know that no matter where you go, no matter how far you run, there is no distance that this spell cannot cover. If you dare to defy me or lie to me, I will melt you from the inside out until you resemble Captain Turner on the floor. As you saw, I have informants everywhere and I will know if you disobey. Guards!"

Four guards lined up on either side of Brett and pounded their chest in salute to the king.

"Escort Mr. Shaw out and remove his shackles. He is free to go."

The guards dragged Brett from the room. He tried to use his legs, but his body, still reeling from the pain, wouldn't respond. At the entrance to the building, the guards removed the shackles, shoved a heavy backpack into Brett's arms, and pushed him out of the castle.

After shuffling a few steps, Brett sat on the steps. He opened his hand to see the bracelet the king gave him, confirming the reality of his freedom. He looked inside the backpack and saw burlap sacks inside. Brett pulled out one of the bags, untied its drawstring and discovered numerous gold coins within. He strapped the bracelet on his wrist and looked out to the city.

# Jonas

Jonas entered the Commander's Council. Six of the seven men stood tall and hit their right fist to their chest. The metal clanging of the men's armor stunned the seventh man who had been staring out the window. Startled, the man spun around and saluted Jonas, his long brown ponytail whipping around him as he turned.

"I apologize, High Commander, I was focused on watching out for the safety of the people and did not hear you enter." The man named Adam Garrison stated in a sarcastic tone.

"You mean you were too busy watching that arena fighter we released to die in the streets, Adam." Jonas returned. "You always had a soft spot for him, didn't you?"

"Well, that's just it. I wanted to watch him die, but right now, a doctor is tending to him. If that stupid wild elf lives, I'll lose my mind! I might pay a visit to that doctor later." Garrison unleashed in the ramblings of a lunatic.

"You lost your mind a long time ago Garrison! The king ordered us to leave the wild elf and anyone who accompanies him alone. You'd do well to remember that."

The man who spoke, Paul Cormac, stood a little taller than average with a medium build. His shaved head revealed the scars of past battles, and his thick, black beard formed a point beneath his chin. A double-sided ax, with a blade that resembled a bat wing, was strapped to his back and a row of three daggers sat sheathed on his belt. In the socket where his right eye should have been, a fire runestone with a runic engraving shined in the reflection of the morning sun. Jonas did not know how or why the runestone replaced his eye, nor did he care to ask.

"Shut up, Cormac! I am willing to bet that the good doctor won't accompany him for very long. I'll wait until…"

"Enough!" Jonas interrupted Adam. "Leave the doctor alone. I am sure we will receive our orders from King Thomas soon enough."

"Oh, I cannot wait! Another day of patrolling the city to ensure the safety of the kingdom." Adam replied, sarcastically. "I may as well get started now." As he began to leave, an enormous man stepped into his path to block his way.

The man, Scott Bell, easily towered as the tallest person Jonas had ever seen. The only doorways within the castle that he did not need to duck beneath were those intended for the entry of horses and carriages. His broad shoulders spanned near the length of Jonas's height, with muscles that forced him to have his armor custom made. His gray eyes and ebony skin likened to storm clouds on a dark night, and his shiny, hairless head revealed the bulging veins that ran beneath the surface. In his hand, a long staffed warhammer made of steel looked too heavy for an ordinary man to lift, let alone wield. An earth runestone was imbued at the center of the hammer's head, and cross-patterned leather ran the length of the shaft. Jonas knew Scott for many years, but not once heard the man speak, although he followed orders better than any other soldier in his service.

Adam Garrison, Paul Cormac, and Scott Bell, the members of the elite group of knights known as the Three Heads of Cerberus, took orders from Jonas alone, although Garrison often followed his own desires over the commands of his superior. The other men in the room, the second, third, fourth and fifth division commanders, waited in anticipation to receive the day's orders, eager to escape the threatening presence of the three elite warriors. The division commanders, all members or former members of noble houses, held no claim to become a lord. Each enlisted in the king's guard to achieve a semblance of glory they could not have otherwise obtained.

"Get out of my way you big dumb oaf before I cut you down to normal size!" Warned Adam as he grabbed the sword handle on his hip.

"Adam, I said that's enough!" Jonas sternly ordered.

"I was only kidding, High Commander." Adam released his sword and raised his hands with a sly smile.

A knock at the door cut the tension in the room. "Enter!" Jonas called out in a frustrated tone. The young messenger entered the room. The boy looked no more than fifteen years and wore an expression of terror, due to the cruel, deadly reputation the Three Heads of Cerberus commanded. For years, Jonas attempted to extinguish the threatening stigma of the elite group, wishing only outsiders felt the fear of their reputation and not the citizens in their charge for protection, but madmen like Garrison made the task impossible. With trembling hands, the messenger handed a rolled parchment to the high commander. Jonas snatched the paper, causing the boy to jump and shrink away, which made Jonas immediately regret his stern action.

252

Unfurling the message, Jonas's eyes widened in shock.

"Well? Are those today's orders? What does it say?" Paul asked.

Jonas read the message from the king. "Today's orders shall be given directly by the King as they are of great importance. The High Commander is hereby summoned to appear before the King in the war room posthaste."

Jonas looked up from the parchment, feeling the same astonishment as presented on the faces of his company. For time beyond remembering, the order remained the same: "Follow the orders of the High Commander." Receiving a direct summons from the king meant that either something terrible happened, or the king felt an imminent danger would soon befall the kingdom.

"You better get moving, High Commander!" Paul said, breaking the awkward silence.

Without reply, Jonas rushed out the door. Entering the courtyard, the soldiers stopped for a salute again, but the urgency he felt from the king's message wouldn't allow him to waste time with formalities. He crossed the courtyard, as quickly as a man forcing himself not to run could, and entered the throne room through the side entrance.

"High Commander, the…" Began a rat-faced man

Jonas knew as the royal attendant named Putnam Callidus, but he did not let the man finish.

"Move!" Without pausing his stride, Jonas shoved Putnam out of his path with one arm and continued to his destination. Jonas felt a fraction of satisfaction to disrespect the royal attendant, as he despised the man.

Jonas entered the war room to see the king standing with his hands folded behind his back, staring out the window. "Your Grace," he said, lowering himself to one knee.

As he bowed, waiting for the king's permission to rise, he detected a familiar and unmistakable aroma lingering in the air. An aroma he would have been happy never to smell again, that of burnt flesh. He wanted to look around the room to locate the source of the foul stench, but he knew that moving from his knelt position without permission would be a sign of disrespect, and his desire to remain in the realm of the living outweighed his pension for curiosity.

"You may rise." The king said, keeping his gaze fixed on the window before him. Jonas rose, silently looking around the room. Spotting a large red stain on the floor, Jonas deduced the events that transpired which left the horrid stench lingering in the room.

The stain served as the last remains of Captain James Turner for disobeying the king's orders, handed down from Jonas himself, to quell a skirmish between two marshals. After receiving intelligence that Turner accepted a hefty bribe to allow the assassination of Marshal Paisley, he reported the events to King Thomas. At the time, the king seemed uninterested in the blatant treason, but the ensuing imprisonment of the young captain revealed his true feelings on the matter. The smell only further interpreted the king's resolve. Assuming the king melted Captain Turner from the inside out utilizing the mandatory Branding Spell burned into the flesh of every member of the king's guards, himself included, Jonas couldn't understand how greed could trump common sense.

"High Commander, I appreciate your expedient arrival."

"Of course, Your Grace."

The king moved to the table in the center of the room. "Please, have a seat. I have received two disturbing reports this morning that demand immediate attention. I called you so that I might assign the appropriate personnel to handle the tasks at hand."

The perplexing situation moved from mysterious to

confusion. The king frequently trusted Jonas to assign tasks to soldiers, and for the king to take command meant circumstances beyond the high commander's understanding unfolded. His mind raced to imagine circumstances dire enough to demand the direct attention of the king.

"At your command, Your Grace."

"First, I received a report that the city of Tenebris has been attacked."

"Attacked? By whom, Your Grace?"

"Centaurs."

"Centaurs? I thought…"

"Yes, as did I." The king interrupted. "After the Beast Wars from twenty-five years ago, I, too, thought that most, if not all, of the centaurs, had been removed from the continent along with the orcs, trolls, cyclops, and any other of the reprehensible beasts. I expected some stragglers to remain. One or two popping up here or there, and yet, according to the report, hundreds of centaurs, along with a handful of trolls, attacked Tenebris and nearly brought it to ruin."

"Your Grace, I shall ride immediately!" Jonas said, rising to his feet.

"Be calm, High Commander. I know you must be

worried about Tenebris. After all, it is your birth city, but for now, the threat has passed."

"Yes, Your Grace, I was born in Tenebris, but I hold neither allegiance nor nostalgic connection to that place. I wish to provide support in case there is another attack."

"Yes, and we shall provide support. However, I have another critical job I wish you to undertake. For now, let us discuss the task at hand. I want you to send the second division commander with half of his troops to help defend Tenebris while the citizens heal their wounds and make their repairs. Also, I would like the commander to investigate the validity of the claim. We must be sure that this is not a ruse to draw our troops from the capital."

"Half, Your Grace? Will that be enough?" Jonas asked. The king looked at him with intensity in his eyes. Instantly realizing he questioned the orders of the king, Jonas grew concerned. "My apologies, Your Grace. I did not mean to offend."

"Also," the king continued as he resumed pacing. "If the claim is true, we must consider how it is possible that hundreds of centaurs and twenty-stone-tall trolls were able to enter the kingdom without notice. Unless you believe it is possible that they have been hiding in the kingdom for the past twenty-five years?"

"No, Your Grace. I have been throughout the entire kingdom during that period. If a regiment of that size were on Preclarium, we would know."

"Just as I suspected. That is why I want you to send the fifth division commander to bring a quarter of his division to Baxis to perform an inspection. I want him to see if it is possible that Lord Hardwood is allowing the centaur's safe passage into the kingdom."

"Your Grace, may I make a suggestion?"

"Proceed."

"The fifth division commander is Cassius Drake. His father was the Lord of Baxis before the Marshal's Rebellion seven years ago. Cassius was set to be the next Lord of Baxis before that unfortunate event occurred, and he may not be objective in his inspection."

"Precisely why I have chosen him. Cassius Drake will leave no stone unturned to discover that Lord Hardwood has rebelled against the kingdom."

"Yes, Your Grace. Shall I send another commander to inspect Prasillo?"

"While it is true that Prasillo is the only other way that the centaurs could have entered the kingdom, it is unlikely that the beasts could have built ships large enough to get there, let alone sail ships that size to Prasillo without anyone noticing. If centaurs have invaded, it is imperative that we have as many troops as possible remain in the capital for defense. Spreading out our troops may have been the purpose of the attack on Tenebris."

"Yes, Your Grace."

"The explanation for this attack can be only one of three things. The Lord of Baxis has revolted against the kingdom, he is negligent in his duties of protecting the kingdom from outside invaders, or perhaps Lord Regent Richter of Tenebris is lying in some foolhardy attempt to remain in his seat of power. Whatever the reason, someone will pay dearly."

"By your command, Your Grace. What about the task you have in mind for me?"

"Ah yes, the task I have for you may sound trivial, but I cannot understate its importance. I have learned that the son of the Liber family, the caretakers of the royal library, has been sneaking books outside the city walls for the illegal study of magic. I want you and the Three Heads of Cerberus to hunt down this boy, kill him, and bring any books he may have directly to me. Have caution though, I fear the boy may have accomplices and may have learned some powerful forbidden wizardry, given the books he has taken."

"Yes, Your Grace," Jonas responded, thinking that this did seem like a trivial task for the high commander. A small squad of troops could handle such a mission, and one he definitely could handle by himself. Sending him and the Three Heads of Cerberus seemed excessive, and any task that included Adam Garrison always ended in chaos and bloodshed, but he dared not debate with the king.

Jonas thought about his wife and the request she made if he were to see the king. He prepared to address her inquiry about a promise made long ago, but the king gave his command before Jonas could speak.

"You are dismissed, High Commander."

# Clarissa

A chill consumed the evening air. Clarissa sat near the fireplace to keep warm, nibbling her fingernails and shaking her nervous leg. Bags hung heavy beneath her bloodshot eyes. The sleepless night did little to relieve her anxiety as she awaited the inevitable message from the king. Not knowing how the king would react to her treasonous actions threatened to drive her into madness. She anticipated another visit from her beloved brother, but after sending several attendants to locate him, his whereabouts remained a mystery. The last time they spoke, he promised that he would talk to everyone he knew to alleviate the storm of fury that would come from her insubordination. She wondered if he found a way to get himself into trouble through his meddling acts.

Loneliness was not new to Clarissa. Ever since her appointment as high priestess of Sanctum, family and friends felt distant. Only her responsibilities mattered to them. She would give up her title and all its benefits for a shoulder to cry on and an eager ear to listen.

A knock on the door snapped her from the reverie. Clarissa nearly jumped out of her skin from the unexpected rapping. Her anxiety soared since the trial, leaving her on edge and easily startled, revealing the scared young woman beneath the regal facade. Taking a deep breath to calm her pounding heart, she rose from her chair and smoothed her dress before calling out. "Enter!"

The young messenger boy opened the door and entered the private chambers. "Your Holiness, a message has come from the King."

"Thank you," Clarissa replied, taking the parchment from the boy and sending him on his way.

Breaking the wax seal, she unrolled the document. Her hands shook, forcing her to spread the message onto the table to keep it still. Tears rolled down her cheeks and dripped onto the parchment as she slowly read the king's official response.

*High Priestess, Clarissa Bright:*

*You are hereby summoned to appear before King Thomas Magicent by sunset of the morrow to plea your case against the accusation of treason. If you do not appear, King Thomas Magicent shall make his judgment without the benefit of your testimony.*

*Signed, His Royal Highness,*

*King Thomas Magicent*

Clarissa dropped the parchment to the floor. Her heart shattered to pieces from despair. Before she could rise and unleash her sorrow into the pillows on her bed, another knock at the door drew her from her anguish.

"Your Holiness, is everything alright in there?" Sir Gabriel called.

Wiping her face on the sleeve of her dress, she

opened the door of her chambers to answer the call. Sir Gabriel stood at attention in his massive armor ensemble. His usual duty partner, Sir Kenneth, appeared to be absent, a highly unusual occurrence.

"Yes, Sir Gabriel. Please send a message to prepare a horse and carriage for a trip to Regiis tomorrow morning."

"Yes, Your Holiness. But…"

"Where is Sir Kenneth? Aren't the two of you on the post together?"

"He is not far. I asked him to step away for a moment so that I may speak with you privately."

"Continue."

"I thought you may like someone to talk to right now."

"And why would you think that? Am I not still the High Priestess of Sanctum? I have received very similar training as the paladins of Sanctum. I, too, was taught to expel both negative and positive emotions to see only truth and justice. I am not some harlot who needs comforting!"

"Yes Your Holiness, but you are…"

"What? A woman? You think my gender requires you to…"

"I was going to say you are a person." Sir Gabriel

politely interrupted. "I know you receive the same training as us. We are the light that expels the shadow. I just wanted to let you know that I, Gabriel Caldwell, not Sir Gabriel the paladin of Sanctum, am here if you need someone to talk to."

Clarissa fought back the tears. She had never heard Sir Gabriel speak in such an affectionate and personal manner. His words touched her heart, leading her to consider opening up to him. She longed to lay her pain and unrest unto sympathetic ears, but her mother's words echoed in her mind. *Never allow yourself to be seen as anything other than a strong, independent woman who bears the title of High Priestess, or risk losing all the respect and authority that comes with that title.*

"Thank you for your kind intentions, Sir Gabriel, but I am fine. Please ensure that my carriage is prepared for departure at dawn."

That night, sleep eluded her again. Tossing and turning on her down stuffed mattress and sheets of silk, the dread of her fate overwhelmed her thoughts.

When morning arrived, the usual rapping at the door came followed by a group of three chambermaids entering her room. "Your Holiness, your carriage awaits. Shall we prepare you for your journey?" One of the chambermaids asked.

Clarissa could only nod her head as she stood. One of the chambermaids began straightening and smoothing her bedsheets, as another rummaged through her closet to pick out the perfect dress for her meeting with the king.

"Would you like some breakfast before you travel, Your Holiness?"

"I'm not hungry," Clarissa hoarsely replied.

The chambermaid returned from Clarissa's closet to present the dress she chose for approval, one of Clarissa's favorites. The golden material came up from the waist, and tied behind her neck, exposing the smooth ivory skin of her back. The white silk midsection, covered in lace, hung to her ankles. She had only worn this dress once before during her coronation as High Priestess of Sanctum. She felt it fitting that she wore it on what could be her last day.

Nodding her head in approval, Clarissa stepped into her dress. The women tied, strapped, and adjusted her clothing while she stared blankly, contemplating her fate. When they finished dressing her, Clarissa sat while one of the women styled her hair into a pair of braids wrapped into a bun at the back of her head, ensuring not a single strand escaped placement.

Clarissa dismissed the chambermaids once they completed their duties. Outside the door, her paladin guards clanked their boots against the stone floor as they snapped to attention. "Let us proceed," she ordered, cueing Sir Ryan and Sir Kenneth to escort her to the carriage.

The lavishly etched carriage dazzled with white paint, trimmed in gold. The plush purple velvet seats looked new even though generations of her family sat on them. Curtains made of the same exquisite material covered the windows, and infrequent use combined with routine maintenance kept the carriage looking new.

Clarissa expected to see her brother before she departed, but the mystery of his location remained. She yearned to hear his words of encouragement; his absence further crushed her spirits.

The journey began. Sir Gabriel led while Sir Kenneth trailed on horseback to ensure a strong defense against any surprise attackers. Sanctum, only an hour's ride from the Capital, provided for safe passage on well-maintained roads, but when those of noble blood travel, no precaution is spared. Clarissa enjoyed any chance to travel, but the dread of her final destination kept any delight at bay. She tried to hide the anxiety, but her chewed fingernails offered evidence of her unease.

The ride proceeded without incident until near half completion. The carriage's unexpected halt snapped Clarissa from her stupor. Typically, when Clarissa traveled, she preferred to leave the curtains open to enjoy nature. She loved to look at the trees and smell the spring air perfumed with wildflowers. Today she kept the curtains closed, wanting the dark interior to match her mood. Not bothering to peek out the window, Clarissa stood and threw the carriage door open to find the reason for the abrupt stall in their journey.

Dirty men dressed in tattered clothing surrounded the carriage. Each brandished a rusty weapon. Clarissa could smell the body odor wafting from the unkempt men, even though the closest ones to her stood more than fifteen stones away.

"Step aside now!" Sir Gabriel shouted.

The man nearest Sir Gabriel stood with a wood chopping ax resting against his shoulder. His greasy brown hair hung in strands and a cloud of gnats encircled his head. Matted patches of hair covered his shirtless body, glistening with sour sweat. As the man smiled, even from this distance, Clarissa could see the jagged and rotting teeth between his dry, cracked lips.

"Oh, yes, sir! No problem, sir! You jus gonna hafta give us all yer gold first is all."

Sir Gabriel chuckled at the audacity of the man. "Do you not know who we are?"

"You be paladins of Sanctum. And dat one back dere be High Priestess of Sanctum." The man said, pointing at Clarissa. "Which mean, ya prolly got enough gold ta feed us fer a year in dat dere buggy."

"If you know who we are, then you must understand the folly of this errand."

"Oh, I understands. If ya wanted, you and yer friend back dere would tear us apart quick, but ya won be doin dat." He replied, nodding his head in the direction of Clarissa.

One of the men, seemingly emerging from nowhere, grabbed Clarissa, pinning both of her arms to her side in a one-armed hug that pressed her back up against his body. With the other arm, the man brought an old rusty dagger to her throat and held the blade against her skin.

"Your Holiness!" Sir Gabriel called out as he saw Clarissa's predicament.

"Now, ya be handin over all yer gold, or da princess ere be gettin a whole new place ta smile from."

The guards dismounted from their horses. "You know," Sir Gabriel began, "most people know that paladins are one of the few warriors who are proficient in both magic and sword skills. It is why most people fear the paladins of Sanctum. The mere mention of our holy name can quell rebellions and bring armistice to war. We are known for our shield and barrier spells, but did you know that there are those of us who can do more? Some of us can use our magic to move at lightning speed in small distances."

Moving faster than the eye can comprehend, Sir Kenneth disappeared for a blink's length of time. Three assailants flew into the air, struck by an attack they never saw. Two men hit the ground twenty stones from where they were standing, while the third man hit a tree hard enough for Clarissa to hear the man's bones shatter.

"Kill her!" The leader shouted to the man holding Clarissa.

"I c-can't... I can't move my arm!" The man cried.

"Some of us," Sir Gabriel continued, "can cast a Barrier Spell so small and precise that we can render a man unable to move. Some of us can shift our barriers around a person to control them like a puppet."

As Sir Gabriel spoke, the arms of the man holding

Clarissa opened, allowing her to step away and face the bandit.

"Sir Gabriel, could you please remove your barrier from this man's head?" Clarissa asked while fixing her gaze on the man who had captured her.

"Yes, Your Holiness." Sir Gabriel responded with a slight bow.

Clarissa slapped the man's face with all of her strength and then turned to walk toward Sir Gabriel.

"Y-ya be monsters! Retreat!" The leader man shouted as he ran away, leaving his hurt and captured friends behind.

"Shall we pursue?" Sir Kenneth asked.

"No, we only need the one," Clarissa responded while staring at the man still entrapped by Sir Gabriel's Barrier Spell.

Clarissa walked to the trapped man and glared into his eyes. "This one dared to place his hands on me! I feel the need to bathe from just being in his presence, let alone being within his grasp. He must be made an example of!"

"N-no I-I just, I have a family! Th-they were hungry is all. Please!" The man begged.

"Do you know who I am, or how humiliating it is for filth like you to lay hands on me? You will learn. You and your friends will learn. Sir Gabriel, you know what to do." Clarissa said, shooting a look of disgust at the man before retreating to the safety of her carriage.

Sitting in the darkness of the carriage, Clarissa waited to hear the familiar sounds of execution. The sounds of breaking bones and spilling blood had become commonplace in her life, but she never learned to be unaffected by them as her mother promised she would. She did not want to take the man's life, but the standards of social status demanded payment to the atrocity this commoner committed. To lay hands on a noble was a crime of the highest offense, but this vile reprobate dared to threaten her life, and she would not stand for such disrespect.

For a short time, Clarissa heard nothing. Parting the curtains to discover the source of the delay, she saw the criminal on hands and knees with Sir Gabriel hovering his blade above the man's neck. Tears splashed to the dirt as the degenerate begged for his life, claiming to have only committed the crime to feed his starving family. Sir Gabriel's apparent reluctance to finalize the execution-only further fueled Clarissa's frustration.

"Sir Gabriel! Why the delay?" Clarissa shouted.

Through the visor of his helmet, Clarissa could see

his apprehension. A paladin's pride was paramount to the holy knights, and killing an unarmed man challenged his moral convictions, but his duty took precedence over honor. The judgments of the high priestess are both divine and absolute. Binging his weapon down, Sir Gabriel removed the man's head clean from his shoulders.

"Your Holiness, what shall we do with the body?" Sir Kenneth questioned.

"Leave it! Let his friends discover what happens to those who dare attack the High Priestess!"

The rest of the journey proceeded without incident. Arriving at the palace, they discovered a gathered crowd on either side of the entrance steps. Clarissa emerged from her carriage to meet a slanderous onslaught from the angry gathering. The citizens screamed and jeered, "how dare you!" and "the king will have your head!" They mocked her with names like, "harlot," and "blasphemer," and other insults she had never heard before. Some people threw rotten food and garbage at her as she proceeded up the stairs, but Sir Gabriel and Sir Kenneth blocked every throw with their shields. The climb seemed to last an eternity as the disgraced high priestess went to face the consequences of her actions. Clarissa wiped the splattered garbage from her face as a palace guard opened the doors to allow her and the paladin guard's entrance.

A rat-faced looking man scurried toward them bearing a devious smile. "Your Holiness, the King is almost ready for you. Please wait before the throne."

Large enough to fit a thousand people, an ominous presage filled the empty throne room. Since her youth, Clarissa attended many banquets, balls, and feasts in the ornate hall, but never had she felt such dread upon entering the room she normally equated with celebrations. Windows spanned from floor to ceiling, all topped with stained glass in the shape of a crowned heart. Portraits of past rulers hung across the stone walls, depicting the countless generations of the Magicent family's rule. The polished stone floor gleamed in the light of the surrounding lanterns, and a strip of red carpet led to a platform that supported the king's throne.

The royal seat commanded attention. Constructed in gold and adorned in crimson velvet, the throne represented both elegant beauty and foreboding danger to those who stood before it. Three crowned hearts decorated the seatback; a smaller one at the top of each post, a larger crowned heart enhanced the center. The armrests, a golden lion's mane, extended into a lion's head that roared a silent warning to those brave enough to approach. The curved legs of the chair formed lion's paws at the base with golden claws digging into the red carpet as if it stood upon the blood of its enemies.

Clarissa waited before the throne for hours. Her back ached, her feet throbbed and anxiety brought her to the brink of madness, but she internalized her discomfort. Several times she considered taking a seat on the carpet that looked increasingly cozy as time dragged, but she knew the lackadaisical posture would do her no favors. Instead, she endured the suffering as Sir Gabriel and Sir Kenneth flanked her still as statues, patiently awaiting the inevitable sentencing.

The clicking of boots striking stone echoed in the throne room, preceding the arrival of the king and his council, signaling the trial's beginning. Clarissa and the paladins genuflected as the procession entered.

"You may rise." The king addressed the trio after taking his royal seat.

Returning to her feet, Clarissa bowed her head in reverence. "Your Grace."

Clarissa studied the faces of the King's Counsel. Felix Hardwood of Baxis, Oscar Harken of Prasillo, Silla the elf from Parvus Arbor, Reagan McDohl the dwarf of Durrum and Matias Alcaldo of Villam stood as representatives of the major houses of Preclarium, save for one. Tenebris still lacked representation, and the seat would remain empty until the young Lena Richter became of age to inherit the title of Lord.

Among the many responsibilities of a lord of Province, selecting a representative to the king's counsel demanded careful consideration. The chosen council member held the distinct responsibility of representing the needs of thousands to the king. In times of famine, disease, disaster, or even political unrest, the council member provided all the necessary information to the king to ensure a province's survival. Lena's uncle, Lord Regent Stefan Richter, garnished vast respect as a worthy place holder for the lordship title. However, the authority to name a representative lay strictly with the heir.

Unexpectedly, a familiar face accompanied her own chosen representative. Her brother Aaron stood alongside her Uncle Vincent. Color drained from his face as his eyes darted across the room to avoid his sister's gaze.

A cavalcade of questions flooded her mind. *What was he doing here? Why did he not see her off this morning?*

*Where has he been and what has he been doing?*
Nevertheless, she dared not ask. She knew the protocol when being brought before the king: speak only when spoken to.

"High Priestess, Clarissa Bright." The king began.

"Your Grace." Clarissa responded, bowing her head and placing her fist over her heart. Her brother's presence overwhelmed her thoughts. She wanted to run to him, ask where he had been when she needed him most. She wanted to insist that he be removed from the preceding, but knew she held no position to make demands. Aaron, the person she cared for more than anyone, would soon witness her ultimate humiliation, and the thought tore a hole in her heart.

"I hope your trip was without incident."

"A minor one, Your Grace. Nothing the mighty paladins of Sanctum couldn't handle."

"Well, I am glad you made it through your minor incident unharmed."

"Thank you, Your Grace."

"I apologize for having you wait so long, High Priestess."

"No need for apologies, Your Grace."

"Perhaps, but it is still common courtesy. Wouldn't you agree?"

"Yes, Your Grace."

"Courtesy. I believe it is an integral part of life. Especially for those of noble birth. A simple lack of courtesy can cause hatred, malice, even war. Do you believe that courtesy is important, High Priestess?

"Yes, Your Grace."

"Yet you do not provide your King the courtesy of time to decide the fate of a man's life. Do you have any malice toward me, High Priestess?"

"No, Your Grace."

"Do you believe I have failed you in any way?"

"No, Your Grace."

"Did you know that it is a law to wait twenty-four-hours hours before execution to allow the King time to grant a pardon?"

"Yes, Your Grace."

"So you knowingly disobeyed the laws set forth by your King. That is very troubling, indeed. Tell me, High Priestess, how old are you?"

"I am twenty years, Your Grace."

"How long have you been the High Priestess of Sanctum?"

"Two years, Your Grace."

"Has it been two years already? Did you receive adequate training and education from your mother?"

"Yes, Your Grace."

"So your education and training were adequate, you knew the laws, you have no feelings of malice, nor hatred for me, and you are aware of courtesies. I am sorry, but I do not understand. Could you please explain to me why you have committed treason?"

Her eyes fluttered as she tried to hold back her tears, preparing to answer this inevitable question. For days, no thought entered her mind other than how to respond to this inquiry. After pondering several excuses she could offer the king, she decided on the only feasible explanation. "I have no excuse, Your Grace. For selfish reasons, I moved the execution time of Marshal Bartram. This decision was mine alone, as I believed that there was no reason that you would grant the marshal a pardon."

"So, not only did you think your selfish reasons were more important than the rights of the King, but you also believed that you knew better than the King regarding the subject of who does or does not deserve a pardon. Why do you shed tears, High Priestess? Is it because you fear the decision I must now make?"

"No Your Grace. It is because I have failed you, my mother, and the entire Bright family. For thousands of years, my family has served your line as the protectors of justice and righteousness, yet in a mere two years of service, I have brought nothing but disgrace and dishonor upon a proud name. I do not cry for fear of reprisal. I have committed a crime, and I will serve my sentence with dignity. It is the least I can do to restore what little honor I can for my family."

"Do you know the penalty for treason, High Priestess?"

"Yes, Your Grace. Death"

"And what method is traditionally used to carry out this sentence?"

"The High Priestess casts the Holy Judgment Spell on the offender, Your Grace."

"That is correct, but this situation is different. The only person in the kingdom who knows that spell is the High Priestess of Sanctum, and you cannot exactly cast that spell on yourself." The king shifted in his seat. Lightly stroking his bearded chin, he gave a long pause before continuing. "I am ready to proceed with my ruling. Clarissa Bright, you are hereby stripped of your title as High Priestess. Traditionally, it is the eldest daughter of the Bright family who inherits the position of High Priestess, but since you are the only living Bright daughter, the position will be handed to your brother, Aaron Bright."

The council broke into a murmur. Clarissa could feel the blood rush from her face as she processed the king's words. The sentence was worse than death. For thousands of years, the women of the Bright family stood over the Holy Court. Having a man serve as the head of the Bright family severed an ancient tradition. The responsibility for the custom's destruction would fall on Clarissa, and the history books would relay her humiliation for countless generations. The legacy of Clarissa Bright would be known as the woman who brought ruin upon the house of Bright.

"Your Grace, this is a far departure from what we discussed!" Vincent spoke up.

"Are you questioning my decision?"

"No, Your Grace, it's just…"

"My decision is final. Clarissa Bright, you are hereby banished from the city of Sanctum. Furthermore, you are forbidden from ever performing the Holy Judgment Spell. That spell is cast as means of holy execution. You shall be allowed to visit your chambers to gather any personal belongings, but by nightfall, I expect you to have vacated Sanctum. Should you fail to obey this direct order, the consequences shall be most severe."

Clarissa's head swam, swaying as the room spun around. She could hear people talking, but the voices combined into indiscernible echoes in her ears. Fighting the urge to swoon, she grabbed hold of Sir Kenneth's shoulder to prevent herself from collapsing.

"Your Grace!" Sir Gabriel knelt and saluted the king.

"Yes, Sir..."

"Sir Gabriel, Your Grace."

"Sir Gabriel. What is it?"

"I request that I be allowed to accompany the Hi...Lady Bright."

"Why would I allow a paladin of Sanctum to leave the service of the kingdom?"

"Your Grace, when paladins enter service, they take an oath to protect the city. The oath compels us to be the light that expels the shadow, but a select few take an additional second oath. I took an oath to protect Clarissa Bright, not the High Priestess. I took this oath before her and Matera, the Goddess of Light. If I do not accompany her, I will have broken my oath, and my worth as a paladin will mean nothing."

"It is not often that I do not foretell the outcome of a ruling, Sir Gabriel. I did not foresee this. You are correct. The paladins assigned to guard the High Priestess of Sanctum vow to serve and protect the person, not the position. Tell me, Sir Gabriel, if I were to deny your request, what would you do?"

"I would follow her anyway, Your Grace. Honor demands it."

"I see. Denying your request leaves you with the choice to either break your oath or commit treason. No paladin worth his shield would ever break an oath."

Clarissa looked at Sir Gabriel kneeling on the floor, puzzled by his request. She knew the truth in his words, but could not understand why he would sacrifice the plushy conditions of Sanctum amongst his family and friends for someone who no longer held the title and privileges of the one he swore to protect. She thought about his life and realized she knew little about the paladians who protected her. Too enamored with the responsibilities as high priestess, she never bothered to know the guards who kept her safe.

"Your Grace, I, too, took an oath to protect Clarissa Bright." Sir Kenneth took a knee and saluted the king.

"Either the paladins of Sanctum are very dedicated to their cause, or very dedicated to a pretty face. I sincerely hope it is the former. Arise, paladins of Sanctum. Your request is hereby granted. You may accompany Clarissa Bright wherever she may go. This court is dismissed."

Clarissa watched the king and his counsel depart. The king's verdict swirled in her mind in a tornado of disbelief and fear. Tears felt like an inadequate response to the despair in her heart. Intending to keep her composure, she turned to exit, but she stumbled and nearly fell. Luckily, the quick reactions of her loyal escorts kept her from crumbling to the floor. Sir Gabriel and Sir Kenneth kept a watchful eye on Clarissa as they exited the palace.

Outside, the crowd of people, who just hours ago berated and humiliated her, dispersed. Her carriage was nowhere in sight, leaving her stranded in a city full of people who despised her. The few citizens that remained walked around the courtyard completing their daily tasks, ignorant to the proceedings that dismantled an ancient tradition.

"Shall we go Your, I mean, m' lady?" Sir Gabriel asked.

"No, my brother will be here to see me at any moment." Clarissa waited for her brother for an hour, but he never came.

"He must be too ashamed to see me. We should go. The king wants me out of Sanctum by nightfall, which leaves us little time. Thank you, Sir Gabriel, Sir Kenneth. I could not have asked for better, more honorable paladins than the two of you."

"We are merely doing our duty m' lady." Sir Kenneth responded.

"That may be, but I thank you anyway. You may as well get used to addressing me as Clarissa. It may be a while before any title is bestowed upon me again."

"Again? Do you have a plan m'…Clarissa?" Sir Gabriel's eyes widened beneath his visor.

"Not yet, but I can promise one thing. I will return one day as High Priestess."

# Razuul

Razuul sat, barely conscious. The hunger pains ached as severe as the pain from the wounds covering his body. Two days ago he ripped the heart out of a dragon and earned his freedom, but this feat did not come without a price. Many times he attempted to stand only to crash back to the blood-soaked dirt. Drained, starving and near death, his battered body no longer possessed the strength to support his weight. Willpower alone kept him alive.

Seventy years he spent within the arena walls, and for his entire tenure as an unwilling participant in the deadly game, he survived. He maimed, disfigured, and killed whoever stood in his path to freedom, and now that he earned his liberation, he could do nothing with it. The entirety of his journey into his freedom lasted no more than an arm's length from the arena doors, the cruelest joke of all.

Razuul saw people stare as they passed by. Some stepped over his lifeless carcass without care while others gave him a wide berth as if some incurable disease infected him.

"Ha! I found you!" Shouted a familiar voice. Razuul turned to see who spoke, but his blurred vision allowed him to see only a cloudy visage. A hazy man approached Razuul, crouched beside him, and pressed an object against his lips, allowing the refreshing sensation of liquid to enter his mouth. He swallowed the water in gulps, ignoring the pain in his dry, scratchy throat.

Razuul looked at the mysterious man, striving to identify the shadowy figure. He wanted to snatch the container from the man, but his arm flopped back to the ground with each attempt. Needing assistance from this stranger infuriated Razuul, a situation he silently vowed never to allow himself to experience again if he survived.

"You look like you've been put through a meat grinder! Can you walk?" The shadow man asked.

Razuul could only shake his head. The shadowy face flirted on the edge of familiarity. He tried to speak, but gibberish escaped from his mouth.

"Well, you need a doctor. Lucky for you, I know a guy. Wait right here." The shadow man laughed, knowing full well no other option remained. Razuul failed to see the humor in the man's jest.

The debilitated warrior drifted in and out of consciousness while the shadow man went in search for a doctor. Pain faded into numbness and he could no longer feel his extremities. His weak heartbeat slowed and the ringing in his ears intensified like the bell's toll of death. Teetering between the realms of the living and the dead, Razuul prayed for the man's return, although his faith in the kindness of strangers would not allow his hopes to get too high.

"Here he is, Doc!" Razuul heard the shadow man say as he struggled to see who spoke. His vision, still too blurry to see anything other than shapes and shadows, only allowed him to comprehend the presence of another man much shorter and rounder than the first.

"Is that?" Razuul heard the round man ask. The voice belonged to man drenched with fear, as evidenced by the quake in his speech.

"Yep, time to get to work."

"B-but I c-can't treat…him! I-I-I'll lose my license!"

"Listen, of all the people that owe me a favor, no one owes me more than you! Besides, you're getting well compensated."

"A-alright. But after this, my debt is paid!"

"Yeah, yeah, just get to work, will ya?"

Razuul felt a tingling creep up his legs, returning the pain in his deadened limbs. The burning sensation quickly turned to relief, as if being submerged into a pool of healing. He wondered if the sensation meant the march of death worked its way up on his body, but the reaper never came. The cold, euphoric feeling came and went. He found himself in a heavenly calm as the discomfort in his body seceded and he drifted off into the most blissful slumber of his existence.

Razuul opened his eyes and saw the night sky. Thousands of stars twinkled in the darkness. The chilly evening air wafted with the scents of fires and cooked meals. The pain in his body dissipated, leaving the only ache in his empty stomach. He saw the man he had spoken to in the cell of the arena taking a bite of an apple. Razuul leaned forward, snatched the apple from his hand and ferociously began to devour it, leaving the juices to drip off his chin.

"I would have just given you an apple you know. I have more." The man presented a burlap bag. Razuul tossed aside the half-eaten apple, grabbed the bag, pulled out an apple, and began to eat as he leaned back against the wall behind him.

"Do you remember me?" The man asked. Razuul just

stared, chewing his apple.

"We met in the arena. My name is Brett. It's a good thing I found you. A couple more hours, and you'd have been rat food."

"Why?" Razuul said with a mouth full of apple. "Why did you help me?"

"Can't a guy just help someone out of the kindness of his heart?"

Razuul responded by throwing the core of his apple at Brett, which exploded on the wall next to his head.

"Okay, okay," Brett raised his palms facing Razuul in surrender. "I do have a reason, but we can discuss that later."

Razuul cocked back his arm to throw another apple core at him, but Brett reacted quickly this time. "No, wait! Seriously, let me take you to get some real food and we can talk. Can you walk?"

Razuul looked down at his legs. In place of the charred, bloody flesh, shiny, scarred skin now covered his legs, as if the burn happened months ago instead of days. Touching his side, he pressed against his ribs to reveal the lack of agony. He grabbed his nose, shifted it from side to side, to discover the absence of pain.

Razuul looked at Brett and nodded his head. The

prospect of a meal enticed him. Seeing no harm in listening, he thought he would hear what Brett had to say. If he didn't like it, he would make him wish he never left the arena.

Razuul stood and followed Brett down the alleyway. Emerging from the dark corridor, they came to a street crowded with people walking to destinations, idly chatting and peddling their wares. As Razuul walked, people stared and gave him a wide berth, as if he were a ship parting the ocean's waves. He could hear the people whisper to each other at seeing the first man to earn his freedom walking freely in the streets. One name in particular that he overheard brought a smirk to his face when he heard the man address him with a title, the Dragon Fist.

Before long, they arrived at Brett's intended destination. An old rickety building with a sign hanging above the door stood before them. Razuul spent the majority of his life imprisoned, and never learned how to read, leaving the message of the sign a mystery to him. He followed Brett into the building to see a room filled with round tables, chairs, and a long, tall table at one end of the room with stools in front. Bottles filled with liquids of brown and clear colored fluid lined several shelves, and a barrel stood in the corner with a spigot at the bottom. Packed with people eating and drinking from wooden mugs, the room gave off a plethora of savory scents that made Razuul's stomach rumble. The conversations and laughter that filled the room fell silent the moment they saw who entered the establishment.

Every person in the room stared at Razuul in wide-eyed fear. Brett looked around the room and walked over to a table with three men seated at it.

"Excuse me," Brett said to one of the men. "I see you are finished with your meal. Would you mind moving so that my friend and I can eat and have a conversation?"

The man looked up at Brett, his body shivering in fear. With a bulge of food tucked in his cheek, he nodded and rose to his feet, while holding his gaze on Razuul.

"Come, Razuul! These nice gentlemen here have voluntarily given up their table so that we can sit and eat."

Razuul walked to the table, glancing around the room at the terrified patrons. The men sitting at the table scattered as he approached. Brett gestured to one of the chairs with his open hand and sat in the adjacent seat. As soon as Razuul sat, every person in the room ran out the door, some screaming, others stumbling and toppling chairs as they fled.

Razuul looked at the table to see that the three plates

on top were still half-full of food. Grabbing a handful of a white mushy looking substance, he began bringing it to his mouth before Brett suggested he halt his current course of action.

"I wouldn't do that. You never know where the hands of the previous owner of that meal have been. You can order whatever food they have to offer here and it will come to you fresh and hot."

Razuul looked at Brett and decided that taking his advice would be wise. He had watched prisoners eat after other prisoners only to become ill later, some of which would go on to suffer miserable and painful deaths. Dropping the mushy substance back onto the plate, he wiped his hand on his pants.

"Hey, barkeep!" Brett shouted. "You've got hungry customers here!"

A timid-looking man emerged from a door behind the bar and approached the table while clutching at a dirty towel.

"W-what c-can I g-get you f-fine, gentlemen?" The man asked with a trembling voice.

"Steak!" Brett shouted, making the man jump and cringe. "I could go for a good steak. What about you, Razuul? Do you eat meat? I've heard elves are vegetarians."

Razuul glared at Brett with narrow eyes. "That's the wood elves. Wild elves eat meat."

"Two steaks it is!"

"R-right away, sirs."

"What is all this? What are you doing?" Razuul asked.

"I'm just getting us some food. You said you were hungry."

Razuul picked up the plate in front of him and cocked it back to threaten Brett.

"You don't have to throw anything at me," Brett said, raising his hands. "Look, I am here to get some food and talk with you. Making people run in terror was just a fun little…perk."

Razuul set the plate down thinking that there is something wrong with this man.

"How are you out of the arena? I know you didn't earn your freedom the same way I did."

"You're right. New evidence confirmed I did not commit the crime I was accused of perpetrating, and now the bastard that set me up is in the arena instead of me. I know many people who owe me countless favors and one of them finally came through. The next day I was released."

"How am I healed?"

"You're not. At least not completely. A doctor I know owed me big-time, so I called in a favor. He healed you with water magic, but that magic is limited. If you overdo it, those ribs will crack, and those legs will bleed. You'll have to try to take it easy for a while."

"I thought only nobles used magic," Razuul squinted skeptically.

"Doctors can receive a license granted through the King to practice healing spells, but even that is rare. Most of the medics in Regiis heal with herbs and medicines. Luckily for you, I knew one who uses magic."

"Why? Why are you doing this? And you better not say kindness."

"You're right; I am not doing this out of kindness. It's simple really. If I am seen walking around with *The Razuul*, people will think we are friends, and no one will mess with someone who is friends with the Dragon Fist. People are giving you that nickname now, in case you did not know. I'll become the king of the underworld! Thieves and all manners of dirty underhanded scoundrels will flock to work for the man who has Razuul on his side!"

"And why would I allow that?"

"Because I will help you find your people. I have enough money to support both of us, and I know people all over the continent. There is no one better to help you find them. People see me traveling with you, and you get to find your family. It's a win-win! What do you say?"

Razuul considered the proposition. Brett spoke many truths. He didn't know how to find his people or where to look, and he didn't have money to support himself. Razuul no longer possessed the skills necessary to hunt or gather food, and aside from Brett, people were terrified of him, leaving him unable to inquire how to find his people. With a reluctant nod of his head, Razuul accepted Brett's terms.

"Alright, it's a deal!" Brett exclaimed jutting out his hand. Razuul knew the gesture meant Brett asked for a handshake, he had seen this gesture in the cells of the arena, but he had never shaken anyone's hand before and he wasn't going to start now.

The timid cook delivered two plates, each containing a large steak, fried potatoes, and a small pile of mixed vegetables. Steam and aromas of spices wafted from the silver platters. Ignoring the fork and knife, Razuul devoured his food with his bare hands.

"Barkeep!" Brett shouted across the room.

"Yes, sir?"

"Do you have any rooms available? My friend and I need a place to stay for the night."

"Y-yes, I do, sir b-but I-if I let you stay here; I-I will never get any other customers."

Brett rose from his chair, picked up his pack, and walked over to speak up-close with the man. "Do you think it is wise to deny a room to Razuul, the greatest arena fighter in history? The man who ripped out the heart of a dragon with his bare hands? Besides, here," Brett handed the man a pouch. "This should be more than enough to cover the price of the meal, the room, and the money that you would have earned tonight had we not patronized your fine establishment."

The man greedily grabbed the sack, looked inside, and beamed a smile at Brett. Reaching into his pocket, he pulled out a key and handed it to Brett. "Up the stairs, the door to your right."

Brett returned to the table. With a sideways glare, Razuul spoke with a mouthful of food. "There is something very wrong with you."

Brett chuckled. "I suppose you're right. Come on, get a move on, we have a lot to do tomorrow."

Brett led Razuul up the stairs. Unlocking and opening the door, a musty odor welcomed the guests. Two beds stood in the center of the room. A single window looked out to the street below and a wooden wardrobe sat in the corner. Brett dropped his pack and flopped onto one of the beds.

"As I said, we've got a lot to do tomorrow, so I suggest you get some rest."

"Like what?" Razuul demanded.

"Like get you some clothes first of all. You can't prance around Regiis with no shirt or shoes and holes in your pants."

"Prancing is not something you will ever see me do."

Razuul hadn't considered his appearance. Brett was right, he did not know how far they would have to travel, nor the type of weather they would encounter on their journey.

"What about weapons?" Razuul wondered.

"You want weapons, huh?"

"I can see you enjoy riding the coattails of my reputation, but that reputation can only carry us so far. If I am seen unarmed, some fool will try to bolster their notoriety by taking out the Dragon Fist."

"Ha! I already thought of that. It just so happens that I am good friends with the finest weaponsmith in Regiis,

Thane Kinsman. I've had plenty of mutually profitable business ventures with the old dwarf. I am sure he will give us a great deal on some high-quality weapons. As I said, we've got a lot to do tomorrow, so you should get some rest."

Razuul looked at the empty bed. If he had ever slept in a bed, he couldn't remember doing so. Peeling back the sheets, he laid down. The plush arrangement felt alien. He tossed and turned on the feather-stuffed mattress. Every time he shifted to his side, he could feel the ache of his previously broken ribs. A few hours of attempting to sleep passed. Brett's snoring and incoherent mumbling filled the tiny room. Deciding that he could not sleep on the bed, Razuul laid his blanket on the floor, grabbed his pillow, curled up, and drifted off to sleep.

The next morning, Razuul woke to Brett's snoring. He chucked his pillow across the room, striking Brett in the face. He woke with a jolt and sat up, rubbing his eyes.

"I'm up! I'm up!"

The rising sun and the cloudless sky greeted the duo as they walked down the street. The fragrance of baked goods and simmering breakfasts made Razuul's stomach growl. Scores of people crossed the street to avoid Razuul as he followed Brett.

They completed their morning tasks of eating, purchasing a few outfits, and finding a pair of boots to fit Razuul. Their errands proceeded without incident other than Brett needing to chase after a few store clerks who fled at the sight of Razuul. The one purchase the impatient elf desired most Brett seemed to avoid, irritating him more with every step they took.

The afternoon came and, after several death threats, Brett finally agreed to take Razuul to the weaponsmith shop. Razuul wanted to go there first, but Brett insisted that the owner would not open his shop before the sun was high in the sky. When they arrived, Razuul saw a shop that looked nothing like what he expected.

Dirt covered the weathered wood of the old, run-down building. Pieces of cloth flapped in the wind from the torn awning that covered the decrepit doorway. A thick layer of dust covered the ground in front of the shop, a stark contrast to the swept walkways of the surrounding shops. Grime covered the windows, keeping the secrets of the building's contents hidden. No sign hung on the building, and no pots of flowers beautified the entrance to make the establishment seem more inviting.

"This is it, let's go!" Brett called, walking into the shop. Razuul raised an eyebrow in disbelief. Yesterday, Brett told him the finest weaponsmith in Regiis ran this shop, but suspicion began to creep into his mind over the validity of this claim.

The disparity between the inside and the outside of the store took Razuul by surprise. Shields and weapons of every kind, shape, and size hung on the walls in a neat, orderly fashion. Barrels marked with prices held bundles of stock of varying quality. The freshly washed floors and polished weapons displayed on the walls shimmered from the few rays of sun that peeked through the dirty windows. In the corner of the shop, a short man slept on a stool. Razuul instantly recognized the man as a dwarf.

Seeing a dwarf made Razuul apprehensive. He had fought many dwarves in the arena, and each one hated him for being an elf. He never understood the hatred dwarves bore for the elven race, nor did he care, but he doubted any dwarf would welcome an elf into his shop.

"Thane!" Brett shouted, causing the dwarf to jump awake and nearly fall out of his stool.

"Huh? What? Who's there?" Thane rubbed his eyes, identifying Brett immediately. "Brett Shaw! Get out of my shop right now!"

"What? Why? Is it because of that last deal? I paid over your asking price for those swords."

"Aye, you paid alright. With wooden coins! Now get out! I will not be dealing with you anymore!"

"Oh come on Thane I…"

"No!" Thane interrupted. "I refuse to deal with any more of your shenanigans."

"Just look!" Brett held out a handful of gold coins. "Try to tell me those are fake."

Thane snatched a coin from Brett's hand to examine its authenticity. Smelling, squeezing and biting the coin, he shot Brett an uneasy look. "Fine! But I am keeping this one. You owe me that much at least!" Thane stuffed the gold coin in his pocket. "Now what do you want? And you better not try to swindle me again!"

"I'm here to purchase a sword for my friend." Brett turned and pointed at Razuul.

Thane's jaw dropped open as he looked at Razuul. "Do you know who that is?"

"Yes, it's Raz…"

"It's an elf!" Thane shouted.

"Wait, what?" Brett replied in confusion.

"An elf! You think I would sell any of my high-quality weapons to a limp-wristed elf? I don't think so! No elf could use my weapons properly!"

"Limp-wristed?" Razuul shouted in anger at the insult. He began approaching Thane to confront him; Thane puffed his chest to welcome the encounter, but Brett quickly stepped in-between them.

"Whoa guys, this doesn't need to get violent."

"Then tell this sissy elf to get out of my shop, and there won't be any problems!" Thane shouted from his tiptoes as he stared at Razuul.

"Oh, now I'm a sissy? You fat little dwarf imp! I'll crush you into..."

"Stop!" Brett shouted. "Look, we have money, let's just forget..."

"No!" Thane interrupted again. "I refuse to sell to an elf. Never have, never will."

Razuul looked around at the weapons in the shop. Not even Adam Garrison of the king's guard possessed a weapon of this high-quality and craftsmanship. Razuul refused to accept a weapon from anyone else. Taking a deep breath to calm his anger, a thought entered his mind.

"Hey, dwarf!" Razuul shouted at Thane. "You said

an elf couldn't use your weapons properly, right?"

"That's right elf, so you should just..."

"I bet I could beat your ass with them!"

"What did you say to me?" Thane took a challenging step toward Razuul.

"Now guys, I don't think..." Brett tried to interject, but the two ignored him.

"You heard me! How about this, you and I have a match. When I win, you sell me your swords at asking price."

"That sounds like a terrible idea. I mean when the..."

"What about when I win? What do I get?" Thane cut off Brett.

Razuul thought for a moment about what this man could want from him. At first, he thought to offer Brett's money, but then a far more enticing offer entered his mind. One that a dwarf would enjoy far more than gold. "If you win, and you won't, but if you do, I will stand in the street, and scream at the top of my lungs that dwarves are better than elves."

The wager brought a smile to Thane. Stroking his beard, he stared off into space as he pondered the challenge. He looked at Razuul with a gleam in his eye. "What's your

Dennis Medbury

weapon of choice, elf?"

"Shit!" Brett exclaimed, throwing his arms up in defeat.

"Two single-handed long swords," Razuul replied, ignoring Brett's disdain.

"Ha! Two swords? Do you know how rare it is that a person is proficient at dual-wielding? You are an elf! There's no way you can use two swords properly!"

"Well then, I guess you'll win even faster than you thought, huh?"

"Damn straight! Hold on." Thane walked over to a barrel full of swords with writing on it that Razuul couldn't read. Pulling out two swords, he tossed them to judge the weight. Feeling satisfied with his assessment, he walked over to Razuul and handed them to him hilt first. "Here you go. These are practice swords with no bladed edge. Perfectly balanced and weighted to be identical. Should be perfect for a dual-wielder such as yourself."

Razuul took the swords and looked at Thane in disgust. "Is this supposed to be some kind of joke?"

Brett looked at the swords, then at Razuul, and finally to Thane. "What joke?"

"He said these swords are identical. If he thinks that,

he is not the weaponsmith you think he is." Razuul stated without examining the swords.

To a novice like Brett, the swords appeared identical, from the tip right down to the size and shape of the hilt. To Razuul, the differences were as obvious as night and day.

"He's right!" Thane said, followed by a deep, slow laugh. "The one in his left hand is slightly heavier than the one in his right."

"The one in my right is also a bit longer."

Razuul's statement beamed a smile from ear to ear across Thane's face. "Aye, although I doubt even the most proficient dual-wielder could have caught that detail. You intrigue me. Maybe you're not the standard sissy little elf I thought you to be. Let's find out shall we?"

"My pleasure. Lucky for you there is no blade on these swords." Razuul gave one final jab as Thane picked up a warhammer and exited the building.

"So glad you two listen to me! I would hate to see a transaction turn to violence!" Brett shouted at the two warriors as they readied themselves for the battle.

Thane and Razuul stood facing each other in the middle of the street. People passing by stopped to watch the spectacle. It did not take long before a crowd encircled the unlikely duo.

"You sure you want to do this elf?" Thane taunted. "I've never heard of an elf besting a dwarf in hand-to-hand combat. There's no sissy bow and arrow allowed in these types of matches."

"Don't worry about me, dwarf. You're the one who needs to worry about being beat by a sissy elf! Won't that be embarrassing?"

Razuul rushed in, swinging his swords in rhythm. Each strike followed another in rapid succession. Thane raised his hammer and kept it close to his body, allowing each intercept to catch the sword strike with minimal movement and maximum speed. Razuul attempted several different striking combinations, but Thane's hammer met each one, keeping one foot planted and only pivoting to intercept at the best possible angle. It seemed as though Thane could predict where Razuul would strike next.

The Dragon Fist stepped back. Thane's defense seemed impenetrable and he knew he needed a different strategy. Bringing both swords above his head, he rushed in, leaving himself wide open for an attack.

The ruse succeeded. For the first time, Thane went on the offensive. Thrusting his mighty hammer at Razuul's chest, Thane lunged for a counter-attack, but the wild elf expected the assault. Spinning on the ball of his foot, narrowly avoiding the strike, Razuul swung one of his swords at the weaponsmith's head, but Thane predicted Razuul's plan. Dropping the head of the hammer, the old dwarf pushed off the ground with one leg and spun around using the hammer as a counterweight to avoid Razuul's swing. The dwarf's agility surprised Razuul and the crowd erupted into cheer at the move.

"You move pretty good for an old guy!" Razuul taunted.

"And you're slightly less sissy than I expected!" Thane returned.

The crowd grew immense. People outside of the perimeter jumped to try to catch a glimpse of the action. Some climbed to tabletops and rooftops so they could bear witness to the once-in-a-lifetime match. The cheers and applause filled the street. Razuul could hear some of the attendees root for the Dragon Fist while others called for his head. He felt his blood boil with anger at the thought of fighting for other's amusement again.

"What's going on here? Break it up!" Razuul heard through the roar of the crowd.

Three guardsmen pushed and shoved their way to the inner circle where the battle took place. The guard's eyes met the murderous gaze of Razuul. The foreboding look told them not to interfere.

"N-never mind. Carry on everybody!" The guard called, receiving the wild elf's warning loud and clear. Turning and escaping the danger Razuul represented, the guards disappeared through the crowd as suddenly as they appeared.

Both men breathed deeply, sweat seeping from every pore. The stalemate continued while they labored to land a single blow. Exhaustion forced the warriors to struggle to keep their weapons held high. Ignoring the fatigue, Razuul dashed in again, swinging one sword after the other, but Thane did something unexpected. The first strike met with the head of his hammer, while the handle intercepted the second. Catching him by surprise, Thane stomped on his opponent's foot and drove his shoulder into Razuul's chest, forcing him to stagger. Fast on his feet, Razuul retreated to avoid a follow-up attack. The pain from his broken ribs returned as Brett's warning to "take it easy" echoed in his mind.

"I… finally… got… you!" Thane said, taking rasping

breaths in-between words.

"That was… a good move! Pretty… much… unstoppable!" Razuul returned, taking deep breaths of his own.

"That's… why… I… use it!"

In all his years of fighting, Razuul never faced an opponent with style as polished and proficient as Thane. Every combination, every feint, and every strike the experienced arena fighter knew had failed. Overwhelming an opponent brought victory in previous battles for Razuul, until now.

After contemplating every move that remained in his arsenal, an epiphany dawned on Razuul. Instead of going in for a charge, he would allow Thane to go on the offensive, and for the first time, attempt a defensive counter.

Razuul took his fighting stance, holding both swords at the ready. Waving the sword in his left hand toward himself in a taunt, he dared Thane to come in for an attack.

Scratching his belly, Thane taunted, "Tired already, elf? Fine. Let me show you how a dwarf fights."

Thane darted at Razuul with his weapon held above his head. The blunt end came driving down toward Razuul, but he halted the attack with both swords forming an X underneath the hammer's head. Razuul saw a glint of metal rushing toward his stomach and realized Thane intended to end the match using a hidden dagger. Dropping the sword in his left hand, Razuul grabbed Thane's arm, stopping the advance of the knife while pushing the hammer outwards with his right. Seeing the opening, Razuul struck Thane with a head-butt that forced the old dwarf to close his eyes and stumble. Before the weaponsmith could raise his hammer, Razuul swiftly swung his sword, stopping the deadly attack a breath's distance from Thane's throat.

The onlookers erupted in celebration. The spectacle created a fervor that reminded Razuul of his days in the arena. At the top of his lungs, Razuul screamed, "Don't you cheer!"

The crowd formed a collective silence. The freed arena fighter paced in a circle wearing a snarl, making sure to glance at everyone in attendance to relay the seriousness of his warning. "Get out of here!"

The hordes scurried away like rats. Exhausted and panting, Razuul wiped the sweat from his brow with his forearm.

"You alright?" Thane asked, walking up to Razuul.

"Yeah, I just swore I would never fight for anyone's amusement ever again. Hearing them cheer made my blood boil."

"Fair enough. I cannot believe that the hidden dagger move didn't work. Did you see me pull it from my belt when I fake scratched my belly?"

"No, I didn't see it until you were driving it toward me."

"Well, then that's some amazing reflexes and skills you have there."

"For an elf?" Razuul asked with a crooked smile.

"For an elf," Thane replied with a smile in return. "A deal is a deal. I promised to sell you some swords, and I would be honored to have a warrior of your caliber wield them. Follow me."

Thane led the men in the shop and disappeared into a back room. Sounds of metal clanking against wood and steel left Razuul and Brett curious.

The weaponsmith returned carrying two swords attached to a leather belt. The sheaths drew Razuul's attention. The polished silver on the throat of the scabbards formed an intricate design of interwoven tendrils. The tip of the casings bore the same detailed design, which rose to form a circle in the center, encasing a bird with flowing tail feathers and spread wings. Leather tightly wrapped the handles in a criss-cross pattern, and the pommel formed a silver phoenix's head with its beak open wide as if singing the legendary bird's song of warning to anyone who would challenge the bearer of these swords. The guard resembled the spread wings of a bird with feathers carved in intricate detail and reflected in a hue of blue that made the wings seems realistic enough to take flight.

"These are the swords for you!"

"How much are they?" Brett asked.

"They are perfectly balanced and weighted to be identical to each other. No pair of swords exist that are better suited for a dual-wielder." Thane spoke, ignoring Brett.

"But how much do they cost?"

Razuul tried to remove one of the blades, but the scabbards refused to release the blades.

"That's one of my favorite features!" Thane remarked with pride. "To remove the blade, you have to twist the handle and pull." Thane demonstrated the procedure to Razuul. "This prevents anyone from taking the blade from you if you are caught unaware. The locking mechanism is spring-loaded, so it locks every time you place the sword in the sheath."

"Am I even speaking here? How much?" Brett spoke louder to ensure the old dwarf heard him.

Razuul took the sword from Thane and marveled at the gleaming, single-edged sword. "It's a little heavier than I expected."

"The swords are made of a Hygard steel alloy. They are virtually unbreakable and never need to be sharpened."

"Hygard steel? That stuff is just a myth! What are you trying to pull Thane?" Brett quipped skeptically.

"I'm not trying to pull anything. Not everyone is a scam-pulling scoundrel like you. I made these swords myself. They were intended for a friend who I recently discovered had passed, so I don't think he will mind me selling them to someone else."

"Let me see that." Brett examined the blade.

Razuul handed the blade to Brett, dropping his arm from the unexpected weight. Brett stared at the sword in awe. "It's nice and all, but how do we know it's Hygard steel?"

"Well, if my word isn't good enough for you, I'll show you! Give that back to him." Thane said, referencing Razuul with a nod of his head.

Thane walked over to the barrel and retrieved a sword similar to the ones used in the duel. Raising the blade to a fighting posture in front of himself, he instructed, "Swing that sword as hard as you can at this one, and I will do the same." The two men drew back their swords and swung them toward each other with full force. The swords clashed. Razuul's blade drove through the steel in the weaponsmith's hands, bringing the upper half of Thane's sword to crash to the floor.

"And you know I do not produce shoddy workmanship, even with practice swords," Thane proudly remarked, presenting the broken sword to Brett. "Now look at the blade of the other sword. I guarantee you won't find the slightest nick in the blade."

Brett examined the blade in Razuul's hand, confirming the truth behind Thane's words.

"Hygard steel, huh? Wow. How much?" Brett asked again.

"A true bargain when you consider the rarity of the…"

"Thane!" Brett interrupted. "For the last time, how much?"

"Five hundred gold pieces."

"Five hundred? For two swords?"

"You didn't let me finish. Five hundred gold pieces...each."

"Each? Why you swindling..."

"Brett!" Razuul interrupted, putting his arm around his shoulders. "I need these swords. If we get into any trouble while traveling, I need high-quality swords. I tend to break swords easily. Besides, if people see me traveling around with swords like these, it will only further raise my reputation, and in turn, raise yours."

Brett turned away from Razuul's grasp to face him. "Fine!" He exclaimed in an angry tone and removed his backpack. Reaching inside, he removed two sacks of gold, walked over to Thane and slammed the coins into Thane's hand. "I think we know who the real swindler is here!"

"Pleasure doing business with you," Thane responded with a smile. "And good luck to you, sissy elf!"

"Thank you, you crusty old dwarf!" Razuul gave as a snarky return.

Razuul buckled his new belt and swords around his waist as he and Brett left the shop. "I'm hungry." He said, looking at Brett.

"We'll need to find a different room for tonight. I

doubt the innkeeper from last night would be too excited to see us again. It's not late yet, we should find a place closer to the edge of the city so we can start heading toward Villam in the morning. I know a guy there who should be able to help us find your people."

# Elendor

An explosion echoed from somewhere within the city, followed by the unmistakable crash of a falling building.

"Centaurs! I thought there were no centaurs in Preclerium!" Jocia exclaimed.

"Me too!" Agreed Galain and Vaylon.

"We have to help them!" Elendor pleaded.

"What can we do?" Galain asked helplessly.

"We are the Miracle Three! An elven archer trained by the great warrior Heece, and two powerful earth mages. We can help!"

"What about me?" Vaylon wondered.

"Carry me and protect me Vaylon, and I will protect you!"

"He is right! We should help. We can help! Lord Regent Richter was likely planning to deny Elendor library access. If we help, it may sway his decision!" Jocia exclaimed.

Without a moment to waste, they ran out of the building and down the stairs. Arriving at the gate, they saw the bone wall erected, blocking their path. They called out asking anyone to drop the wall, but no movement came. Interrupting their pleas, the booming sound of doors crashing open echoed in the courtyard.

A man came running down the stairs. "Elves! What are you doing here?"

"It doesn't matter! Drop this wall! We can help!" Elendor pleaded.

"I will, but only because I am going out there to help." The black-robed man drew out a runic symbol in the direction of the bone wall. In an instant the bones disappeared into the ground, revealing the carnage occurring in the streets of Tenebris.

Hundreds of centaurs attacked citizens, summoned skeletons, and zombies. Screams of pain and terror rang from every direction as the centaurs charged through the streets wielding spears and swords. The pungent smell of death competed with the rotting odor of the swamp. The man who let them through the gate turned to re-summon the bone wall. Before he could finish making the symbol, a spear flew through the air and skewered him through the neck, dropping his lifeless body to the cobblestone road.

Three centaurs charged at the elves with spears tucked under their arms. Elendor looked at his panicked friends. Their expressions revealed the terror they felt, frozen in place and unsure of what to do.

"Jocia! Trip them!" Elendor shouted.

Jocia, keeping her gaze on the charging centaurs, drew out a runic symbol. A chunk of earth raised underneath their horse legs, causing the attackers to tumble to the ground.

"Galain!" Elendor shouted.

"I know!" Galain responded before firing three arrows in rapid succession, killing the trio of charging beasts.

The screams, clashing metal and the centaur's rapid hoof beats against cobblestone forced Elendor to shout. "Escort me to the entrance of the city! I can end this battle, but I will need to conserve my energy until we get there. My friends, I must rely on you to continue this fight until that time!"

The friends crouched down and began moving through the city toward the entrance. Galain fired arrows at any centaur that came within range. Jocia raised spike-shaped sections of earth to pierce the centaur's hide and lifted rock walls to halt the advance of charging attackers. By the time the group arrived halfway through the city, exhaustion wore their spirits raw. They ducked into an empty building to catch their breath.

"What are we going to do? We've got a long way to go, and I've only got three arrows left!" Galain asked Elendor.

"Jocia is not looking so good." Vaylon added.

Elendor saw her gulping air into her tired lungs. Her pale skin glistened with sweat. Matted strands of damp hair stuck to her forehead. Elendor knew that the casting of so many spells in succession would tire her quickly, but her fatigue proved much worse than he anticipated.

"I am well. Let us proceed." Jocia panted.

"No, you are not well. I shall cast from here on." Elendor insisted.

"If you do that, you won't have the energy to cast the spells at the gate!" Galain warned.

"Well, what choice..." Elendor stopped speaking. His earth mage powers drew alarm. An enormous section of earth hurtled toward them; he knew the building in which they hid would soon be flattened.

"Everyone! Get out now!" Elendor screamed.

They darted out of the building, escaping destruction in the nick of time. A boulder flew through the air and crumpled the building. The explosion shook the ground and tossed the group into the stone street.

Dust and debris flew in all directions. Vaylon cried out in pain as a piece of splintered wood pierced his thigh.

"Vaylon!" Jocia rushed to him.

Vaylon gripped his blood-soaked leg and moaned in pain. "Pull it out! Get it out!"

"Jocia! You're going to have to pull it out!" A petrified Elendor screamed.

"Hold still, Vaylon," Jocia instructed. "Are you ready?" After a nod of Vaylon's head, Jocia grabbed the wood embedded in his leg and yanked it free in one sharp pull. Vaylon screamed in agony. Resisting the urge to flail, he stiffened his back to prevent himself from crushing his passenger. Jocia tore the sleeve off her tunic and began to wrap the gaping wound.

"He cannot walk with that wound. What shall we do?" Jocia asked.

"Perhaps we can find a horse and cart to carry them!" Galain suggested.

"No!" Shouted Vaylon. "I can't cast magic, and I

can't shoot a bow, but I can carry. Rely on me, Elendor!"

Elendor nearly corrected Vaylon's grammar, but stopped himself, admiring the bravery of his friend.

"Look out!" Galain shouted. Four centaurs rushed down the cobblestone street in their direction, ready to attack the easy prey. Elendor raised his hand and began tracing out a runic symbol, rushing to complete the spell. Before the cold hand of death touched the young elves, reinforcements intervened.

Spears of bone whizzed past them and pierced the charging warriors. A fur-covered beast, moving at lightning speed, attacked the remaining centaur that avoided the barrage. The centaur wailed in agony and fell to the ground beneath the weight of the mighty pouncing beast. Using its teeth, the creature tore the throat out of the last centaur, erupting a gruesome spray of blood from its neck.

The frightened elves stared at the beast in terror as it approached them. The head appeared wolf-like, and its two legs resembled the haunches of a canine. It walked with an awkward gait, steadied by massive clawed feet. Blood dripped from the beast's maw and clawed hands; shredded clothing hung loosely from its hide.

A nearby voice shouted. "Alexander! Change back

before their hearts burst from fear!"

The wolf-man transformed, shifting into the dreadlocked man they met in Stefan's office.

Locating the voice, Elendor turned to see Stefan and Lena with one hand still raised from casting a spell.

"A lycanthrope!" Galain proclaimed, turning back to the beast.

"Master elves! What are you doing out here?" Stefan asked sternly.

"They are here for the fun! Look at all this death! I am going to make so many zombies and chimeras when this is over!" Lena delightfully responded.

Snapping out of his bewilderment from seeing a beast emerge from myth, Elendor became insistent. "We can help! If I can get to the entrance, I can end this battle, I know it!"

"Just how do you intend to do that?" Stefan asked in disbelief.

"Out there, in the swamp, there are enough trees and vines to halt an army, and I am an arbormancer!"

Another boulder flew through the air and crashed into a nearby building. The sounds of war echoed from every direction, forcing the group to yell their communications.

Stefan looked to Lena and Alexander. "We need to

get these young elves to the gate. Protect them at all cost!"
Drawing out a runic symbol in the air, he cast a spell. Five
skeleton warriors rose from the black smoke on the ground.
Each brandished a sword and shield.

"Oh, I want to do that too!" Lena announced as she
drew out the same symbol. Twenty armed skeletons
materialized.

"Show off!" Stefan said, looking at his niece. Lena
stuck out her tongue and childishly blew raspberries at her
uncle.

With raised shields, the skeletons marched toward the
gate. Stefan and Lena cast bone spears above the summoned
skeletons, intercepting any centaur that charged the line of
the undead. Alexander changed back to his wolf-form,
darting across the battlefield, tearing apart the attacking
horde one-by-one.

Vaylon limped as they walked, but with unwavering
determination, marched on. Blood soaked the lower portion
of his pant leg. Wincing in pain with each step, he kept
moving forward while Jocia and Galain helped him retain
balance.

Reaching the battlements, Elendor saw the
deteriorating defensive wall. Three sections of the wooden

barrier crumbled into splintered piles. Squadrons of the city's guard desperately fought to prevent the intruders from charging through. Beyond the broken sections, he saw eight trolls and an army of centaurs charging through the swamp. Summoned zombies and skeletons of the necromancers fought to prevent entry, but were quickly losing ground.

The trolls, as tall as the battlements, loomed in the shallow swamp waters. Their arms, with muscles the size of a horse's torso, hung low, allowing their knuckles to rest on the ground as they stood. The only clothing they wore, a loincloth barely large enough to hide their humility, flapped like a flag in the wind. Metal collars attached to a chain wrapped around their trunk-like necks. The chains, secured to a giant cart loaded with boulders, jangled as the trolls heaved the massive rocks into the city. Tossing the hardened chunks of earth with ease, as if they were pebbles, the trolls served as efficient catapults in the siege.

Alexander sped across the remains of the inside wall, killing any centaur that slipped past the summoned army of the dead.

The fetid odors of the swamp, mixed with carcasses lining the streets, overwhelmed Elendor. The screams of the combatants crossing into the afterlife invaded his ears.

Arrows and boulders flew over his head as he and his company cautiously navigated through the city.

"I need to get a little closer!" Elendor yelled to Stefan.

"Hold on! I have an idea!" Lena began drawing a runic symbol. A whirlwind of black smoke encircled her and covered her with an armor comprised of bones from a litany of creatures. A skull helmet, once belonging to an oversized bull, protected her head and a trident comprised of bone was clutched in both hands. "I'll clear a path!" She shouted before darting toward a crumbled portion of the wall.

"Lena, no! Wait!" Stefan cried.

Lena sprinted toward the crumbled wall. A barrage of arrows bounced off her bone armor as she ran. Arriving at the broken wall, she began casting her spell.

An icy wind blew outwards as she cast her magic. Elendor could feel the massive amount of dark energy emitting from the necromancer. He never imagined a human could possess such power, let alone one so young.

Slamming the fork of her weapon onto the ground, Lena fell to her hands and knees. An enormous skeletal warrior, dwarfing the boulder-hurling trolls, climbed from a void of black smoke before her. A deafening roar erupted from the boney beast as it raised its fists high above its head, and brought them crashing down, crushing all centaurs in its path. The ensuing shockwave shook the ground, threatening to collapse the city.

Rising to her feet, Lena displayed a proud grin. She stepped forward, wavered, and crumbled to the ground. Her bone armor and summoned skeletons dissipated into waifs of black smoke as she succumbed to exhaustion.

"Lena!" Stefan shouted, breaking into a dash to be by her side. Before he could make it past his elven companions, Galain reached out and grabbed Lord Regent's arm.

"Can you erect a bone wall where she cleared the path?"

"Lena! I have too…" Stefan fought to run to her, but Galain yanked him back.

"If we can't get Elendor up there, she will have done all that for nothing!" Galain shouted above the chaos.

Stefan understood. "You are right. Give me a moment," he replied in a shaky voice.

Turning to the crumbled section of the wall, he cast his spell. On command, a curved shaped bone wall emerged from the ground to connect to the two remaining parts of the structure, blocking any further intrusion from the invading force. Stefan fell to his knees, trembling from the exhaustion of casting spells in rapid succession.

"Good job, Lord Regent! This is our opportunity!" Galain called out.

The elves approached the bone wall as fast as their tired, injured legs would allow. Before reaching the erected bone structure, two centaurs charged at them with weapons raised. Galain lifted his bow and shot his last remaining arrow, hitting his mark. He reached for the dagger on his belt with shaky hands, but before he could draw the blade, Alexander ran up from behind the centaur. Swiping his massive claws, he decapitated the remaining attacker.

"Thank you!" Galain called to Alexander, but only received a deep rumbling growl in reply, before the lycanthrope darted off to defend the city.

Arriving at the bone wall, Jocia used her last bit of strength to conjure a wall of stone, connecting to the bone wall to form a full circle of protection around them. Buckling over, Jocia crossed her arms over her stomach and retched. She began to crumble, but Galain caught her before she fell. With fluttering eyelids, Jocia's eyes darted from corner to corner as Galain encouraged her to remain conscious. Looking up from her, he called to Elendor, "Do it!"

Elendor peered through the open spaces between the bones of the wall to see the destruction and carnage. Dead bodies, mangled and disfigured, lay scattered across the battlefield. Weapons stained with blood littered the ground in a sea of crimson and silver. Splatters of blood covered the ground and trees. Limbs and entrails floated carelessly in the swampy waters, giving the cloudy marsh a scarlet tinge.

Having exhausted their supply of boulders, the centaurs released the chains that bound the trolls. Waves of the undead army began disappearing into clouds of black smoke, signaling that leagues of necromancers met their end. Without intervention, the city would soon fall.

Elendor closed his eyes in concentration and began casting, drawing out a runic symbol the entire span of his reach. Opening his eyes, the swamp came into view from every angle, as if he possessed hundreds of eyes scattered throughout the battlefield. His newfound connection to the swamp allowed him to feel every snapped branch and every trampled blade of grass.

Manipulating the roots of the trees, whips of wooden tentacles sprang from the water, wrapping around the legs, arms, and necks of the trolls. They clawed at their timbered bonds, but with the wave of a hand, Elendor pulled them beneath the water's surface. Bubbles of air popped at the water's surface, the sole remnant of their existence. Branches and vines sprang to life. The foliage flogged, impaled, choked and dismembered legions of centaurs.

Elendor felt himself begin to wane. Fighting the sleepy urge with all his might, he pressed on, commanding the vegetation of the swamp to attack with unbridled fury. Centaur after centaur fell to the unleashed rage. Elendor knew the magical energy needed to cast this immense spell would force him into unconsciousness, but his determination to see this battle ended allowed him one final effort.

Using the remainder of his strength, he intended to make a statement that would force the invaders to escape. Grabbing as many centaurs as he could, he raised his prisoners into the air as they struggled and fought to free themselves. In a display of vegetative might, Elendor pulled his captured enemy's limbs taught, denying them any movement. Releasing every bit of remaining power, Elendor dismembered everybody within his grasp.

Elendor collapsed within his harness. Willing a final look at the battlefield, he peered between the bones to see the results of his effort. The regiment of centaurs dropped their weapons and splashed through the swamp waters in retreat of the city.

Darkness encircled Elendor's vision. Before the encompassing shadow could envelop his sight, a glowing pair of red eyes appeared before him. The faceless entity radiated with an aura that felt ancient and malevolent. Its gaze pierced Elendor's very soul. Terror filled the young elf, but he no longer had the strength to fight off the coming wave of exhaustion. The eyes remained fixed on Elendor as he drifted off into slumber.

# Dorian

The sun hid behind dark gray clouds, signaling the ominous message that rain would soon arrive. Dorian stood in front of his father's forge, swinging his new sword that he aptly named Shadowflame. Putting his responsibilities aside, he gave into the desire to keep the weapon within his grasp. Ever since the night he and his friends wreathed the sword in black flames, the sword remained on the forefront his mind, calling to him, as if it possessed a consciousness of its own.

In the days since, he learned many things about his new weapon. The weight, the balance, and the reach of Shadowflame became as familiar to him as an appendage; so familiar that the sword felt like an extension of his body.

Another lesson he learned, through mishap, ended the life of yet another tree near his home. One day, while honing his skills in the woods, he accidentally ran the blade into a sapling, instantly turning it to ash. Later that evening, he dropped the sword onto the floor of his home. The blade left a gouge in the wood, but the floorboard remained otherwise unharmed, leaving Dorian to conclude that the flames only devoured living things.

Dorian practiced until dinner time. The dark clouds rumbled and flashed a symphony of chaos as they drew near. Scarfing his food, he waited for his friends' arrival. Before long, he spotted the four companions walking through the woods, but something seemed different. Nathaniel's overly enthusiastic gait and broad smile relayed a message of excitement. Looking to the sky repeatedly as he hurried along, he stumbled on raised roots from the lack of focus on his steps. Holding his pack close to his chest, it seemed as though he protected something precious inside.

Dorian rushed outside to greet them. Each friend shook his hand and hugged him. They visited nightly for two weeks, leaving Dorian to fall behind on his duties, but he didn't care. The time he spent with his friends meant more to him than his father's approval. He knew there would be repercussions for his negligence, but that was a problem for another day.

Since the incident with the umbra beast, Lukas and Margaret grew close, always holding hands or finding a reason to lay a hand on a shoulder, thigh, or face. Dorian assumed they were courting by the way they acted toward each other. They could not stop themselves from gazing at each other, even when required to have their attention focused on casting a spell or practicing a sword swing. Their distractions caused more than a few accidents. A stray column of flame nearly burned down Dorian's home, and a summoned rock wall almost collapsed on an unsuspecting Elijah.

"Dorian, I cannot contain my excitement! I've been waiting for a night like this for a long time." Nathaniel glanced up as a flash of lightning lit the sky. "Can we go into the forge?"

"That's probably a good idea." Dorian looked up, squinting his eyes as drops of water began to fall from the sky.

Dorian and his friends moved their nightly reunion inside. By the time he finished lighting the torches, the rain shifted from a drizzle to a downpour. Flashes of lightning and crashes of thunder grew closer as Nathaniel pulled a book from his pack and began reading the text fervently.

"I found it!" Nathaniel announced, throwing his hands wide into the air. "The Lightning Strike Spell! It can only be cast by a wind mage on a night like tonight!"

"I've seen you cast lightning spells plenty of times. What's so special about this spell?" Elijah asked.

"A wind mage can cast lightning spells, that's true enough, but the natural lightning that comes from the sky is far more powerful and devastating. It takes a large degree of focus and concentration, but if performed correctly, the spell not only aims the lightning from the heavens, it enhances the power and widens the area of effect." Nathaniel's eyes widened with excitement.

"I've read a story about this spell. A wind mage became a legend for casting this spell. What was his name?" Margaret asked no one in particular, as she racked her brain for the answer to her question. "Euroch!" She announced, pleased that she remembered. "Euroch the Storm!"

"Euroch the Storm!" Lukas added. "I've read about him too. He was an elf that used wind magic. This was before Nakaan united the wood elf tribes to form Parvus Arbor in Cantata Forest and all the elves decided to use earth magic only."

"Never heard of him, but that's probably because he's an elf. My father would never buy me a book that had anything to do with elves." Dorian knew of the rivalry between dwarves and elves, but never understood their animosity.

"Euroch the Storm," Nathaniel spoke excitedly.

"Growing up, he was my hero. I read every story and every historical account of him. Thousands of years ago, during the Dwarf-Elven War at the Battle of the Crossroads, Euroch watched as his people faced extinction. Thousands upon thousands of dwarves advanced toward an elven army that was just shy of a thousand. The battle was nearly lost when the rains came, and Euroch the Storm cast the Lightning Strike Spell, summoning a bolt of lightning so massive, that its light swallowed a thousand dwarves. The massive crater caused by the spell still exists to this day. It is known as Euroch Lake now. The dwarves retreated in fear that another bolt would come from the heavens, but they did not realize the truth. The spell Euroch cast was too large, and it took the entirety of his life force to cast. Euroch died a hero to his people that day. He's the reason I chose wind as my runestone, and the inspiration for me to practice magic in the first place."

Lightning illuminated the room, followed by a deafening clap of thunder.

"I have to try this now!" Nathaniel exclaimed as he walked to the doorway of the forge. Dorian hadn't seen his friend look this intense since the day he helped create Shadowflame.

Nathaniel closed his eyes, extended his arm, and faced his palm toward the damp night air as if feeling something invisible in front of him. Taking a few deep breaths, he concentrated, drinking in the smells of the rain and the nearby wet woods. Lifting his other hand, he began tracing out the runic symbol he studied in his book.

A flash of light descended from the heavens. The beam, broad enough to immerse Dorian's body in its electrifying glow engulfed a nearby tree, bathing it in blinding light. Thunder boomed and shook the forge. The bolt of lightning remained visible for an extended length of time, and vanished, leaving a smoking, deep crater of scorched earth where the tree stood moments ago.

The look on Nathaniel's face seemed foreign to Dorian. With a furrowed brow and an open-mouthed smile, he resembled pictures of fabled monsters and demons from his book collection. The unexpected sight sent a shiver of fear down Dorian's spine.

Nathaniel should have been exhausted and drawn from the intensity of the spell, but instead seemed energetic and alert. His chest heaved slightly but otherwise showed no side effects by performing the devastating magic.

Margaret, Lukas, and Elijah cheered to his success.

"It worked! I can't believe it worked!" Nathaniel exclaimed.

Dorian lit the fires of the forge to bring warmth to the chilly air. Waiting for the storm to pass, the friends jested and laughed late into the night. The frequent topic of discussion, the unfathomable destructive power of Nathaniel's spell, lead the group to pour lamentations on their friend. Uncomfortable with such praise, he offered compliments of his own to divert the attention. Needing to raise their voices over the rhythmic beat of raindrops pounding on the tin roof, the group became lost in conversation. Hours passed before the early morning glow of the amber sun crept upon the woodland home.

Dorian's ears perked to the sounds of snapping branches and rustling leaves. He shot to his feet and drew Shadowflame from the sheath, instantly bathing the blade in black fire. Dorian brought his finger to his lips to signal his friends to remain silent. With the morning sun above the horizon, the possibility of his father's return loomed, and if he found Dorian's friends, the young half-dwarf doubted he would be able to contain the paternal rage.

Dorian softly stepped to the forge's entrance,

scouting the area for danger. Seeing no signs of his father's approaching cart, he gestured for his friends to join him and soon stood in the damp morning air.

Three popping sounds resounded from an unseen source within the woods. The powerful snaps sounded like tree trunks being cracked, as easily as one would break a twig for kindling. Before they could identify the source of this unusual sound, the forge exploded in a whirlwind of fire and smoke. The inferno tossed Dorian and his friends into the air before crashing them back to the ground.

The forge laid in ruin with pieces of stone scattered across the woods. Dorian's hearing rang with a high pitch squeal as if a thousand bats sang a single note in his ears. Scanning the area for his friends, he hoped to find them unharmed. What he found proved to be straight out of a nightmare.

Nathaniel and Elijah laid unharmed nearby. Face-down and motionless, Lukas had a large gash on his shoulder, his shirt drenched in blood. Dorian desperately searched to locate Margaret, only to find her in far worse condition than the rest.

A large section of the forge wall landed on Margaret. The stone covered her from the lower back to her feet, and a puddle of blood seeped from beneath the granite. Dorian screamed for Margaret, but his parched throat only released a breathy, scratchy sound that formed no words. Panic washed over him in a tidal wave of fear as a chill of gooseflesh covered his body. With shaking legs, Dorian struggled to his feet. He scanned the area for the source of this disaster, but with blurred vision and a dizzy head, he found the effort to focus nearly impossible.

"You may have overdone it a bit, Cormac." Dorian heard from somewhere in the woods. The footsteps of armored men rang like someone shaking sleigh bells in perfect timing. Three hazy figures cut through the rising smoke of the ruined forge.

The first man, the size of a cave bear, was dressed in dull, golden armor. He carried a hammer large enough to pound Dorian into the ground like a nail in a single swing. The second man wore black armor with screaming skulls on the shoulders, knees, and waist. Horns poked from the temples of his skull-shaped helmet and curved toward the sky. The third man gave off an even stranger appearance than the first two. Where his right eye should have been, a fire runestone sat embedded in the socket. Tendrils of red smoke rose from the runestone, signaling the source of the explosion that decimated his forge and friends.

"The one with the skulls is the High Commander of the King's guard, Jonas Werner," Nathaniel whispered. "The other two are Paul Cormac and Scott Bell. They are the King's elite, the Three Heads of Cerberus. They did this. They killed Margaret."

"All three of us are here," an unfamiliar voice spoke, followed by a maniacal high-pitched laugh that chilled Dorian to the bone.

An arm's length behind Nathaniel stood a man in black armor, trimmed in red. He held a sword forged with Hygard steel, a feature Dorian instantly recognized. "Oh, and thanks for the giant bolt of lightning. It made it much easier to find you all."

Dorian reached for Shadowflame and swung it at the man, but the man vanished before the blade could make contact.

"Is this one dead already too? Oh, come on. How is a guy supposed to have any fun if you all die so easily?"

Dorian spotted the disappearing man at the edge of the woods, standing beside Lukas. He covered a distance of twenty stones in the blink of an eye. Kicking his unconscious friend in the side, as if he were trying to wake him from slumber, a look of rage and frustration glazed over the mysterious man.

"That one is Adam Garrison. He's known as the fastest man in the realm." Nathaniel informed, sounding angrier with every word spoken.

"You kids are in a heap of trouble," Jonas announced in a deep voice echoing through his skull helmet, giving it an eerie, hollow sound. "I suggest you tell us where the books are before things get worse, and believe me, things can get much worse."

"High Commander, do you see that sword?" Adam began as he appeared next to the leader. "I've never seen anything like it. I want that thing. I call the first claim on it after we pry it from his cold, dead hand."

"That's a mul," Cormac interjected. "There was nothing in the mission report about a mul."

"That's true, but he is an accomplice. We'll have to..."

"Margaret!" On his hands and knees, Lukas crawled to her. Blood trickled down his head, forcing one of his eyes shut.

"Oh, that one is still alive!" Adam announced excitedly, and dashed at Lukas with blinding speed, driving his armored knee into Lukas's face before he could reach Margaret. The force of the bash tossed Lukas into the air. After landing, he rolled many lengths away, unconscious once again.

"You were so close!" Adam broke into an evil cackle as he called out to Lukas, mocking his effort.

Dorian could hear Nathaniel breathing deep beside him. He could feel the anger and hatred seething from him, vile contempt pouring from his very soul. Nathaniel raised his hand, drawing out a runic symbol. Recognizing the spell, Dorian flung himself onto the ground and covered his head.

The spell, Razor Wind, shot hundreds of sharp entrails of wind, like the blades of a scythe, in all directions. Far from inexperienced in dealing with mages, the high commander and his cohorts easily dealt with the deadly spell.

Scott took two steps forward, a distance equal to six paces for an ordinary man. Driving his hammer into the ground, a wall of rock rose to form a barrier in front of himself, the high commander, and Paul Cormac, protecting them from the ensuing attack. Dorian looked to see if the spell found its mark on Adam Garrison, but once again, he disappeared. Dorian turned in every direction, expecting a blinding speed attack from Adam, but it didn't come. The wall of rock exploded as Scott struck it with his mighty hammer. Shards of the wall flew at Dorian and Nathaniel. A chunk of earth blasted Dorian in the chest, knocking him to the ground, forcing all wind from his lungs. He clutched at his chest as he tried to breathe.

Dorian located Nathaniel, who took the brunt of the damage. The debris from the exploding wall flung him into a tree. He writhed on the ground with a dislocated shoulder, leaving his limp arm to dangle at his side. His leg fared even worse. Visibly, no blood surfaced through his clothes, but his friend's crooked and mangled appendage laid awkwardly in the dirt.

Dorian next found Elijah. He was able to avoid the exploding debris, but not able to escape the fear of the situation. He curled up in a fetal position, sobbing uncontrollably.

"I told you things could get worse," Jonas said as he approached Dorian and Nathaniel, his armor clanking with each step. "You need to understand. You have broken the law, and your punishment is nigh. Tell us where the books are before your misery escalates."

"Or don't, I love escalating misery!" Adam added,

suddenly appearing next to Jonas.

Jonas squatted down in front of Nathaniel, who squirmed to lean against the tree behind him, his mangled leg making jagged trails in the dirt as he moved. "What books?" Nathaniel asked defiantly.

Dorian knew why Nathaniel resisted giving Jonas the information he desired. His friends told the tales of the high commander and the Three Heads of Cerberus. Stories of cruelty and punishment that left ordinary folk like them terrified of their unyielding justice. The moment these men acquired the information they desired, they would execute them.

"Well, you certainly have a lot of guts, don't you? Alright, I guess we'll have to use other methods to get you to talk." Jonas said in an exaggerated mocking tone, rising to his feet and placing the tip of his massive sword near Nathaniel's eye.

Dorian squeezed Shadowflame's handle. He could no longer take the torment these men dealt to his friends. The ache in his chest throbbed from the effort to stand. Drawing his sword back, he made his first step to attack Jonas, but the giant man intercepted Dorian, driving the handle end of his colossal hammer into Dorian's gut.

Buckling over, a weak pair of coughs escaped his lungs. Dorian dropped Shadowflame and fell to his knees, wrapping both arms around his stomach. He could feel his dinner attempting to flee his mouth, as the intense pain from Scott's hammer strike seared into his abdomen.

"That was unwise." Paul Cormac held his ax at the base of Dorian's neck. "Why don't you toss that strange sword of yours aside, just to make sure you're not tempted to do anything that stupid again."

Dorian complied with Paul's order with reluctance. Tossing Shadowflame aside, pain radiated throughout his body from the effort. He began to fall but managed to catch himself with both arms before hitting the dirt.

"This is becoming tedious," Jonas announced. "If you don't care about yourself, maybe I can persuade you another way." Jonas walked to Elijah and gave him a swift kick. "Sit up, fat-boy!"

Elijah sat and pulled his knees to his chest. His tear-soaked face, flushed as red as his bloodshot eyes, trembled with fear.

"Now, I am going to start cutting pieces off of this fat little cow unless you tell me where the King's books are." Jonas pointed his sword at Elijah.

Nathaniel relayed with a silent glower aimed at Jonas.

"Would you look at that!" Jonas sighed, turning his attention to Elijah. "Apparently, dusty old books are more important to him than your body parts. What do you think of that?"

Elijah attempted a reply, but only a couple high-pitched squeals escaped, sounding like a mouse dying in a trap.

"If that's the way you want to play it," Jonas threatened, "hold out your arm, tubby. You heard me. Hold out your arm, or you're going to find out what my sword tastes like." Jonas bent over toward Elijah's ear and spoke in a hushed voice, "I don't mean to ruin the surprise, but it tastes awful. Especially after it pierces out the base of your skull."

Elijah's crying became hysterical. Slowly, he extended his shaking arm out in front of him. Jonas raised his sword and hovered it above Elijah's wrist to line up his strike. "Now whatever you do, don't move. If you move, my sword is going to get stuck in the bones of your arm, and then I will have to step on your face to wrench it out, and your blood will get all over my armor, and I'll have to clean it up. It'll be a whole mess, and no one wants that."

Jonas raised his sword to lop off Elijah's hand, when moans in the tone of a female voice, hardly loud enough to hear, distracted him. Margaret shifted her arms and head groggily as if waking from a deep sleep.

"That one's still alive!" Adam marched over to Margaret and crouched next to her. Her arms moved in an attempt to rise, signaling the ignorance of her predicament.

Seeing the opportunity, Nathaniel took advantage of the distraction. Lifting his uninjured arm, he drew out a runic symbol, releasing a torrent of electrical streams at the four adversaries. The bolt of lightning, aimed at Adam Garrison, veered off course and struck the ground. Scott Bell tried to deflect the charge with his hammer, leaving him to drop the weapon and clench his electrified hand. The shot aimed at Jonas Werner would have found its target, but the darkness runestone embedded in his chest opened a void that absorbed the attack.

The last shock found its destination, striking Paul Cormac in the chest, sending him flying backward, as small arcs of electricity crawled across his body like a swarm of insects.

Seizing the moment, Dorian tucked and rolled toward

Shadowflame. Scott picked up his hammer and stepped in front of Dorian to block him from his intended target, Jonas.

Raising his sword to attack Scott, he stopped when he heard the unmistakable sounds of steel piercing flesh. Dorian looked to where Adam Garrison stood and saw him holding his sword, the blade piercing through the back of Margaret's skull with the tip jutting from her gaping mouth.

Rage and hatred boiled within Dorian. He no longer felt the aching pains of his bruised and beaten body. The power of Shadowflame coursed through his arm and bathed his body in unnatural disdain and wrath, void of empathy. Swinging his sword in a horizontal arc, black flame trailed the tip of the weapon and jettisoned forth in a crescent wave of fury.

Jonas's chest absorbed part of the Defensive Spell's wave, but the power of the flame proved more than he could handle. Dropping to one knee, he squeezed his hand to his chest, his face winced in obvious pain. Adam Garrison avoided the wave with his blinding speed, but the giant, Scott Bell, did not possess the same swift instincts.

The wave passed through Scott's body unhindered, turning trees and shrubs to ash as it proceeded. Scott's face lit with horror as he dropped his hammer to the ground.

Cracks emitting purple light spread across his body like a volcano breaking the ground before the eruption. Purple beams of light shot from his eyes and mouth as he raised his head in silent prayer to the Gods above. With an explosion of light, the giant crumbled into a pile on the ground, leaving ash, soot, an empty set of armor, and a hammer fit for a giant, as the only remains of Scott Bell.

The power of the spell Dorian cast drained his strength. Sweat covered his skin. His head felt like an invisible vice squeezed his brain inside his skull. Heaving deep breaths, the pain returned to his body, a stark reminder of the damage done to him. Searching for his friends, to ensure they avoided the devastating spell, he found they escaped Scott Bell's fate.

Nathaniel leaned against the tree with his mangled leg and limp arm. Elijah checked his body to make sure the spell left him with all his body parts before bursting in a sprint away from the carnage. Margaret remained beneath the massive stone lying in a pool of blood that encased her head like a log floating at the bank of a lake. A black mark seared across the top of the boulder that pinned her danced with black flames. Dorian searched for the one person unaccounted for, but could not locate Adam Garrison.

Dorian rose to his feet using Shadowflame as a crutch. "Gods be damned!" Jonas shouted as he rose to his feet with far less effort than Dorian required. "Forget him, Garrison, get the fat one! The mul is mine!"

Dorian turned to see Adam Garrison creeping up on him to stab him in his back. Grunting his disapproval, Adam followed orders, streaking past Dorian in pursuit of Elijah.

In the blink of an eye, Adam found his mark. Driving his shoulder into Elijah's back, the portly young man struck the ground, giving him a face full of dirt in the process. Elijah flipped to his back and saw Adam looming over him with his sword raised in preparation for execution. Raising his hands in front of his face in defense, Elijah squeezed his eyes shut, expecting the inevitable killing blow, but before Adam could bring the blade down, another sword pierced through Adam's shoulder from behind. Adam's face folded in a mixture of pain and shock as he grabbed at the protruding steel blade.

Adam turned to see who attacked. Standing before him, Lukas swayed back and forth as he struggled to remain standing. Lukas's eye, swollen shut and covered in blood, looked like a ripe peach. Blood trickled down his face, his body trembling as he staggered from the pain and effort.

"Damn it! I was aiming for your heart," Lukas said with an attempted smile, but the swelling on his face would only allow one corner of his mouth to rise. Adam's face twisted in fury as he grunted and swung his sword, sending Lukas's separated head to roll in the dirt.

Dorian tried to scream Lukas's name, but only a choked, raspy "Lukas" escaped from his parched throat. Refocusing his attention to Elijah, Adam saw Dorian's chubby friend tracing out a runic symbol with his finger. Drawing the Ice Shard Spell incorrectly, the spell backfired, launching a chunk of ice deep into the flesh of his own bicep, but his intentions did not go unrealized. The broken spell caught Adam unaware, and the ensuing explosion sent him flying through the air, unconscious and covered in frost.

Jonas advanced with his sword drawn high. A surge of adrenaline shot through Dorian as he raised Shadowflame to block Jonas's deadly attack. He squeezed his eyes closed with the expectation that Jonas would overpower him for the final time. The clash of steel against steel rang like a bell, but Dorian felt nothing. Opening his eyes, he saw a familiar warhammer blocking Jonas's sword. Dorian followed the handle of the warhammer to see his father standing before him with a wide grin beneath his shaggy beard.

"Father?" Dorian uttered in a weak voice.

"Thane! What, in the name of the Gods, are you doing here?" Jonas asked in a shocked voice.

Dorian felt just as surprised as Jonas. Not only by his father's timely arrival, but also by the familiarity in which Jonas spoke.

"Hello Jonas, it has been a very long time." Thane put Dorian's suspicion to rest. Jonas did know his father. The past few days proved that he knew little about his father's life outside their small cottage home.

"Did this whelp just call you father? This mul is your son? That means..." Jonas's words trailed off as if he figured out the answer to his next question. "Alora! That means Alora is dead! You bastard! What could you have been thinking?"

Jonas spoke his mother's name with a familiarity that proved he knew both of his parents, and by the sound of his tone, they were once friends!

"Dorian," Thane smiled, ignoring Jonas's questions and accusations. "That is the most magnificent blade I have ever seen. I am so very proud of you. Do you remember where the emergency bag is?"

Thane's eyes, glazed with tears, showed a gentle

kindness Dorian had not seen since childhood. Feeling responsible for the trouble they were in, he wanted to apologize, but could only manage a nod of his head in response.

"Good. Grab the bag, gather up your tubby friend there, and go. Do not wait for me, and never come back here under any circumstance. Do you understand?"

Dorian began to protest, but his father cut his words short. "Do you understand?" Thane's gaze intensified after repeating himself. Dorian felt as if his father meant to look stern, but he only seemed happy and proud.

Nodding his head again, he turned to go. After a single step, Jonas blocked Dorian's path with an extended sword. "The boy isn't going anywhere, Thane. I can't allow that."

"Well, you can try to stop him, and you may succeed, but then you'd have to take your focus away from me. How do you think that will turn out for you?" Thane leered at Jonas with an arrogant smile, bringing his hammer in position for attack.

Jonas stared at Thane, frustration and, contempt plastered across his face. Lifting his sword, he refocused his attention on the threat Thane presented, allowing Dorian to pass.

"Dorian, do as I said and go. Jonas and I have to…talk."

"You can't win, Thane! I have grown much since last we met!"

Thane responded by patting his belly and saying, "As have I!"

Jonas tapped the runestone on his chest, and Dorian felt his strength abate. For a moment he stumbled, but caught himself and continued to follow his father's instruction. Reaching the door of his home, he felt his strength return once he arrived at a safe distance from Jonas.

Inside his house, he heard the clashing of steel and knew that Jonas and his father were amidst the battle. Dorian went into his father's room, pulled up the loose floorboards, grabbed the backpack hidden beneath, and left.

Outside, Dorian could not help but watch his father fight. Thane moved quicker and more agile than he had ever seen him move when they sparred. Walking to Elijah, who still grasped at his arm where the ice penetrated, Dorian helped his friend to his feet. With arms wrapped around each other's shoulders, the two young men began to limp up the hill that ran west, away from both the Capital city and his home.

The clank and clash of steel rang loudly as Dorian and Elijah reached the top of the hill. Dorian turned around to see his father, but the two battling men looked like shadows, no larger than a child's doll.

Unable to see who the victor of the fight would be, Dorian closed his eyes as the battle between two great warriors raged on.

# About the Author

Dennis is a veteran of the United States Navy after serving in his country for fourteen years. During his service, Dennis developed PTSD, which resulted in insomnia. Not willing to take prescription or over-the-counter-medication, he began constructing a story in his mind to find a natural method to fall asleep. After fifteen years of development, and countless sleepless nights, he finally decided to put the story into words. This story is the result of him turning a debilitating condition into something positive.

Dennis is a native of the Buffalo, New York area where he was raised by his parents, Lawrence and Barbara, alongside his sister, Kelly. He currently lives in the Atlanta, Georgia area with his loving and supportive wife Kimberly and three children, Hailey, Joseph, and Breanna.

Excerpt from Book Two

The gleam of the two swords on Razuul's hips caught
Dorian's attention, filling him with dread. The silver
pommels of the swords, in the shape of phoenix heads, was
instantly recognized as his father's work. Thane had worked
on these swords for days, ensuring that the craftsmanship
was of the highest quality. When Dorian asked about them,
his father had replied that they were for a very special
customer. He did not know who the customer was, but he did
know his father would never craft swords for an elf, leading
Dorian to come to the only conclusion that made sense. He
must have stolen them!

"Where did you get those swords?" Dorian insisted,
knocking his chair to the floor as he stood.

The tavern's occupants scattered, leaving Dorian,
Elijah, Brett and Razuul alone in the center of the room.
Dorian breathed deeply, his nostrils flaring with each gulp of
air. He could feel heat radiating from his skin as the rage
burnt from deep within. He kept his menacing stare fixed on
Razuul's unwavering eyes.

"Have you lost your senses? Do you know who this
is?" Brett asked with a cynical chuckle.

"Aye, he's the Dragon Fist, and I might be frightened if I believed the story," Dorian replied to Brett, keeping his gaze set on Razuul. "What I do believe is that those swords are stolen and that you better give them here or taste my steel!" Dorian drew his sword. The black flame that had once bathed the blade every time he held his sword remained absent.

Brett let loose a hearty laugh in disbelief of Dorian's audacity. Wiping a tear from his eye, Brett began an attempt to deter Dorian from his course of action by stepping between them.

"If you are in a hurry to die, I…" Brett stopped mid-sentence when he felt the sharp clasp of a hand on his shoulder. He turned to see Razuul staring at Dorian with intensity in his eyes.

"Shut up, and move!" Razuul demanded, shoving Brett aside. Drawing his swords, he shifted into a fighting stance, waiting for Dorian to make his move.

"D-Dorian, I-I don't think…I-I m-mean, you…." Elijah stammered, too frightened to interject.

Dorian let loose a scream and rushed at Razuul.

Contact Dennis Medbury:

dpmedbury@gmail.com

Instagram @dpmedbury

Twitter @dpmedbury

Made in the USA
Monee, IL
18 September 2020

42945115R00215